Devil's Homecoming

Book Six
The Blackout Series

A novel by
Bobby Akart

Copyright Information

© 2017 Bobby Akart Inc. All rights reserved. Except as permitted under the U.S. Copyright Act of 1976, no part of this publication may be reproduced, distributed or transmitted in any form or by any means, or stored in a database or retrieval system, without the prior written permission of Bobby Akart Inc.

This is a work of fiction. Names, characters, places, and incidents are either the product of the author's imagination or are used fictitiously and any resemblance to any person or persons, living or dead, events or locales is entirely coincidental.

Other Works by Amazon Top 50 Author, Bobby Akart

The Doomsday Series
Apocalypse
Haven
Anarchy
Minutemen
Civil War

The Yellowstone Series
Hellfire
Inferno
Fallout
Survival

The Lone Star Series
Axis of Evil
Beyond Borders
Lines in the Sand
Texas Strong
Fifth Column
Suicide Six

The Pandemic Series
Beginnings
The Innocents
Level 6
Quietus

The Blackout Series
36 Hours
Zero Hour
Turning Point
Shiloh Ranch
Hornet's Nest
Devil's Homecoming

The Boston Brahmin Series
The Loyal Nine
Cyber Attack
Martial Law
False Flag
The Mechanics
Choose Freedom
Patriot's Farewell
Seeds of Liberty (Companion Guide)

The Prepping for Tomorrow Series
Cyber Warfare
EMP: Electromagnetic Pulse
Economic Collapse

Dedications

To the love of my life, thank you for making the sacrifices necessary so I may pursue this dream.

To the *Princesses of the Palace*, my little marauders in training, you have no idea how much happiness you bring to your mommy and me.

To my fellow preppers—never be ashamed of adopting a preparedness lifestyle.

Acknowledgements

Writing a book that is both informative and entertaining requires a tremendous team effort. Writing is the easy part. For their efforts in making The Blackout Series a reality, I would like to thank Hristo Argirov Kovatliev for his incredible cover art, Pauline Nolet for making this important work reader-friendly, Stef Mcdaid for making this manuscript decipherable on so many formats, John David Farrell, who together with Marshall Davis has brought my words to life, and The Team—whose advice, friendship and attention to detail is priceless.

The Blackout Series could not have been written without the tireless counsel and direction from those individuals who shall remain nameless at the Space Weather Prediction Center in Boulder, Colorado and at the Atacama Large Millimeter Array (ALMA) in Chile. Thank you for providing me a portal into your observations and data.

Lastly, a huge thank you to Dr. Tamitha Skov, a friend and social media icon, who is a research scientist at The Aerospace Corporation in Southern California. With her PHD in Geophysics and Space Plasma Physics, she has become a vital resource for amateur astronomers and aurora watchers around the world. Without her insight, The Blackout Series could not have been written. Visit her website at http://www.SpaceWeatherWoman.com.

Thank you!

About the Author

Bobby Akart

Author Bobby Akart has been ranked by Amazon as #55 in its Top 100 list of most popular, bestselling authors. He has achieved recognition as the #1 bestselling Horror Author, #2 bestselling Science Fiction Author, #3 bestselling Religion & Spirituality Author, #6 bestselling Action & Adventure Author, and #7 bestselling Historical Author.

He has written over twenty-six international bestsellers, in nearly fifty fiction and nonfiction genres, including the chart-busting Yellowstone series, the reader-favorite Lone Star series, the critically acclaimed Boston Brahmin series, the bestselling Blackout series, the frighteningly realistic Pandemic series, his highly cited nonfiction Prepping for Tomorrow series, and his latest project—the Doomsday series, seen by many as the horrifying future of our nation if we can't find a way to come together.

His novel *Yellowstone: Fallout* reached the Top 50 on the Amazon bestsellers list and earned him two Kindle All-Star awards for most pages read in a month and most pages read as an author. The Yellowstone series vaulted him to the #1 best selling horror author on Amazon, and the #2 best selling science fiction author.

Bobby has provided his readers a diverse range of topics that are both informative and entertaining. His attention to detail and impeccable research have allowed him to capture the imaginations of his readers through his fictional works and bring them valuable knowledge through his nonfiction books.

SIGN UP for Bobby Akart's mailing list to receive special offers, bonus content, and you'll be the first to receive news about new releases in the Doomsday series:

eepurl.com/bYqq3L

VISIT Amazon.com/BobbyAkart, a dedicated feature page created by Amazon for his work, to view more information on his thriller fiction novels and post-apocalyptic book series, as well as his nonfiction Prepping for Tomorrow series.

Visit Bobby Akart's website for informative blog entries on preparedness, writing, and a behind-the-scenes look into his novels.

BobbyAkart.com

About the Blackout Series

WHAT WOULD YOU DO
if a voice was screaming in your head - *GET READY* . . .
for a catastrophic event of epic proportions . . .
with no idea where to start . . .
or how, or when?

This is a true story, it just hasn't happened yet.

The characters depicted in The Blackout Series are fictional. The events, however, are based upon fact.

This is not the story of preppers with stockpiles of food, weapons, and a hidden bunker. This is the story of Colton Ryman, his stay-at-home wife, Madison, and their teenage daughter, Alex. In 36 Hours, the Ryman family and the rest of the world will be thrust into the darkness of a post-apocalyptic world.

A catastrophic solar flare, an EMP—a threat from above to America's soft underbelly below—is hurtling toward the Earth.

The Rymans have never heard of preppers and have no concept of what prepping entails. But they're learning, while they run out of time. Their faith will be tested, their freedom will be threatened, but their family will survive.

An EMP, naturally generated from our sun in the form of a solar flare, has happened before, and it will happen again, in only 36 Hours.

This is a story about how our sun, the planet's source of life, can also devastate our modern world. It's a story about panic, chaos, and the final straws that shattered an already thin veneer of civility. It is a warning to us all ...

never underestimate the depravity of man.

What would you do when the clock strikes zero?
Midnight is forever.

Note: This book does not contain strong language. It is intended to entertain and inform audiences of all ages, including teen and young adults. Although some scenes depict the realistic threat our nation faces from a devastating solar flare, and the societal collapse which will result in the aftermath, it does not contain graphic scenes typical of other books in the post-apocalyptic genre.

Previously in The Blackout Series

The Characters

The Rymans:

Colton – Colton Ryman is in his late thirties. Born and raised in Texas, he is a direct descendant of the Ryman family which built the infamous Ryman Auditorium music hall in downtown Nashville. His family migrated to Texas from Tennessee with Davy Crockett in the 1800's. The Rymans became prominent in the oil and cattle business and as a result, Colton inherited his skill for negotiating. After college, he landed a position with United Talent, the top agency for the country-western music industry. He eventually became managing partner of the Nashville office. He is married to Madison and they have one child, Alex.

Madison – Madison, in her mid-thirties, is a devout Christian born and raised in Nashville. She grew up a debutante but quickly set her sights on a career in filmmaking. But one fateful day, she was introduced to Colton Ryman and the two fell in love. They had their only child, Alex, which prompted Madison to give up her career in favor of a life raising their daughter and loving her husband—two full time jobs.

Alex – Fifteen-year old Alex, the only child of Colton and Madison Ryman, was a sophomore at Davidson Academy. Despite inheriting her mother's beauty, Alex was not interested in the normal pursuits of teenaged girls which included becoming the prey of teenaged boys. Her interests were golf and science. It was during her favorite class, Astronomy, in which the teacher encouraged his students to become *solar sleuths* that Alex learned of the potential damage the sun could cause.

Supporting Characters of Importance:

Dr. Andrea Stanford – Director of the Joint Alma Observatory (JAO) Science Team at the Atacama Large Millimeter Array (ALMA) in the high-mountain desert of Peru. She is a graduate of the Harvard-Smithsonian Center for Astrophysics in Cambridge, Massachusetts. Her long-time assistant is Jose Cortez.

Members of the Harding Place Association (HPA) – In 36 Hours, book one of The Blackout Series, Shane Wren and his wife Christie Wren make their first appearance. They have two daughters and live just to the north of the Rymans. Shane Wren is the President of the HPA. In Zero Hour, two other members of the HPA are important players in the saga. Gene Andrews, a former director of compliance with the Internal Revenue Service, and Adam Holder, a former banker, make their appearance. Jimmy Holder, Adam's stepson, is a key player in the story as well.

Betty Jean Durham – In Turning Point, we are gradually introduced to Betty Jean Durham, the only child of the infamous former sheriff of McNairy County, Tennessee, Buford Pusser. Betty Jean had a tragic childhood that shaped her into a hardened woman—Ma Durham. Following the murder of her husband which resulted in her banishment from the sparsely populated southwest Tennessee county, Betty Jean and her two young sons relocated across the Tennessee River to Savannah in adjacent Hardin County. She rose to political power the old fashioned way, via luck and trickery, and became the iron-fisted Mayor of Savannah. The solar storm wreaked havoc on the world, and ruined the ambitions of many a politician, but nobody stops Betty Jean Durham. No sirree.

Leroy Durham Jr. – But his friends call him Junior, all five of them. Junior is the youngest son of the now deceased Leroy Durham, and Betty Jean Durham. Likened to Deputy Barney Fife, Junior was elected to become sheriff of Hardin County, Tennessee at the age of twenty-seven, just like his grandfather—Buford Pusser. Junior missed out on the Pusser genes somewhere in the process. While his grandfather was nicknamed Bufurd the Bull, during his short-lived wrestling career, Junior stood five-foot-eight and weighed one-hundred-fifty pounds soakin' wet. Now, Junior didn't have a big stick like his grandfather, but he wielded power nonetheless, with the aid of his Ma, who was very encouraging. Like all great antagonists, Junior always thinks he's right.

Coach Joe Carey – Unless you've lived in Smalltown, U.S.A., it's hard to appreciate the importance and grip high school football has on a community. While some may look up to their political leaders for inspiration, most will see the coach of the local high school football team as their guide to the Promised Land. In Turning Point, we are introduced to Joe Carey, former Head Coach of the Hardin County Tigers who has taken on a far more important role—leader of an underground resistance comprised of the brave young men and women of Hardin County High who stand opposed to the tyrannical actions of Ma Durham and her son Sheriff Junior Durham. The Tiger Resistance will play a big role in the Blackout Series.

Beau Carey – son of Coach Joe Carey and QB1, captain of the Hardin County Tigers football team. He is also the undisputed leader of the *disdants*, as Junior Durham calls 'em, those members of the Savannah community that fight back against the tyrant Mayor—Ma Durham. By the way, Beau is sweet on Alex, but then, what high school boy wouldn't be.

The Bennett Brothers, Jimbo and Clay – twin adopted sons of Coach Carey and therefore the brothers of Beau. Jimbo and Clay's parents passed away in a tragic accident and as Beau puts it, "they were left to us in their parent's will". Now the twin starting linebackers of the Hardin County Tigers join with the Carey's as an active thorn in the side of the Durhams.

Russ Hilton and family – Retired country crooner who found his way to the tiny town of Saltillo, Tennessee located on the west side of the Tennessee River in upper Hardin County. Hilton was of Colton's first clients and the two were surprised to run into each other toward the end of the Rymans' journey to Shiloh Ranch. Saltillo immediately accepted Hilton as their adopted son so he rewarded the community with its own honky-tonk, The Hillbilly Hilton.

The Tennessee River – Wait, hey Bobby, shouldn't this be under the next section titled Primary Scene Locations? Not in my book. You see, throughout history, bodies of water have played major roles in the development of mankind. They are the sources of life, providing hydration and food to all species on the planet. Bodies of water are also significant geographic boundaries, or barriers, to the movement of man. Before there were boats, planes and rocket ships, the vast oceans blocked man's migration. Then the new world was discovered, but for those without the ability to sail her waters, the rivers and lakes separated whole communities of people. The Tennessee River is one such body of water, dividing Hardin County in half both geographically, and politically.

As The Blackout Series continues, and pay attention my friends because this is important, you'll find that life is like a river. It's always easier to flow with the current. To turn against the current takes effort and fortitude.

Sometimes, going against the flow was necessary.

Jake Allen and family — Jake Allen is a country music star who began his career like so many others, in a honky-tonk on Printer's

Alley in Nashville. Like Russ Hilton, Jake hired Colton to be his agent and the men remained close friends for years. The Allens live halfway between Springfield and Branson, Missouri where Jake performs in his newly created music venue. Emily Allen went to nursing school before marrying Jake and becoming a full time mom to their son, Chase. Chase is in his late teens and has a bit of a wild streak, as most boys his age have.

Stubby Crump and his wife, Bessie — The Crump family has resided on the west side of the Tennessee River for many years. The small town of Crump was founded by Stubby's grandfather and the family ran a farming operation for many years. Following high school, Stubby embarked on a two year stint in the St. Louis Cardinals baseball organization during which time he married the love of his life, Bessie. He realized baseball wasn't for him and like so many other young men in the Hardin County community, he enlisted in the military. Stubby's military career as an Army Ranger found him in the jungles of Cambodia, an experience which deeply affected him. Now in his late sixties, Stubby has converted a lifetime of experiences into making Shiloh Ranch a prepper haven.

John Wyatt and his wife, Lucinda – The Wyatt's own a cattle farm just to the north of Shiloh Ranch. Their land borders the Shiloh National Park.

Primary Scene Locations

Ryman Residence – located on Harding Place in Nashville. It is located approximately two miles east of historic Belle Meade Country Club and just to the west of Lynnwood Boulevard. It is a two-story brick home similar to the one depicted on the cover of Zero Hour.

Harding Place Neighborhood – The portion of the Harding Place Neighborhood depicted in The Blackout Series is bordered by Belle Meade Boulevard to the west, Abbot-Martin Road to the north,

Hillsboro Pike to the east, and Tyne Boulevard to the south. Generally, this area is southwest of downtown Nashville in an area known for its historic homes—Belle Meade.

ALMA - the largest telescope on the planet—the Atacama Large Millimeter Array, or ALMA. It's located at an altitude of over sixteen thousand feet in Atacama, Chile.

The Natchez Trace — Well, this scenic route developed in the mid twentieth century was ordinarily a leisurely trek from Nashville to the Mississippi River. In Turning Point, it became the proverbial highway to hell. In our pre-apocalyptic world, don't let the experiences of the Rymans during their bug-out influence your decision to enjoy a long drive on this four-hundred-forty mile stretch of southern hospitality. But know this, you never know what lies around the bend.

Savannah, Tennessee — the county seat of Hardin County, Tennessee, population six thousand (pre-collapse) and lies on the east banks of the Tennessee River. It is a beautiful southern town with gorgeous antebellum homes and lots of friendly faces. Historically, Savannah has played a role in the Civil War. Fictionally, Savannah represents a microcosm of the small towns across America which chooses a path after TEOTWAWKI to be feared by every prepper. Beauty is only skin deep, but evil cuts clean to the bone.

Saltillo, Tennessee — the perfect prepper hideout. Sitting on the west side of the Tennessee River in the uppermost corner of Hardin County, Saltillo still maintains its local charm from two hundred years of sleepy isolation. Larger than life country music star Russ Hilton moves there with his beautiful family and now Saltillo has a claim to fame. Russ built his own music venue, the *Hillbilly Hilton*, and the town enjoys a close knit relationship centered around country music, southern comfort food, and the Tennessee River. Prepper Utopia.

Shiloh Ranch, Tennessee – the Rymans' bug-out destination. That's all you get for now my friends. You must read on.

Previously in The Blackout Series
Book One: 36 HOURS

The Blackout Series begins thirty-six hours before a devastating coronal mass ejection strikes the Earth. Dr. Andrea Stanford and her team at ALMA identified the largest solar flare on record—an X-58—hurtling toward the Earth.

This solar flare was many times larger than the Carrington Event of 1859, widely considered the strongest solar event of modern times. Alarm bells were rung by Dr. Stanford and soon eyes at NASA and the Space Weather Prediction Center, SWPC, in Boulder, Colorado, were maintaining a close eye on Active Region 3222—AR3222.

AR3222 was a huge dark coronal hole which has formed on the solar disk. It had grown to encompass the entire northern hemisphere of the sun. As the story begins, AR3222 had only fired off a few minor solar flares, but as the hole in the sun rotated out of view, Dr. Stanford knew it would be back.

That same evening, Colton Ryman was in Dallas, Texas on business. One of his country music clients was being considered for a spot on the upcoming Super Bowl halftime show. Colton participated in a dog-and-pony show hosted by Jerry Jones, owner of the Dallas Cowboys which included tours of the Cowboys' stadium and a concert in downtown Dallas.

Via news reports and text message conversations with Madison, Colton became aware of the unusual solar activity. At first, he brushed off the threat, but as time passed he became more and more convinced.

Madison and Alex were in Nashville going about their normal routine. Alex was the first to ring the alarm that the threat they faced from a major solar storm was real. She tried to raise the level of awareness in her mother, but Madison initially brushed it off as the overactive imagination of a teenage girl.

By noon the next day, all of the Rymans were beginning to see the signs of a potential catastrophic event. While the rest of the country went about its normal routine, Colton, Madison, and Alex made their decision—*Get Ready*!

The initial reports of the solar event were widely downplayed by the media. Even the President refused to raise the alarms for fear of frightening the public unnecessarily. But the Rymans were convinced the threat of a catastrophic solar flare was real, and the three sprang into action.

Colton, unable to catch a flight back to Nashville from Dallas, rented a Corvette and began to race home. Madison, using a valuable resource in the form of a book titled *EMP: Electromagnetic Pulse*, studied the *preppers checklist* contained in the back of the book which enabled her to apply a common sense approach to getting prepared in a hurry.

Madison pulled Alex out of school and they immediately hit the Kroger grocery store for food and supplies. It was during this shopping expedition that news of the solar flare broke. Society began to collapse rapidly.

After forcing her way out of the grocery store parking lot using her Suburban's bumper to shove a KIA out of the way, Madison and Alex made their way to an ATM. The lines were long, but Madison waited until she could withdraw the cash. However, she let down her guard and was assaulted by a man who tried to steal her money. While the rest of the bank customers stood by and watched, Alex sprang into action with her trusty sand wedge. She beat the man repeatedly until he crawled away—saving her Mom, and the cash.

Meanwhile, Colton's race home—doing over one hundred miles an hour in the rented Corvette—was almost red flagged when he was stopped by an Arkansas State Trooper. While he was waiting for the trooper's deliberation of what to do with Colton, a gunfight ensued between two vehicles in the southbound lane of the interstate. Having bigger fish to fry, the state trooper left Colton alone, who promptly hauled his cookies toward Memphis.

Madison, despite being battered and bruised, elected to make another *run* with Alex. They added to their newly acquired preps but encountered a group of three thugs on the way home. Frightened for their safety, Madison once again used her trusty Suburban bumper to pin one of the attackers against the car in front of her. This brought an abrupt end to the assault.

As Colton drove home, he listened to the scientific experts on the radio broadcasts talking about the potential impact an EMP would have on electronics and vehicles. He learned pre-1970 model cars were more likely to survive the massive pulse of energy associated with an EMP. This knowledge served him well when he stopped at a gas station in eastern Arkansas.

Colton was confronted by three men who took a liking to the shiny red Corvette. Not wanting any trouble, Colton made the deal of a lifetime. He traded the new 'vette for a 1969 Jeep Wagoneer. The good ole boys thought they'd gotten the better of the city slicker, but it was they who were hoodooed. Colton took off with his new, old truck and sufficient gas to make it to the house.

Madison's and Alex's exciting day was not over. After dark, a knocking on the door startled them both. It was their friendly neighbors, Shane and Christie Wren. Madison attempted to keep her conversation with them brief, and her newly acquired preps hidden, but the simple mistake of turning on a light revealed her bruised face to the Wrens. The couple immediately suspected Colton of being a wife abuser despite Madison's explanation to the contrary.

After Madison sent the nosy Wrens on their way, she and Alex settled in to watch CNN's coverage of Times Square and the Countdown to Impact Clock. Thousands of people had gathered in New York to witness the apocalypse's arrival. The drama was high as the scene in Times Square was reminiscent of a New Year's Eve countdown without the revelry and deprivation.

The girls anxiously waited as they were unsure of Colton's whereabouts. Then they heard the kitchen door unlock, and Colton entered—reuniting the family. They began to move into the living room when Alex exclaimed, "Hey, look! The clock stopped at zero and nothing happened."

The CNN cameras panned the mass of humanity as a spontaneous eruption of joy and relief filled the packed crowd. The trio of news anchors couldn't contain themselves as they exchanged hugs and handshakes. Jubilation accompanied pandemonium in Times Square, the so-called Center of the Universe, as the bright neon lights from the McDonald's logo to the Bank of America sign continued their dazzling display. Then—

CRACKLE! SIZZLE! SNAP—SNAP—SNAP!

Darkness. Blackout. It was — *Zero Hour.*

Book Two: ZERO HOUR

The central theme of The Blackout Series is to provide the reader a glimpse into a post-apocalyptic world. Book One, 36 Hours took a non-prepping family through a fast-paced learning curve. In the period of a day, they had to accept the reality that a catastrophic event was headed their way and accept the threat as real. Once the decision to *GET READY* was made, then the Rymans scrambled around to prepare the best they could with limited time and resources.

Book two, Zero Hour, focuses on the post-apocalyptic world in the immediate hours and days following the collapse event.

Zero Hour picks up the Rymans' plight immediate after the collapse of the nation's power grid and critical infrastructure. First, they accept the challenges which lie ahead and then they apply common sense to establishing a plan.

First order of business was security. Colton recalls a story from his grandfather who reminds him to never underestimate the *depravity of man*. While they accept their fate, and attempt to set up a routine, there are neighbors who have other ideas about what's best for the Rymans.

Under the pretense of banding together to help the neighbors survive, the self-appointed leaders run a survival operation of their own. Using the intel willingly provided by unsuspecting residents, the three leaders of the Harding Place Association loot empty, unguarded homes and keep the contents for themselves.

When a rift forms between the Rymans and some of their neighbors, things turn ugly. There are confrontations and arguments. One of the leaders attempts a raid on the Ryman home at night with plans to steal the generator and some supplies. A gunfight ensues which wounds several of the attacking marauders. One of the three HPA leaders later dies due to lack of sufficient medical care.

There are also undercover operations including one involving Alex and a teenage boy. Alex recognizes the family's weakness in not having sufficient weapons to defend themselves and this boy's stepfather has an arsenal ripe for the pickins. Alex befriends the boy, procures weapons and ammunition, and everything is going smoothly until she finds the stepfather abusing her teenage friend. In self-defense, Alex shoots and kills the man, who happened to be one of the HPA leaders.

The death of the other two leaders has a noticeable effect on Shane Wren, the ringleader of the HPA who is the cause of the rift between the Rymans and the other neighbors. We're left in the dark as to whether the death of his cohorts resulted in the turnaround, or simply the knowledge that the Rymans are capable of defending themselves with deadly force, if necessary.

As a new threat emerges, the HPA and the Rymans come together to repel the vicious group of looters as they make their way deeper into the neighborhood. It was, however, too little too late for the majority of the neighbors in the HPA. Many, because they were out of food, and scared, opted to leave their homes and walk to one of the many FEMA camps and shelters established in the area.

The Rymans debated and considered their options. Madison stepped up and set the tone for the next part of their journey by making a large meal and announcing that it was time to go. The family gathered their most valued belongings to help them survive. It was time to go.

Here are the final paragraphs from ZERO HOUR:

Madison shed several tears as she closed the kitchen door behind them. Colton opened the garage door, revealing the trophy received for the most cleverly negotiated deal in his career—the Jeep Wagoneer. This old truck was their lifeline now. It was their means to a new life far away from the post-apocalyptic madness of the big city.

Colton eased the truck out of the garage and worked his way down the driveway until he had to veer through the front yard to avoid the Suburban. As he wheeled his way around the landscaping, all three of them looked toward the west where fire danced above the tall oak trees. Reminiscent of a scene from *Gone with the Wind*, the magnificent antebellum homes of Belle Meade were in flames.

Madison began to sob now. "Will we ever be able to return?"

"What about our things?" asked Alex.

"Having somewhere to live is home. Having someone to love is family. All we need is right here in this front seat—our family." With that, Colton drove onto the road and led the Ryman family on a new adventure and to a new home.

They'd reached their turning point—a point of no return.

Book Three: TURNING POINT

If you've come this far, you know The Blackout Series is designed to provide an imaginative journey into life after a major collapse event. Not everyone is a prepper, and the Rymans certainly fell into the non-prepper category. However, they're learning—the hard way.

At the end of book two, Zero Hour, they'd reached a consensus as a family that Nashville and the areas surrounding their home were unfit. The unknown destination of Shiloh Ranch seemed less dangerous than the known perils threatening them on Harding Place. So they bugged-out.

The perils of bugging-out are on full display in Turning Point—especially if (a) you wait to long and (b) you don't plan for all unforeseen contingencies. My goal in writing Turning Point was to provide the reader many of the realistic scenarios one might face as they're forced to leave their home.

In our busy lives, we scurry to and fro, using the highways and the byways to move from Point A to Point B. We take this freedom of movement for granted. In a post-apocalyptic world, everything changes, especially freedom of movement.

You see, in a grid down scenario like the one experienced by our characters in The Blackout Series, your world gets much smaller. The center of your universe starts with where you live, and can only expand as far as your means of transportation will carry you—feet, horse, bicycle, old car, canoe, etc.

The Rymans, thanks to some forethought and the art of negotiation on the part of Colton, were fortunate to have a pre-1970 vehicle which was immune to the massive blast of electrical energy released by the solar storm. The old Jeep Wagoneer served them well throughout the truck, showing its ability to get shot at with both bullets and arrows.

During their bug-out expedition, the Rymans faced a number of obstacles. There were the marauders who manned overpasses, underpasses, bridges, and town boundaries. They experienced natural roadblocks including fallen trees, horrendous storms and an important factor in this saga—The Tennessee River.

Above all, they experienced the depravity of man, and child. Children will grow up fast in the post-apocalyptic world but they will still need the guidance of an adult. The boy scouts at the Devil's Backbone were led down the wrong path of survival by their scoutmaster, who paid the ultimate price at the hands of Madison, who notched a couple of kills in Turning Point. Alex has grown into a woman with nerves of steel and an eye for trouble. She has an intuition that has developed throughout her post-apocalyptic experience. She also has learned that her fellow teens are prepared to step up as well.

The quaint town of Savannah has a problem—Ma Durham and her offspring, Sheriff Junior Durham. Like every tyrant before her, she takes over everything for the *greater good* and the *protection of Savannah's citizens*. However, it's not Savannah's citizens who benefit. There are those who are prepared to resist Ma Durham's tyranny.

Enter the *disdants*, as the dissidents are referred to by Junior Durham. Led by beloved football coach Joe Carey of the Hardin County High School Tigers, local students and athletes went into hiding for the sole purpose of fighting back against Ma Durham, and surviving. A few of these young men play an instrumental role in saving Colton from discovery and assisting the Rymans in escaping the grasp of Junior and his Ma.

But, despite their successes and evasion of imprisonment, or worse, the Rymans still have a major obstacle to overcome—the Tennessee River. The route through Savannah was out of the question. The Pickwick Dam to their south was closed and blocked by the National Guard. The bridges farther north were either blocked by locals or manned by ransom-seekers.

As luck would have it, there was another option, one that hadn't been used regularly in decades. Old Man Percy, an elderly black gentleman pushin' a hundred years old, owns the dormant Saltillo Ferry. He agrees to fire up the old vessel and tote the Rymans to Saltillo, a small town of three-hundred-three inhabitants.

And one very dear friend, one of Colton's earliest clients, Russ Hilton. Hilton and his family moved to the tiny town to make a home for themselves as his country music career faded. They constructed the Hillbilly Hilton as a hangout for their neighbors and friends. The Rymans enjoyed a night of their southern hospitality, which included a song by Colton and Russ, and a respite from the travails of the road.

Invigorated by their fun, relaxing evening in Saltillo, the Rymans head south for the final thirty miles to Shiloh Ranch. It was intended to be an easy trip until a brutal thunderstorm collided with their progress.

The Rymans had lost their windshield wipers on day one of this bug-out when a marauding woman attempted to bash in their windshield with a tire iron. Madison, who was the family expert in using a vehicle as a weapon, shook the woman who was holding onto the windshield wipers for dear life, back and forth. Finally, utilizing the age-old technique of punching the gas and abruptly stopping,

Madison threw the woman, and the windshield wipers, to the asphalt pavement. The wipers were ruined, as was the skull of the marauder.

In any event, wiper less, the Rymans elected to ride out the storm after a bolt of lightning brought a tree down right in front of them. In Colton's attempt to hide the truck, he got it stuck.

So they decided to hoof it—a fifteen mile hike to the Promised Land—Shiloh Ranch.

From Turning Point …

They made their way onto Federal Road and once again took in the smells emanating from the Tennessee River. The sounds of overflowing, rain-swollen creeks became deafening as they entered the canopy of trees which enclosed the quickly narrowing road that ended at Shiloh Ranch.

Excited, yet nervous, Colton could sense Madison and Alex picking up the pace. Madison giggled a little as she broke out into a slight jog. Alex laughed as she began to run and pass her mother.

Not wanting to be left behind, Colton joined them and grabbed his girls' hands as they rounded the bend to the entrance of Shiloh Ranch, giddy with excitement—until they stared down the barrels of half a dozen rifles.

Book Four: SHILOH RANCH

The Rymans made a decision to leave their home and chose a path into the unknown. They loved one another and they loved their life together. They made a decision to survive rather than succumb to a certain fate. Madison said it best around the campfire one night—*I survived because the fire inside me burned brighter than the fire around me.*

Thus a new chapter in their lives began at Shiloh Ranch, the vacation home of their friends Jake and Emily Allen. Jake, a country singer with an entertainment venue in Branson, Missouri, had been a long-time client of Colton's as well as a family friend.

By sheer coincidence, Jake, Emily, and their teenage son Chase happened to be at their two hundred acre cattle ranch located on the west bank of the Tennessee River in Hardin County. Shiloh Ranch, which was maintained by Stubby Crump and his wife, Bessie, was ideally suited for bugging out. Over the past couple of years, Stubby and Jake had added dairy cows, extensive gardening, and alternative-energy sources with an eye towards off-grid living. Their steps toward sustainability and self-reliance paid off when the power grid collapsed at Zero Hour.

The Rymans quickly assimilated into the extended family at Shiloh Ranch and a normal routine was established. One of the aspects of life in a post-collapse world was foraging. The inner debate between looting and foraging will always be a part of the prepper conundrum. The same applied to the activities of Chase and Alex who had become a team. They would explore areas within the Shiloh / Pittsburg Landing area to find empty homes and requisite supplies.

Their rules were simple—only get what we need and be careful. Rule one was followed but rule number two, be careful, was difficult for teenage Chase to abide by. Whether it was because he was trying to impress the pretty girl, or because he was raised largely unrestrained, Chase pushed the envelope constantly. In a world where danger lurks in the form of your fellow man, unnecessary risks could get you killed.

Although Colton assumed that Junior Durham was angry over the Rymans' escape from Savannah, he didn't expect it to become an obsession. For Junior, he'd become determined to find the Rymans and punish them for embarrassing him. Determination turned to obsession, which then became *all that matters*.

When Chase and Alex let down their guard and placed themselves in a compromising position, Junior's men pounced and kidnapped Alex. She was taken to Savannah where Junior tormented her. The women of Savannah had not fared well since the blackout. Junior and his friends were sadistic. Alex faced a certain fate.

But a rescue effort contrived by ex-Army Ranger Stubby, together with the assistance of the Rymans' rescuers—the Tiger Resistance led by Coach Joe Carey and his sons Beau, Jimbo, and Clay, was mounted to save Alex. The plan was working flawlessly when the wild card inserted itself into the game.

Chase, perhaps wanting to make up for the mistake that put Alex in harm's way, or in an effort to be the *big hero*, once again threw caution to the wind. In the chaos and darkness which surrounded Cherry Mansion during the rescue effort, he undertook an ill-advised shot in Alex's direction.

He missed his target, the two men who were dragging Alex towards Junior's home, but ruptured a propane tank instead. His second shot punctured two nearby gas cans. His final shot ignited the fuel mix creating an explosion that sent fire into the darkness and which engulfed Junior's bungalow on the Cherry Mansion property.

The scene was surreal as the devastation froze all the participants in the battle, except *one*. *One* who was watched through the eyes of Ma Durham and her new companion—the spirit of a Civil War hero.

From Shiloh Ranch …

Burgundy. It was Hardin County Tigers burgundy. Number 1. Gunfire continued to fill the night air from all directions. The young man was undeterred. He'd reached his destination. Briefly, he crouched down and lifted up a lifeless body.

Number 1 began running towards the neighborhood to Ma's left. He was fired upon but escaped unscathed with the blonde hair of the young woman flowing over his shoulder.

Ma stared into the fire, mesmerized. The roof of Junior's home collapsed to the ground, causing a rush of sparks and flames to gush out in all directions. Despite the intense heat created by the burning home and the surrounding vegetation, a chill came over her body. Ma unconsciously balled up her fists, unaware that a figure had joined her in the window. It wasn't Junior.

It was an aberration — a ghost who had been in a similar position one hundred fifty years before. The hissing sounds coming from the flames provided a voice for Union Major General William Wallace, who whispered in Ma's ear.

Fight fire with fire. Fight fire with fire.

Ma gritted her teeth and set her jaw. She mumbled the words but only loud enough for General Wallace to hear.

"When you poke the hornets' nest, ya better make dang sure you kill 'em all. If you don't, you're gonna suffer their wrath."

Book Five, HORNET'S NEST

Hornet's Nest opens where Shiloh Ranch left off — the chaotic scene resulting from the explosion of the propane tank. Chase decides to take an ill-advised shot at Alex's captors and misses, puncturing, and then igniting, a five-hundred-pound propane tank.

The resulting explosion engulfed Junior's bungalow in flames and knocked Alex free from Junior's men, but left her unconscious with a likely concussion.

Beau and the Bennett brothers race to the rescue. Beau scoops Alex up in his arms and hustles her to safety. When he realizes the seriousness of her injuries, he admits her to the hospital (after running over one of Junior's men).

As Junior's army of rogue deputies descend upon the hospital to lick their own wounds, Beau, with the aid of Colton, Jake, Chase, and Coach Carey, escape deep into South Hardin County where they take Alex to recuperate.

This is where Mrs. Rhoda Croft is introduced and her dairy farm for wayward girls, so to speak. Following the solar storm, Junior began to round up the young woman of Savannah for nefarious purposes. Many escaped to Miss Rhoda's place and other surrounding farms. The girls, all of whom know Beau from high school, immediately become intrigued with Alex's heroics and she develops a loyal following.

Meanwhile, back at Shiloh Ranch, Stubby realizes that a war is coming. The Durham's will be furious and they have to prepare for the inevitable battle. Stubby rallies the ranchers on the west side of the Tennessee River while Coach Carey readies his Tiger Tails in Savannah.

Alex, who has recovered, mostly, suggests that the displaced young women of Savannah are ready to join the fight. She believes Chase is the right man for the job of training them to help in the task. Her call turns out to be correct as Chase steps up — and out — of the large shadow of his father to create the Feisty Fifteen, Alex's platoon of loyal young women ready to take their town back.

The plan is developed and implemented. The first phase is to set up sniper positions for Charlie Koch, an expert marksman, on the north side of the bridge leading into Savannah, and for Alex, who creates a hide atop an ancient Indian burial mound.

As Junior and his men begin to cross into West Hardin County, Charlie and Alex unleash a barrage of high-powered rounds on the men. Many were killed and some of the vehicles were disabled, but Junior pressed on because he had the numbers.

Phase two of the resistance kicks in at this point. Alex travels with Colton to Croft Dairies to meet up with Chase and the Feisty Fifteen. While they are traveling to Savannah to join Coach Carey's Tiger Tails, Stubby and his men take up positions along the ridge on both sides of Shiloh Church. Just like General Beauregard did at the Battle of Shiloh, Stubby hoped to stop Junior's advance towards Shiloh Ranch and defeat Junior and his army of rogue deputies.

The battle begins on both sides of the river. The Tiger Tails pair off with the Feisty Fifteen to conduct insurgent-style actions on Junior's skeleton crew left behind to defend the town. Alex, Beau, and Colton take out the guards and secure the Hardin County Detention Center.

They turn their attention to the blockade at the west bridge leading over the Tennessee River. During the gunfight, one of Junior's men escapes down an embankment and runs toward Cherry Mansion. Beau and Alex, despite her recent injuries, hunt the man down. They both focus their eye on the prize — Ma Durham who is inside the mansion.

The second Battle of Shiloh is fierce. Stubby's men have driven the remaining deputies into a hasty retreat. While they are chasing them down in The Woods, Stubby isolates Junior who attempts to flee through the Hornet's Nest back to Savannah.

The hunter stalks his prey through the thick underbrush and the ghosts of the many who died in that very spot during the Battle of Shiloh in 1862. Stubby, using his excellent tracking skills, captures Junior and resists the urge to kill him. The townspeople of Savannah deserve to face this tyrant, thought Stubby.

Meanwhile, Alex, using her knowledge of the inside of Cherry Mansion from her prior captivity, sneaks up the stairs towards Ma's bedroom with Beau in tow. They immediately surprise Ma and Bill Cherry in her bedroom watching over the gunfight between Junior's men and Coach Carey with Colton's assistance.

Beau raises his weapon and fires at Ma, but she grabs Cherry and pulls him in front of her as a human shield. Cherry is killed by Beau and Alex immediately pounces on Ma. With every fiber of her being, Alex wants to kill Ma and the evil within her. But like Stubby, she chooses to keep her alive to face the people she's tormented for these many months.

By the next morning, the word had spread of the destruction of the Durham's tyrannical hold over Savannah. The residents cheered as they learned Ma and Junior would face justice. Immediately, plans were discussed to make Savannah great again.

Elections were scheduled, a barter economy was established, and finally, the Durham's had to face the town. A debate raged among the town leaders and the citizens. Some wanted to hang the Durhams from the highest tree. No trial, no judge. Just do it. Others thought a formal process should be followed. Some believed the Durhams should be turned over to the Federal government at the FEMA facilities in Jackson.

In the end, the passionate plea for forgiveness provided by Pastor Bryant spared the Durhams lives and they were delivered to FEMA by Coach Carey, Beau, Colton, and Alex.

A huge weight had been lifted off the town's shoulders as the evil was purged from Savannah. A big Thanksgiving celebration was planned and Coach Carey even suggested a scrimmage between the Hardin County High School football players.

The day was beautiful and the comradery between all was apparent. Savannah was on the right track to creating an oasis in a post-apocalyptic world. The football game was underway to the delight of all. The guys hammed it up for the crowd while Alex and Beau emerged as the *it couple* of Savannah.

Then, Alex heard it first — the steady rumble of large vehicles approaching town. As the roar grew louder, Stubby heard it as well, and then the others. One-by-one, the people of Savannah migrated back to Main Street in front of the gazebo at Court Square. As the citizens filled Main Street, a voice boomed though a loudspeaker:

"*Attention, attention. You are conducting an unlawful assembly in violation of the President's Declaration of Martial Law. You are to cease and desist immediately. Place any weapons on the ground and stand still with your hands up! You are all under arrest by orders of Major Roland Durham, commander of the Federal Emergency Management Association headquartered in Jackson.*"

My friends and dear readers, it appears Hell is empty and the Devils are all here.

The saga concludes in — DEVIL'S HOMECOMING
Enjoy!

Epigraph

The next time satan reminds you of your past, remind him of his future.
~ Matthew 25:41
*****

We shall not fail or falter; we shall not weaken or tire. Give us the tools and we will finish the job.
~ Winston Churchill
*****

The only way to deal with an unfree world is to become so absolutely free that your very existence is an act of rebellion.
~ Albert Camus, French philosopher
*****

Death leaves a heartache no one can heal. Love leaves a memory no one can steal.
~ Albert Einstein
*****

I am the storm.

Devil's Homecoming

Book Six
The Blackout Series

Prologue

When a deer stares into the headlights of an oncoming vehicle, its eyes fully dilate to capture as much light as possible. There is a brief period of time when the deer stares into the beams, seemingly paralyzed—mesmerized by the threat hurtling towards it. In reality, the deer cannot see at all during this brief moment and freezes until its eyes can adjust. As the vehicle closes the gap between it and the helpless deer, what happens next is in the hands of the driver.

Like an animal frozen in fear, humans have a similar *deer in the headlights* reaction to certain stimuli. Our mental state can cause a form of temporary paralysis from anxiety, fear, panic, surprise or confusion. Like the deer that freezes instead of running safely out of the vehicle's path, humans become stuck in time. While they perceive the threat, the fear response of standing still is a natural defensive reaction. Our bodies become rigid, our heart rates decline, and muscles become stiff.

In theory, our bodies are freezing as a defensive mechanism to make us less noticed by a potential predator. That's the theory, anyway.

If the driver slows to avoid a collision, the deer's eyesight will adjust and it will quickly bound off the road into the relative safety of the woods. But how does a human react when sensory perception processes the threat, clearing the way for a reflexive reaction?

Much has been written about a human's fight-or-flight response to a perceived event, attack, or threat to its survival. In animals, the reaction varies from escape, to fight when cornered, and in some cases, like the Myotonic, Tennessee Fainting Goat, they faint to *play dead*. In humans, the consensus is that men tend to fight while women tend to flee. It's just human nature.

However, in large groups, humans tend to follow the leader—especially when faced with an imminent threat to their survival.

From Hornet's Nest …

As the citizens filled Main Street, a voice boomed through a loudspeaker.

"Attention, attention. You are conducting an unlawful assembly in violation of the President's Declaration of Martial Law. You are to cease and desist immediately. Place any weapons on the ground and stand still with your hands up! You are all under arrest by orders of Major Roland Durham, commander of the Federal Emergency Management Association headquartered in Jackson."

Chapter 1

Afternoon
Thanksgiving Day, November 22
Court Square
Savannah, Tennessee

"RUN!"

The gaping open mouths of the residents of Savannah couldn't speak, but one managed to find the word that brought them out of their collective semiconscious state. That simple word triggered a complex series of reactions.

"RUN!" repeated another.

Like popcorn kernels boiling in hot oil on a stove, eventually the kernels succumb to the heat and explode. In the blink of an eye, the psyche of the citizens of Savannah detonated, sending them scurrying in all directions.

Women and children were knocked down and trampled. Men momentarily stood in defiant disbelief at the disruptors of their Thanksgiving Day celebration. A few, however, kept a clear mind throughout and quickly analyzed their options.

"Colton," said Stubby, grabbing the arm of his new, trusted friend, "quickly, go to the horses. Take Bessie and Madison and return to Shiloh Ranch. Prepare to leave immediately. Begin taking as many things to the Wolven place at Childer's Hill as you can."

"What about you?" asked Colton.

"And Alex?" added Madison.

Stubby searched through the chaotic crowd, seeking out Jake and his family. His short stature prevented him from seeing over most of the people running in all directions. Then his eyes were drawn to the vehicles that slowly rolled onto Main Street.

The scene was reminiscent of his days in Cambodia when U.S. troops would descend upon a small village, frightening the children, to the dismay of its residents. Over time, the villagers became used to the intrusion, but their fear subsided when they learned the battle would take place elsewhere.

Now, in Savannah, Tennessee, it appeared FEMA had brought the battle to Smalltown, U.S.A. A convoy comprised of black MRAPs bearing the logo of Homeland Security coupled with several tan-colored Humvees spread out on both sides of Main Street. Camo-laden soldiers filled in the gaps with their automatic weapons pointed in all directions. Thus far, no shots had been fired.

"I need her and we've got to go!" he replied, shaking the parallels to Cambodia. He turned to Alex. "Do you still have the keys?"

"In my pocket," she replied without hesitation. "Are you thinking what I'm thinking?"

"Yeah, but we gotta go while they're distracted."

Stubby kissed his wife and Alex hugged her parents.

"I'll be fine," she whispered to them and then immediately began to run around the gazebo toward the Detention Center. Then she added over her shoulder, "Take Snowflake home too."

Stubby checked for the Allens one more time and took off after Alex. The two had a brief window of opportunity and they had to hurry.

*****

Colton grabbed Madison firmly by the hand as she attempted to protest Alex's decision. Both parents maintained concern for their daughter, who was still recovering from a concussion, but they had grown to accept Alex's new role in the community. She was a freedom fighter in a way, respected by everyone for the challenges she'd faced and overcome. Mostly, she was revered as the hero who took down Ma Durham.

"Maddie, she'll be fine," said Colton as he tugged her toward the bridge. "Bessie, are you okay?"

"Oh yeah, let's get out of here," Stubby's wife replied as she led the way through the throng of panicked people.

"This is Major Roland Durham, commanding officer of FEMA in Jackson. Pursuant to the President's Declaration of Martial Law, I command you to halt, drop any weapons, and put your hands over your head!"

Colton glanced over his shoulder as the three began to run toward the horses. Either the masses didn't hear Rollie's commands or their intense desire to flee overrode any consideration of compliance. This was fine with Colton because every moment the standoff continued, he and the women would be closer to safety.

They approached the grassy area where over a dozen horses had been tied off during the Thanksgiving Day festivities. The horses were spooked by the high energy emanating from Court Square. Their lack of cooperation and anxiety almost got Colton kicked as he retrieved Snowflake first and then the others.

"Halt!" Rollie bellowed over the loudspeaker. "No one is authorized to leave this area. Drop your weapons and put your hands in the air, or we'll shoot!"

Colton urged his horse up the embankment and onto the bridge. He pulled Snowflake behind him and, likewise, Bessie brought along Stubby's horse. The three riders made their way through the maze of concrete barriers, hoping that FEMA wasn't waiting for them across the bridge.

CLIP-CLOP—CLIP-CLOP—CLIP-CLOP.

The horses picked up the pace along the concrete bridge, which crossed over to the west. Both sides of the highway were cluttered with the debris of battles fought. The dead bodies had been removed, but the hulls of destroyed vehicles remained.

When Colton cleared the bloody stains of Junior's men shot by Charlie and Alex, he turned the group off the road and onto the fields leading into the Shiloh Battlefield National Park. He led the entourage into a patch of woods and stopped, allowing everyone to catch their breath and release their emotions.

The shouts and the booming voice of Rollie over the loudspeaker was barely discernible from this distance. The comfort of safety allowed Madison to gather her thoughts and realize that once again, her teenage daughter was at risk. She slid off her horse and collapsed in a heap in the cool grass.

"Colton, I thought this was over," she said as she began to cry. "I thought we could get our lives back to normal. I thought …" Her words trailed off as she began to openly sob. She was losing control.

Colton dismounted and joined his wife. "Maddie, I know. Me too. None of us anticipated this."

Madison was breathing rapidly to the point of hyperventilation. "Alex. Colton, she's just a kid. She plays golf. She's on Facebook. She studies algebra. She's not a soldier!"

Bessie came to Madison's side as well and tried to comfort her new friend. "Honey, Stubby will take care of her. He won't let her get hurt."

Madison shot back, "Stubby keeps putting her in the line of fire! She's not an Army Ranger. She's a kid!"

The words stung and Bessie subconsciously wrapped her arms around herself, providing a comforting hug.

Colton tried to comfort her further. "Maddie, please calm down. Alex is an extraordinary young woman who has grown throughout this entire ordeal. You've said it yourself. We have to trust in her abilities and Stubby's wisdom. Also, you've got to trust that God will protect her and Stubby in doing …" Colton paused and then continued as he looked into Madison's eyes. "Well, in whatever they're doing, okay?"

Madison nodded, although she didn't appear to have her heart in it. "What are they doing?"

"God only knows," said Colton as he looked back to Savannah, searching for answers.

Chapter 2

Afternoon
Thanksgiving Day, November 22
Court Square
Savannah, Tennessee

"Round 'em up, boys! We've got runners!" shouted Rollie over the loudspeaker. "You people have one last chance to stop where you are, or I'll consider your actions as hostile against the United States government and the power vested in me by the President under martial law. Do not make me shoot you!"

Two dozen men poured into the crowd from behind the convoy of FEMA military vehicles. They slapped people to the ground and physically beat anyone deemed uncooperative.

During the melee, Jake, Emily, and Chase had slowly retreated in a wooded area near the football field. They hid behind the three-foot-wide trunks of hundred-year-old oaks to weigh their options.

"We wasted too much time looking for everyone else," said Chase. "We've got to get to the horses now. This way!"

Chase hooked his arms inside his parents' and led them down a well-worn trail through the patch of woods towards Cherry Mansion. It was a path he was familiar with, having used it the night he accidentally blew up the propane tank that nearly killed Alex.

He was sure of himself—confident in his abilities. But what he'd learned was that his overconfidence was the most dangerous form of carelessness. Chase simply didn't consider the possibility of a missed shot and where the projectile would land if it didn't hit its mark. His desire to right the wrong that had landed Alex in the hands of the Durhams in the first place blinded him to the likelihood that he might miss with his second shot or his third. Confidence was good but overconfidence always sank the ship.

"This way." Chase encouraged his parents toward the bridge and the horses. Jake's chest was heaving and he was clearly winded. They reached an opening as they approached the rear of a group of local businesses, which gave Chase an opportunity to glance back toward Main Street. The soldiers had driven a wedge within the center of the crowd, effectively dividing them down the middle. They were systematically handcuffing people, who lay prone on the ground.

"Son, I've gotta catch my breath. Just gimme a minute." Jake immediately stopped before receiving a response and bent over, clutching his knees.

"Dad, we don't have much time," said Chase. "I hate to tell ya, but we're gonna have to run the last hundred yards or so to get to the horses. We'll be exposed on Main Street the whole time."

Emily pointed to the western horizon and nodded toward the setting sun. "It'll be dark soon, can't we wait 'til then?"

"Maybe, but it's a matter of time before the soldiers make their way to the bridge to lock it down," replied Chase. "Plus, they'll confiscate the horses. I don't think we can chance it."

Jake stood up and put his hand on Chase's shoulder. "You're right, son. We've gotta go. We don't wanna get stuck on this side of the bridge."

Chase nodded to his dad and he led the way along the alley littered with empty boxes and trash cans. In between buildings, he'd look to see if the soldiers had made a move toward the bridge. Thus far, they were still preoccupied at Court Square and the immediate vicinity in front of the courthouse.

The Allens eased along the back side of the last commercial business in line and faced the charred, skeletal remains of the Hickory Pit BBQ Restaurant across Main Street.

"They're coming," whispered Chase, immediately causing Jake and Emily to snap their heads to the east. "I see three men, all armed. We've got to go."

"Son, they're too close," said Jake. "If they don't run us down, they may just open fire and cut us down."

Chase looked at the approaching soldiers and then to the horses, which were tied up by the bridge. They needed a distraction. He immediately cursed himself for coming to this Thanksgiving shindig unarmed. *I let my guard down. We all let our guards down.*

Still a teenager, Chase was as unprepared for this post-apocalyptic world as anyone. Heck, he was still unprepared for life. He was mature enough to know that he couldn't carry the guilt of the danger he'd placed Alex in. He also didn't want to disappoint his dad. He needed to relieve himself of this burden. Self-redemption was the first step to exonerating himself from this guilt.

"I'm going to distract them, which will give you guys a chance to get away," started Chase. "Once I start, don't hesitate and run to the horses. Get out of town."

"Chase, no," his mom pleaded. "We're not gonna leave you here. We'll stick together and figure out another way."

"There is no other way, Mom," said Chase. "I'll be fine. Now, we have to act quickly."

"Son, what are you gonna do?" asked Jake.

Chase leaned out from behind the corner of the building. The three soldiers were getting closer.

"We don't have time, Dad. I'll be fine. I'll make my way to Miss Rhoda's and then I'll cross the river by boat. Get ready."

Before either of his parents could question him further, Chase was off, backtracking his way toward the alley. He darted from building corner to building corner, watching for the armed men walking toward the west.

Then he saw them. He caught a glimpse of the trio passing the third building from the end, dangerously close to his parents' position. He had to act.

Chase ran through the alleyway toward Court Square and then found what he was looking for—the distraction that would do the job. He reached into a trash can and began hurling empty beer bottles toward Main Street.

With a rapid-fire motion, Chase broke the bottles on the sidewalk, the sides of the building and onto Main Street. The shouts from the soldiers gave him the response he'd hoped for. Now, he had to lure them in his direction.

The sounds of heavy footsteps crunching glass and kicking debris filled the alleyway. Chase counted three soldiers. *Perfect!* He tossed three more bottles in their direction, breaking them at their feet.

"Stop!" shouted one.

"Halt!" yelled another.

Chase decided to get in one more lick. He grabbed a wine bottle by the neck and jumped into the opening. He hurled the bottle toward the lead soldier. The heavy bottle crashed against his riot helmet, temporarily stunning him.

Time to go. He began running back toward the woods adjacent to the neighborhood, backtracking into familiar territory.

SPIT—SPIT—SPIT!

Suppressed automatic fire erupted behind him as the soldiers attempted to shoot him. Chase ran like the wind, zigzagging through the woods to avoid the bullets. However, darkness had set in and he was running without regard for the low-hanging branches of the oak trees. His instincts allowed him to avoid the first branch, but his attempt to turn and check on his pursuers prevented him from seeing the second one.

THWACK!

The oak clotheslined Chase, sending his legs out from under him and landing his back against the ground with a thud. He tried to regain his footing and stand, but only made it to one knee. His vision was blurred and then he tasted the salty blood flowing out of his forehead into his mouth.

He tried to get up again.

THUMP!

The buttstock of a rifle came crashing down at the base of his skull, sending him face-first into the pine needles. He made one last feeble attempt to rise on one hand until a boot crashed into his ribs, sending him to the ground. Another boot stomped into his side, followed by another to his stomach.

Chase couldn't breathe, nor could he see, as his vision was blurred by the pain and the blood gushing from his forehead.

CRUNCH!

He was kicked in the face. Chase tried to cover himself with his arms, using his innate defenses to shield his body from further harm. Another buttstock crushed his hand into his nose. Another kick. And then another.

Chase was holding onto consciousness, his mind wandering from his parents' faces and then ultimately to Alex. The blows were relentless as Chase paid a hefty price for his redemption. Then his mind slipped into darkness.

Chapter 3

Afternoon
Thanksgiving Day, November 22
Hardin County Detention Center
Savannah

Alex slowly opened the glass door and entered the lobby of the Detention Center. The only light within the building was coming from the end of the hallway to her right, where the setting sun illuminated the sheriff's office and the adjoining conference room. She drew her sidearm, having left her beloved AR-15 at Shiloh Ranch because everyone thought it was *over*. The building was eerily quiet. *Where is our new sheriff? What about the deputies?*

She eased down the hallway toward the sunlight, her shadow stretching twelve feet behind her along the tile floor. *Something doesn't seem right.* Sometimes, silence said a lot more than you think.

Creak.

Alex resisted the urge to call out like they do on television shows. The character would ask *who's there?* That was so stupid, thought Alex. Of course the bad guys aren't gonna tell ya *who's there*. They really needed to get some new scriptwriters in Hollywood, she thought as she laughed under her breath.

Creak.

The noise was emanating from the end of the hall near the sheriff's office. Alex's palms immediately became sweaty as she recalled being left alone in there with Junior. He was vile and he smelled. Alex knew what he'd had in store for her. She'd narrowly escaped the barbarity he'd wanted to inflict upon her.

Alex lowered herself into a crouch as she inched closer, her gun pointed toward the open doorway of the conference room. She took a quick, deep breath to steady her nerves and then she burst into the room, slamming the partially closed door against the wall with a thud.

She checked the corners of the room and crouched lower to observe the space under the conference table. The room was empty.

Creak.

Alex spun around, pointing her gun in all directions. *Where is the noise coming from?* She approached a bathroom door and looked inside. The steel-bar-covered window had been broken and the cool breeze was blowing a sheriff's deputy's uniform on a hanger suspended from a fire sprinkler.

Alex laughed out loud as she released the tension. She mumbled, "That's what we should have done to Junior. Hanged him."

Then she heard heavy footsteps coming down the hallway. She gathered her wits and stood against the wall next to the door. She pointed her pistol at the center of the opening and waited.

The sounds stopped. Slowly, through the opening, Stubby entered the room.

"Hey," said Alex.

Stubby jumped and flung himself against the door jamb. "Jeez, Alex!"

"Sorry, Stubby," Alex said, laughing. "Did I scare you?"

"Yeah, maybe a little," he replied. "You're lucky I didn't shoot you."

"You would've never had a chance. I think we're clear, but the sheriff is missing," said Alex as she slid past Stubby and headed for the sheriff's office. "I think he slipped out the back."

Stubby holstered his weapon. "We don't have time to play around, Alex."

"I'm not playin'. I'm just not panickin' either."

Alex entered the office. She surveyed the wall of keys and looked at each in the diminishing sunlight. "We're gonna need wheels. Whadya think, big for more hauling room, or fast to get away from those guys out there?"

Stubby glanced out the side door into the adjacent parking lot.

"Look for one labeled Ford Bronco."

Alex ran her fingers along the wall until she stopped and pulled a set of keys off the hook. She tossed them to Stubby.

"Do you remember the layout from when we were here the other day?" asked Stubby.

"Yeah, admin is in this wing. Jail is on the opposite end to the east. The kitchen, intake, and the armory are in the south wing of the T."

"I'm glad you remembered the armory keys this morning," said Stubby.

"Yeah, I planned on giving them to the sheriff after the game. So what's the plan?"

"I'm gonna drive around to the loading docks for the kitchen. The truck will be shielded from the prisoner intake on the other side of the T. You go to the armory and start hauling weapons to the loading dock through the kitchen. Focus on long guns first—battle rifles, not hunting weapons. I'll help you with the ammo. Those ammo cans could weigh fifty pounds each."

"Got it. Should we lock the front door?" Alex surveyed the wall for the keys to the double glass doors. Once they were located, she tucked her pinky finger through the ring. "Good. If they have to break in, at least we'll hear them coming."

Alex took off down the hallway and locked the doors. She stared for a moment at the activity around Court Square. People were lying on the ground everywhere with armed soldiers pointing guns at them and kicking their spread-eagled limbs. "Unbelievable," Alex muttered.

She strained to see through the waning daylight for any signs of Beau. He and Coach Carey had still been on the playing field with most of the Tiger Tails when the armored vehicles had rolled onto Main Street. Through the hectic few moments before she'd raced to the Detention Center, she'd forgotten about Beau and had lost track of his location. Now, as she had an opportunity to take a breather, she realized how much she missed him.

Alex shook off the thoughts of Beau and the others and got back to the task at hand. After Ma and Junior had been taken into custody,

Alex's first thought was to secure the armory. She didn't trust anyone and was concerned that the guns would fall into the wrong hands. Also, she was fully aware of how scarce and valuable ammo was.

She had rustled through the desk drawers of Junior's office that day and found the keys to the solid steel doors protecting the cache of weapons. Alex then slipped them in her pocket and didn't tell anyone except Stubby. He'd appreciated her way of thinking, whereas she knew her parents would encourage her to return the keys to the new sheriff.

Alex had a different perspective and outlook on the world following the collapse of the power grid. Some people might call her cynical or pessimistic, but Alex understood early on how mean people were. There was a reason for the old saying *desperate people will do desperate things*. Alex had grasped the concept immediately in those hours before the solar flare hit, and the events of the last three months only reinforced her convictions.

She made her way down the unlit hallway, using an LED-lit keyring she and Chase had found while scavenging. She missed those days. There was a certain thrill of going through abandoned homes to see what you could find. It sure beat lurking through a dark, abandoned jail where, if the walls could talk, the screams of untold horrors performed by Junior's men would fill the air.

Alex really liked Chase and felt everyone was overreacting in blaming him for her capture. Alex knew the risks every time they went outside of Shiloh Ranch. Chase was a good guy, and Alex saw the potential in him. She pulled her hair out of her face and tossed it behind her. *Back to business.*

For the next ten minutes, Alex and Stubby emptied the armory of the Hardin County Sheriff's Department. Several dozen weapons and thousands of rounds of ammo were removed and placed in the back of the old Bronco. They were impressed with the number of weapons still available considering Junior's propensity to hire deputies. The ammo cache was a huge help, as the ranchers on the west side of the river had spent so many rounds on Shiloh Ridge the day of the battle with Junior.

"Let's grab the radios," said Alex.

"We need to go, Alex," Stubby whispered back.

"C'mon, they're near the intake window," Alex said as she hustled into the dark kitchen.

Stubby followed and the two made their way down the hallway to retrieve the Motorola two-way units, which they crammed into a small gym bag found in a property locker.

As they returned to the kitchen entrance, they heard a crash of glass and muffled voices. The two froze and crouched against the wall. Stubby handed Alex the gym bag full of radios and drew his pistol.

They listened to feet crunching glass on the floor. Then there was a momentary silence. Nobody moved until Alex heard a chuckle, followed by a louder maniacal laugh.

"Well, I'm baaack! Did y'all miss me?"

It was Junior Durham.

Chapter 4

Late Afternoon
Thanksgiving Day, November 22
Savannah

"Tigers! Follow me!" shouted Coach Carey when he realized that the government had arrived in the form of FEMA. He was certain they were not there to help.

As the rest of the town was drawn to the spectacle on Main Street like bees to honey, Coach Carey sensed trouble and immediately gathered his young charges, who were wise beyond their years. The Tiger Tails and several of the girls from Croft Dairies gathered around him in the cover of the oak trees near the end zone of their makeshift football field.

Over twenty teenagers waited, many on one knee, waiting for their coach, and probably former mayor, to give them direction. Coach Carey removed his cap and wiped the sweat off his forehead. Despite the chill of evening coming on, the stress and anxiety caused him to break out in a sweat.

"Listen up," he started. "I don't know what's happening, but it ain't good. The way they've rolled into town, throwing Junior's brother's name around, I feel like we've taken two steps forward and three steps back. We have to put the Tiger Tails back into play."

"We're ready, Coach!"

"Yeah, just tell us what to do!"

Coach Carey clapped his hands softly and then moved closer to the group so that he wouldn't be overheard. "Everybody go back to your original assigned areas. Ladies, stick with the guy you were paired up with. Does everyone still have their radios?"

"Yes, sir," many of them replied.

"Beau, where do you wanna start the channel rotation?" asked Coach Carey.

"Let's start at the top and work backwards," replied Beau. "Today's channel designation will be number 99, Joel Case. Tomorrow will be number 95, Don Scott. Got it?"

"Yeah, QB1!"

Coach Carey surveyed their surroundings and then stuck his head back into the huddle with the Tiger Tails. "The first thing we have to do is assess the situation. It's just like those first few days when Junior and Ma took over our town. We're gonna do recon and surveillance. Report to me periodically, but keep radio chatter to a minimum."

"Coach, is there anything in particular you'd like us to monitor?"

"First, let's establish a pattern of activity. Determine the number of soldiers being used. How often do they rotate? What are they protecting? Are they conducting specific operations?"

Beau added, "In other words, count 'em and tag 'em."

"Exactly, son. Something like that. Avoid engagement, but get close enough to determine their intentions. Try to pick up their radio chatter. Gather intel."

"We'll do it, Coach!" said one of the boys.

Coach Carey stood and gave the scene one more good, hard look. He shook his head in disbelief. His friends and neighbors were being handcuffed and dragged to a central location in the middle of Main Street.

On the far end of the football field, he saw three dark figures dragging a fourth, lifeless body across a gravel parking lot before losing their grip and dropping it in a heap. After hurling several curse words, they yoked the body up by the limbs and started toward Court Square.

Savannah was on solid footing now, he thought to himself. This wasn't necessary. *Just leave us alone!*

Coach Carey's thoughts were so loud in his head that he immediately looked to the faces of the Tiger Tails to see if he'd expressed his inner rant aloud. All he saw in return were several sets of eyes looking to him for guidance and strength.

"Okay, before we break, let's do a quick head count and make sure everyone is accounted for."

The group looked around and several began to count heads. Beau walked around the outside of the group and then became frantic.

"Hey, wait a minute," said Beau. "Has anyone seen Jimbo and Clay?"

"No," said one.

"No, come to think of it, we never saw them again after they started dancing in the other end zone," replied another.

Coach Carey walked into the middle of the field, exposing himself to the FEMA soldiers if they were to look in his direction. He circled around, desperately looking for a sign of his two adopted sons, whom he loved as his own. In the commotion, he'd lost track of the Bennett boys.

He jogged back to the group, worried that the body being taken by the soldiers might be one of the Bennetts. "Okay, let's stick to the plan, except now we need to keep an eye out for Jimbo and Clay. If your post is in the northwest quadrant, search through the woods and also for any known hiding places Jimbo and Clay liked to use. The rest of you, keep your eyes open for them as well. Please report to me immediately if you see anything."

"Dad, do you want me to go looking for them?" asked Beau. "We hung out together all the time, so I know their favorite spots."

"You and I will do it together, son. We'll find your brothers."

Chapter 5

Dusk
Thanksgiving Day, November 22
Shiloh Ranch

Colton heard the sound of horses approaching and he immediately grabbed his rifle. Bessie and Madison were moving through the rooms upstairs, packing a minimal amount of clothes for everyone into olive drab military duffle bags. The clothing would be included in the first run of supplies taken to the Wolven place at Childer's Hill.

"Maddie! Bessie! Horses are coming from the Wyatts' direction," shouted Colton up the sweeping stairwell. "Come on down!"

Colton heard a thud as one of the bags of clothing was dropped to the floor, and then the sounds of footsteps came rushing down the hallway.

"Is it Alex?" asked Madison frantically.

Colton peered through the back windows but couldn't see. He moved to the kitchen door and cracked it open. Javy and two ranch hands were running toward the approaching riders.

"Come on!" shouted Colton as he bolted out the door and into the cold night air.

A horse whinnied as the riders slowed to a stop. "Mr. Jake! Miss Emily! You're home!"

Jake and Emily dismounted as they received hugs from Javy and Maria plus a couple of the ranch hands. Colton stopped and his shoulders drooped. Dejected, he found himself torn between being glad the Allens were safe and the fact that the riders did not include Alex.

"Alex?" asked Madison as she ran to join Colton's side. "Is she safe?"

"I dunno, honey," said Colton. "Jake and Emily made it back. Let's go see." Colton took his wife by the arm and they walked to greet the Allens. After Bessie joined the group, Jake and Emily relayed their experiences in town before they escaped. They'd assumed Alex was with Colton and Madison.

Madison buried her face in Colton's shoulder and began to cry. He reassured her and told her not to read anything into Alex's absence. She and Stubby would take care of each other.

The group went back inside while Javy and Maria tended to the horses. They planned on riding to Childer's Hill at first light and they had to also take extra horses with supplies. It was gonna be a long day tomorrow.

"I assume Alex and Stubby were doing something at the jail," said Colton. "Those two appear to be able to read each other's minds. I swear it wasn't thirty seconds after FEMA's arrival that they were off and running."

"What about Chase?" asked Madison. "Where did he go?"

"After he created the distraction, we ran to the horses," replied Jake. "Chase is resourceful. He'll find a way to get safe and back home. He also knows the area around Childer's Hill better than any of us. Chase will be fine." Jake looked down into Emily's face, who began to well up in tears. It was a tender moment between the two parents, who'd had a difficult time recently dealing with their son. Colton decided to reassure them.

"Let me say this about Chase, my daughter thinks the world of him and has the utmost confidence in his ability to survive. Whatever plan Chase employed, it'll work out fine. Don't worry, guys."

Jake patted Colton on the shoulder and then kissed his wife on the cheek. "I think we need to go over our plans."

"Agreed," said Colton. "Why don't you all join me by the fire and warm up. Maddie, do you wanna whip up some coffee?"

"I'll do it, Colton," replied Bessie. "You guys talk and I'll catch up in a moment."

Bessie left for the kitchen and Madison leaned in to whisper to the group, "Bessie is rock solid and unemotional. Do you think she's putting on a façade to hide her true feelings? She has to be worried about Stubby."

Jake led them to the eight-foot-long stone hearth and everyone sat down with their backs to the fire. Colton felt the heat soak into his lower back, which he'd twisted sometime in the last few hours.

"Stubby is a soldier despite all of these years out of the military," said Jake. "Bessie will always have a soldier's wife's mentality. She learned to trust in her husband's abilities to survive."

"I wish I was strong like her," said Madison. "Sometimes I feel like I can rise to the occasion, but others, I'm just a ball of mush." She laughed as she began to shed a few tears. Colton knew his wife was afraid for Alex. Madison had acquiesced to Alex's involvement that placed her in danger, but that didn't mean she liked it.

"I thought it was all behind us," added Emily. "I was settling into a pioneer-style life where we could all live off the land and take care of each other without threats of bullets flying everywhere. Who cares if it was the 1800s again. I was kinda liking it."

"We can have that feeling again," started Jake. "We just have to regroup."

"Regroup and retreat," said Madison. "I feel like we're gonna be on the run forever."

Colton slowly twisted his back as the warmth loosened it up. "Stubby was confident that the Wolven place was a good backup to Shiloh Ranch. He was always thinking ahead like that. I've learned about his survivalist mind-set in the short time that we've been here. He told me that while we can't anticipate every contingency, we have to accept the reality that our plans have to change based on conditions around us."

"Exactly," said Jake. "If we have to leave Shiloh Ranch, then we'll go to Childer's Hill. And if that doesn't work out, we'll all go somewhere else. We're family now, which means we'll stick together, fight together, and survive as a result."

"What if nothing happens?" asked Madison. "When we left

Nashville, I knew our days, or even hours, were numbered. I mean, here at Shiloh Ranch, we don't have an immediate threat from FEMA."

"I look at it the same as when we left our home," answered Colton. "We have to consider the threat from FEMA to be real. As I see it, if nothing happens, we can always come back."

Bessie returned with a pot of black coffee and a tray of mugs. As everyone warmed their bones with the hot brew, Jake reiterated the plan.

"Tomorrow, I'll ride to the Wolvens' with Javy and a couple of men. We'll load up packhorses with gear and supplies. It's been a while since I hunted down there with Chase, but I'll get a handle on things."

"We have a lot of bodies to take with us," interrupted Colton. "Between the existing ranch hands and the Mennonites, we're well over twenty. Where are we supposed to house all of these folks?"

"There are a couple of campgrounds near there that should have RVs, campers, and some small bungalows available. We'll scope it out tomorrow."

"What about food?" asked Madison.

Bessie took that question. "You and I, together with Emily and Maria, will load up the wagons tomorrow and send them down the next day. I'm sure Char has a root cellar, so we'll stock it up. We can always dig another."

"Stubby would say focus on beans, Band-Aids, and bullets," added Emily. "That's what we'll do."

"I have to ask this question, y'all," started Jake. "We all heard them mention Rollie's name over the loudspeaker. I'm assuming that Ma and Junior are a part of this too. Right?"

"I'm afraid so," replied Colton.

Chapter 6

Dusk
Thanksgiving Day, November 22
Hardin County Detention Center
Savannah

"Are you kidding me?" Alex whispered into Stubby's ear. "All of that for nothing? I'm so pissed off right now."

"I'm not surprised," muttered Stubby. "We should've put those rabid dogs down the first time."

Stubby inched closer to the main hallway to listen. Alex carefully set the bag of radios into the kitchen entrance and pulled her gun. The two moved in silence, walking heel to toe. Alex was cognizant that her sneakers squeaking on the tile floor could give them away.

The crunching of glass was heard once again as more people entered the Detention Center. "Unlock these dang doors, Junior! I'm in no mood to cut myself on this glass."

Alex mouthed the word *Ma*. Stubby nodded his head and inched closer, attempting to catch a glimpse of the front entry.

"Let's take them out and end this," hissed Alex. "We should have done it to begin with."

Stubby raised his finger to his lips and shook his head side to side. He held up four fingers, indicating Junior and Ma had at least two soldiers with them. Alex squeezed the grip on her pistol. They needed their rifles to deal with the FEMA soldiers. Handguns wouldn't be enough.

The sound of the steel door rolling up in the intake garage startled them both. While they were focused on the Durhams, the soldiers were entering the Detention Center from the rear. Stubby quickly motioned for them to back down the hallway to the kitchen. They were about to be trapped.

Alex walked hurriedly to the doorway and picked up the bag of radios. As she fumbled her way through the dark kitchen, she bumped into a stainless steel prep table and groaned. Stubby moved past her to lead the way to the loading dock.

Where she was loose and nonchalant before, Alex was now visibly nervous. Their vehicle was on the other side of the wall from the intake entry. As soon as it started, they'd be heard. She was mad for not having a sense of urgency before, silently admonishing herself for lollygagging.

Stubby held the door for her as she slid into the open night air. They could hear voices on the other side of the wall and the sound of shuffling feet on the pavement.

"Move it along!" a man's husky voice bellowed.

A woman could be heard crying as another voice asked, "Why are you doing this?"

"Shut up!" ordered another voice and a thud was heard as the questioner received a blow of some kind.

"Stop! You're hurting him," a woman's voice begged.

"Let's go! Keep moving!"

Alex quietly slipped the bag into the backseat of the Bronco and whispered to Stubby, "I'm gonna get a look. When it appears they're inside, we'll go for it."

Stubby nodded and got behind the wheel.

Slowly, she moved along the ten-foot-tall brick wall that separated the kitchen loading dock from the prisoner intake area of the Detention Center. When she reached the end of the wall, she carefully glanced around the corner. The headlights of a camo-painted M35 Deuce and a Half cargo truck illuminated the large intake entry. A dozen people were handcuffed and standing in the doorway. Alex counted at least three guards watching over them. One of the men was pounding on the steel doors, demanding that someone grant them entry. Alex couldn't make out the words because the big Cummins diesel engine was still running.

She turned and jogged back to Stubby and the Bronco. She slid into the front seat and closed the door.

"They're taking prisoners inside. I saw three guards, with another one trying to get into the building. He apparently didn't have the keys."

Stubby laughed. "I have them."

"You do?" asked Alex.

"Yup, sure do. I removed all the keys from the wall and shoved them into my pockets and this small bag." Stubby reached into his pockets and began to empty keys into the backseats. "I took the ones for the cars, too. Ya never know."

"Very true." Alex laughed. "That truck is pretty loud. I think we can ease out of here. It looks like this driveway leads to the left around that fenced-in area with the razor wire. If you hug the left side, they won't see us."

"Let's roll, then," said Stubby. He turned over the Bronco and steered it along the fence. Alex turned in her seat and watched their rear, looking for any signs of pursuit. She began to breathe easily when she realized they were in the clear.

As Stubby turned south onto Cherry Street, Alex sat up in her seat and said, "Much better."

"We'll head down to Rhoda's. Do you remember the way?"

"Pretty much," she replied. "It was daylight when we came up before. I'll just have to remember where to turn off. The main road is more to our left."

Stubby continued to drive through the neighborhoods until he reached a dead end. He turned left toward County Road 128, which led to South Hardin County. As they approached the intersection, a vehicle raced past and Stubby hit the brakes. Then another followed it.

"I'm glad you left the lights off," said Alex.

"It's hard to see without them, but at least we can't be easily seen."

"Those looked like Hummers," quipped Alex.

"Yeah, military Humvees, like the Hummer H1. They're headed south too."

They reached the intersection and Stubby stopped the truck. "I'm gonna take a look," he said as he exited the Bronco. "Open up the back and grab a couple of those M16s. We might need some real firepower."

"No prob," said Alex as she happily obliged. While she loved the AR-15, which she had relied upon for months, the thought of having the fully automatic M16 as her protector gave her the warm and fuzzies.

Moments later, Stubby returned and met Alex at the back of the truck. She was fumbling through ammo cans, looking for extra magazines and ammo. She held her LED light for Stubby while he got their weapons ready.

"Those Humvees are either going to Miss Rhoda's because they caught one of the girls and coerced information out of her, or they're going to block access in and out of south county. Either way, we're gonna have to deal with them."

Alex and Stubby both entered the truck and sat silently for a moment. Then Alex chuckled and told Stubby about her idea.

Colton had mentioned in passing that they'd passed the airport on the way to Miss Rhoda's after they'd taken her from the hospital. He'd noticed a large banner read *American Barnstormers Tour: Fun Fly Savannah*. Several vintage aircraft were parked on the tarmac near the small terminal. Alex thought it might be a stretch, but what if those planes worked despite the solar flare? They were old looking.

"Who's gonna fly the thing?" asked Stubby.

"I don't know. Maybe the pilot lives around there," started Alex. "The way I see it, we're not gonna get through that roadblock tonight. We don't have a map and have no idea how to get around it. Without some recon, we might just get ourselves caught."

"Well said, grasshopper." Stubby chuckled as he started up the Bronco.

"Grasshopper?" asked a puzzled Alex.

"Yeah, you know, from the *Kung Fu* show," replied Stubby.

"What? *Kung Fu?*"

"Never mind, *young lady*," said Stubby sarcastically. "Keep an eye out. The airport is straight down this road."

Chapter 7

Dawn, November 23
Wolven Place
Childer's Hill

Some towns find it necessary to create a claim to fame. You know, Nashville is the Music City, and Lauderhill, Florida, is the home of the world's largest rubber band ball. Claxton, Georgia, is the fruitcake capital of the world, while Albertville, Alabama, proudly boasts that it is indeed the fire hydrant capital of the world—*male dogs of the world rejoice!*

But for most small unincorporated communities in Tennessee, they're just fine being anonymous and nondescript. They have a *we'll do our thing and you do yours* mentality. Childer's Hill was one such community. Like so many scattered throughout the state, their claim to fame was no fame at all, and that was the way the residents liked it.

"This way," said Jake as he led the caravan of riders, which included Javy and two ranch hands who spoke perfect English. Each rider had a horse in tow, laden with supplies. "Their place is up on the hill on the other side of the Lick Creek Canal."

The Lick Creek Canal was a manmade river created by the Corps of Engineers during the construction of the Pickwick Dam. It was designed to connect several small tributaries to the Tennessee River for flood control. These early efforts had created a vibrant farming community in the area of Childer's Hill.

The horses' hooves clapped along the floor of the wooden covered bridge that crossed over the creek leading to the Wolvens' home. Although shallow in points, a flat-bottomed boat could navigate Lick Creek directly to Shiloh Ranch.

As the group started up the incline to the log house owned by the Wolvens, Jake recalled their history. Fred and Char Wolven were interested in farming as they approached retirement. Living near large cities in Indiana all their lives, they woke up one day and said they wanted to try something totally different. The Wolvens had always dabbled in their small gardens, but Char's love for animals wasn't feasible near the city.

On a whim, they loaded up their retirement vehicle, a Winnebago, and started to tour the southeast. By sheer fate, Fred turned down Lick Creek Road and found his way to the covered bridge, where they were prevented from continuing. Char, always the adventurous one, encouraged Fred to walk to the other side of the canal through the bridge and they found their way to the top of Childer's Hill. They sat there for hours, admiring the view and listening to the sounds of birds. This was their spot.

When they returned to their motorhome, they immediately began to study maps and make phone calls. As it turned out, the property was available for sale and a deal was struck. Fred called Fifth Third Bank, liquidated his retirement, and the Wolvens' retirement home came to fruition.

Now it was about to become the refuge for a couple dozen folks in fear of their lives. Char and Fred wouldn't have it any other way.

Jake led the way through the tree-lined driveway until they reached a clearing at the top of the hill. He stopped the group and paused to take in the view. Childer's Hill was an aberration compared to the rest of the landscape. It rose out of the ground a couple of hundred feet higher than the flatlands below it. Jake, whose only experience in any type of battle had come in the last month, was astute enough to see how easily defendable this property was. They'd be able to see anyone coming for miles.

"Hey, Jake!" shouted Fred as he walked out of a storage building to the left. He wiped his hands off on his overalls and he approached the group. "Y'all movin' in?"

"Fred, how are you?" replied Jake as he dismounted. The two old friends shook hands. Stubby had introduced the two men during a chance meeting at the feed store. The families had hit it off and became friends.

"I'm doin' just fine, but I'm guessin' somethin' must be goin' on over your way," replied Fred.

"Yeah, we've stirred 'em up over in Savannah. I know you and Stubby have discussed this before, but we're gonna need a place to hang our hats for a while until things settle down."

Fred shook Javy's hand and motioned for them to follow him. They strode toward the house as Char exited the entrance, waving as she recognized Jake.

"Hey, Jake, I've got a pot of stew started. Did you come to sing for your supper?"

"I reckon so, Char," he replied. "We'll have to do somethin' to earn our keep."

Fred showed Javy where to unload their supplies, and then Jake filled him in on what had happened in Savannah. The two men found a couple of Adirondack chairs on the porch overlooking Lick Creek.

Fred shook his head in disbelief. "We've been insulated from that mess over there and glad of it. Listen, y'all are welcome to stay here as long as you want, but I'm afraid for your ranch, being left unattended and all."

"Me too, Fred, which is why we intend to bring as much as we can to keep it safe here. If they destroy the house, then we'll just rebuild it. Our lives are more important than trying to fight a military led by the devil."

CHAPTER 8

Dawn, November 23
Hardin County Airfield
Savannah

After they cleared the airport and deemed it secure, they elected to get some sleep before getting an early start. The next morning, they inspected the vintage airplanes, which were parked in an open hangar. In addition to a ticket office, which also contained a number of vending machines, the building contained a large room with a movie screen, theater-type seating, and several exhibits around the perimeter of the room. A beautiful mural adorned one wall with a blown-up photograph of Savannah and the Tennessee River.

"You know what I find odd about all of this," said Stubby as he looked around the hangar containing three vintage aircraft. "It's undisturbed, even tidy. If I didn't know better, someone is looking after the place."

"Do you think the pilots are still here?" asked Alex. "It's our only hope of getting around FEMA's blockades."

Stubby led Alex outside and looked around. There were no houses nearby. The only option was down the road a half mile. Stubby pointed toward the south.

"Let's check it out."

Stubby hustled across the road into the vast parking lot of the Clayton Mobile Homes manufacturing plant. The facility assembled double-wide homes in two parts, each of which were side by side, awaiting furnishings. The plastic wrap covers of the partially constructed units were gently flapping in the breeze as storms and high winds took their toll on the protective measure.

Alex joined him and they took cover behind the first mobile home. They both peered under the plastic sheeting. This half of the manufactured home contained the kitchen, a small bath, half the living room, and part of a bedroom.

They darted from spot to spot, taking cover as they got closer to the administrative offices. When they were only a hundred feet away, they stopped to observe the area. Stubby didn't want to walk up on trouble.

"Do you think they're here?" asked Alex.

"It's possible. A facility this large probably has a cafeteria with food storage. I see several model homes that somebody could hide out in. From what I saw across the street, it doesn't appear that Junior's men showed any kind of interest in this area."

A curtain fluttered in the window of one of the homes. "Stubby, did you see that? Did you see that curtain move?"

"No, which building?"

"That one, with the wooden stairs leading to the front door," replied Alex.

"Okay, listen up. I don't know if they saw us, but we have to assume they did. I want you to run through the parked cars to the other side of the building while I cover you. I'll watch for movement. Once you're in position, I'll try to talk them out. Okay?"

Alex gave Stubby a thumbs-up and prepared to run through the cars. She was off in a flash and ran a zigzagged pattern through the parked vehicles. When she was in position next to a partially constructed home, she waved to Stubby.

Stubby took off for the parked cars and placed himself behind the hood of a pickup truck. He studied the building and didn't see any movement.

"Psssst!" Alex was trying to get his attention. She pointed to her eyes and then the end of the building that Stubby couldn't see. She gave him another thumbs-up.

Stubby nodded and raised the M16. "Hey, inside! We need to talk. Come out with your hands up. We are not going to harm you. We just need your help."

There was movement behind the sheer curtains to the right of the entry door. Stubby swung his rifle to take aim on the shadow of a figure that paced back and forth in front of the window. The occupant was nervous.

"Hello. You inside. Please come out. We will not hurt you. We're looking for the pilots of the old airplanes. Can you help us?"

Two faces emerged in the window, older men wearing glasses. For a moment, they were gone and then suddenly the window was pushed open, allowing the wind to blow the sheers.

"What do you want?" yelled a voice with a heavy German accent.

Stubby glanced at Alex and nodded.

"We're looking for the pilots of the barnstormer airplanes. Can you help us?"

"*Warum?* Why?" asked the German.

Stubby slung his rifle over his shoulder and looked toward Alex, who had him covered. He trusted her implicitly and knew that she would shoot anyone who threatened him. With his arms raised, he walked out into the open space between the parked cars and the model home.

"My name is Stubby Crump and I live across the river in Shiloh. I was hoping you'd give us a ride home."

Stubby could hear their muffled voices as he carefully approached the steps leading to the front door. He studied his cover options. If a gun emerged, he'd hit the ground and roll under the building, which was mounted on wheels.

Stubby inched forward. "Can we talk about it?" he asked just as the front door slowly opened.

An older, heavyset man emerged onto the landing, nervously holding a small gun.

"Drop the gun!" yelled Alex, who maintained her cover behind the corner of the manufactured home.

The man swung his weapon in her direction and then back towards Stubby.

"Hold on! Hold on!" Stubby repeated. "Nobody has to get hurt here. Lower your weapon, sir. Alex, stand down!"

"Drop it!" Alex yelled again.

"Is that a Luger?" asked Stubby, trying to diffuse the situation. "You'll never get off a shot before my friend drops you. Please lower your weapon."

"*Ja*, no sudden moves, *Verstehen?*" the man asked.

"I understand, and so does my friend with her automatic weapon. Now, I've come to you in good faith, so please stop pointing that gun at me."

Reluctantly, the old man nodded and tucked the Luger into his waistband. "My apologies, sir. One cannot be too sure."

"Thank you," said Stubby. "May we come in?"

"*Ja, wo sind sie freunden?* Your friends?"

Stubby waved to Alex, who came around the partially built home. As she trotted, carrying her M16 at low ready, her blond ponytail swished back and forth across her back.

"*Ah, Wunderschön!* She is a beautiful young woman. Please, both of you, come in."

*****

Gunther Splinter and his younger brother, Horst, were the proprietors of the American Barnstormers tour although their touring days had come to an end when the solar storm had caused the collapse of America's power grid. They were a product of post-World War Two Germany, a nation torn apart both during and after the war.

The Splinters had lived in Berlin, and like so many German families, they found themselves foraging for food and supplies in order to survive. After the war, Germany was divided into four sectors, with the Allies—the U.S., France, and England—controlling the west, and the old Soviet Union controlling the east.

The war-ravaged capital of Germany, Berlin, was isolated from the west sector because it was located one hundred miles within the heart of Soviet-controlled East Germany. Food was scarce and the Russian soldiers were brutal in their treatment of Berliners who wandered out of the confines of the city.

Horst and Gunther were young boys at the time, but they recollected how their sisters would have to sneak out of their homes at night to look for food. At times, the girls would have to venture into the forest in search of farmhouses, where they might be given a loaf of bread and some cheese. The entire family developed a survival mind-set as a result of those difficult years.

The boys would frequently go to Tempelhof Airport, where they would watch the Americans fly in food and supplies during the infamous Berlin Airlift. They vowed to become pilots one day, and when their family emigrated from Germany to America, they immediately got jobs on a farm in Wisconsin, where they learned to fly crop dusters.

With the growing popularity of the *Peanuts* cartoons—especially Snoopy and the Red Baron—the Splinters purchased a Spartan three-seater biplane. The aircraft, which resembled the legendary Sopwith Camel, became so popular around Milwaukee that the Splinter brothers quickly became an attraction in local air shows. They eventually added a Bristol Primary Trainer so that each of the brothers could fly and perform aerial acrobatics for their paid onlookers.

The brothers eventually settled down in Savannah because of its idyllic location on the Tennessee River. It reminded them of the Rhine River, which meandered from Switzerland, across Germany, and into the North Sea.

"When the Berlin Wall was constructed by the Russians, the city was cut into two parts," said Gunther. "Families were torn apart as the Russians refused passage from East to West Berlin. The Russians were trying to contain the flood of Germans who fled the east sector and its socialist government."

"The Iron Curtain," interjected Stubby.

"Symbolically, yes," replied Horst. "My brother and I will never forget the joy we felt in 1989. After many years of political pressure from President Reagan, the Berlin Wall was removed."

"I learned about this in my history class," said Alex. "The

President said, 'Mr. Gorbachev, tear down this wall.' Right?"

"You are correct," replied Gunther. "It was a symbol of freedom that Germans will never forget. On that day, Horst and I became proud Americans."

The group sat quietly in the middle of the Clayton model home, sipping bottled water. When the grid collapsed, the Splinters had remained in hiding in their downtown home for several days until Junior's men came around and discovered them. They had been bullied and beaten down while their home was disgorged of its food and medical supplies.

The brothers had discussed the situation and considered flying to another location, but there was too much uncertainty. They'd foraged for a couple of days and then made their way into the cafeteria at Clayton's plant. Horst and Gunther said they'd cried when they opened the dry good storage room in the kitchen. There was enough food to feed them both for six months or more.

With a new sense of commitment to living, the brothers drew on their upbringing and heritage to gather strength to survive. They'd disbursed the canned goods throughout the vast Clayton complex, using hidden storage compartments in the partially built homes. Within the confines of their model home, they kept the bare minimum in case they were confronted by someone. They'd give up a few cans of food to preserve the rest.

Stubby fidgeted in his chair as he nervously glanced out towards the highway. Unlike the Splinters, who were comfortable in their surroundings, Stubby knew Savannah was abuzz with activity.

"Will your planes fly?" asked Stubby.

"Absolutely," replied Horst. "We have kept them maintained and they're full of fuel. Gunther and I understood that at some point, if things did not get better, we would be out of food. Also, these Durhams are like the SchutzStaffel, um, the SS. They were the Nazi criminals capable of unspeakable acts. The Durhams are no different."

Gunther stood and put his hands in his pockets as he paced the floor. "Our family has experienced tyranny by Der Fuhrer and the

Soviets. We will not live under the thumb of these tyrants."

"Come live with us," Alex blurted out. "We have a farm and dairy cows. You can fly us home and we'll find you a place where you can be safe."

"Alex, that's a decision that has to be made by more than the two of us," Stubby admonished.

Gunther patted Alex on the shoulder. "Thank you, young lady. My brother and I must make a decision, as our supplies will run out eventually. We would prefer to be a part of a safe community, but only if we're welcome."

Stubby thought for a moment and considered the importance of getting these weapons and themselves across the river. These men and their airplanes could be assets. His mind raced as he considered whether to fly to Shiloh Ranch, where there wouldn't be a sufficient landing area, or to Childer's Hill, which was their bug-out location.

"No, you know what? Alex is right," said Stubby. "Gentlemen, our group, our extended family, will welcome you with open arms. If you will fly us home, then our home can become your home as well."

CHAPTER 9

Dawn, November 23
Court Square
Savannah

Major Roland Durham, Rollie as his adoptive stepfather preferred to call him, stood next to the gazebo where just the day before, the people of Savannah had rejoiced in their freedom with a Thanksgiving feast. The Welcome Home banner hung by a thread, tattered and torn by the FEMA soldiers as they rounded up the violators of the martial law declaration.

Unlike his brother, whom Rollie considered to be a mama's boy, he'd paid his dues. When one seven-month tour of duty in a Middle Eastern theater ended, he'd insist upon having it extended or being sent to another. When the Corps forced him to return stateside, he hadn't visited Savannah, a town he'd never considered home. Rather, he'd fulfilled his annual training requirements and undertaken additional training on the side with his buddies in survivalist schools. He'd become a jarhead in every sense of the word while serving in the United States Marine Corps.

Rollie was recalled from overseas like many others when the solar storm hit. Initially, he was sent to FEMA Region One to help stabilize Washington. As the city came under the control of the military, he was reassigned by a pencil pusher to Jackson because it was close to home.

Rollie protested the redeployment to his commanding officer, to no avail. He'd said to Rollie, "The country has bigger problems than your preferred deployment, Marine. Besides, by accepting this command, you earn your gold leaf, Major Durham."

It was hard to argue with that, Rollie had thought. He could suffer a tour in West Tennessee while the President got the nation back on its feet. Besides, as a major, he could have some influence over his future back in the Middle East, killing terrorists.

It was three days after Rollie arrived in FEMA's Jackson headquarters that he discovered Ma and Junior locked up in a holding cell. They were about to be transported to the federal penitentiary in Atlanta to stand trial when Rollie released them into his custody. The next day the evidence against them disappeared and the two began planning their revenge on those responsible for his family's arrest.

Much to Junior's chagrin, Rollie was not prepared to roll into Savannah with tanks and helicopter gunships. Rollie tried to impress upon his family that despite the fact that he controlled a sizable military contingent, his activities were still monitored by his superiors. He was also a new commander to this unit. He needed to get to know his men and determine who would be on board with any type of military takeover of a small town.

Rollie began to lay the groundwork for a proposed military occupation of Savannah under the martial law declaration. He gained favor and loyalty by quickly promoting several men to the ranks of second lieutenant and platoon sergeant. Under the circumstances, the men within his unit were largely made up of Tennessee National Guardsmen from various military branches of service. First, he sought out his fellow Marines, especially those without Tennessee ties. After his selective promotions, he allowed these chosen few to pick out the rest of the thirty-man platoon.

While Rollie agreed to clean up Junior's mess, he wasn't gonna destroy his career in the process. However, if the good people of Savannah didn't cooperate, then by the power vested in him by the *good old U. S. of A.*, he'd clamp down hard. One thing Rollie wouldn't tolerate was disrespect.

Now, as the sun was rising over the deserted downtown, Rollie began to feel the power that rank provided him. In just over twelve hours, he'd arrested hundreds of residents and locked them up in the Detention Center. By last count the jail, which usually held fifty or sixty inmates, was now packed to the gills with nearly three hundred locals.

Based upon the affidavits provided to his predecessor, Rollie and Junior created a list of those who might have the most knowledge surrounding the raid on Savannah and Cherry Mansion the night of their arrest. At Rollie's insistence, Junior would start his interrogations with the locals before they executed arrest warrants on the *real perps*, as Junior called the ranchers on the west side of the river.

The worst of the *disdants*, Junior said, *can get the heck out of his town and rot in the FEMA camp*. Rollie expected others to volunteer for that fate. That was fine by him because his pay structure with the Department of Defense included a bonus based upon the number of refugees he managed. Rollie asked Junior to *encourage* as many townspeople as he could to volunteer themselves to FEMA's protection.

"Major?" asked a young pimple-faced corporal.

"Yes," replied Rollie, slightly annoyed at the corporal for interrupting the serenity he was enjoying.

"Sir, the prisoners are secured and we have commandeered several homes in the neighborhood five blocks north of our position. One home is ideal for you, sir."

"Thank you, Corporal," said Rollie. "Let's get a few hours' sleep and then let's see what we're dealing with around here."

Rollie spun around and took one final look at Court Square. *Actually, I could get used to this—my own town.*

CHAPTER 10

Morning, November 23
Hardin County Detention Center
Savannah

The roars and howls of the three hundred plus people crammed into the Detention Center were deafening, yet it was music to Junior's ears. If it were up to him, he'd line them up against the wall and shoot them for their insubordination and disloyalty. In his mind, he and Ma had gone through a lot of effort to secure their town from outsiders and protect these people from starvation or murder. *Some might not agree with our methods*, Junior thought to himself, *but you people are still alive as a result of our actions.*

He and Ma got settled into Cherry Mansion once again after they cleaned the blood off Ma's bed. Junior hoped to find the killer of Bill Cherry so he could thank him for the favor. Then, of course, the murderer would be immediately executed for committing a capital offense.

Once again, Junior was frustrated by Ma, and now his brother, for preventing him from going after the big prize—the rich folks across the river. He knew they were behind this and he would exact his revenge with the help of the military. *They're not gonna outgun my guys this time.*

Junior leaned back in the leather chair that occupied the head of the conference room table. He munched on a partially thawed Egg McMuffin-type sandwich that was part of the MRE supplies provided by Rollie for the prisoners. Junior didn't intend to feed anybody until he got his answers. If they knew nothing and were of no further use to him, he'd force them to sign a request to be admitted to the

FEMA camp. Going back to their home wasn't an option.

He dropped a few crumbs out of his mouth as he scratched another name off the list. The next two names were James and Clayton Bennett, brothers and teenage boys, according to his notes. As he ordered his only deputy to retrieve the boys from their cell, he wondered to himself why they hadn't been part of his work crew at the Vulcan Quarry.

"Sheriff, I have the Bennett brothers here," announced the deputy from outside the doorway. "Do you want to see them one at a time?"

"No," said Junior with a mouth full of food as he stuffed the rest of the sandwich inside it. "Let's see them both."

The deputy forcibly shoved the stout young men into the room and then grabbed them by the collars to keep them upright.

"Well, lookie here." Junior cackled. He stood up and circled the boys. "We've got us a couple of football players. Well fed, too. Whadya make of that?"

"They are pretty hefty, sir," replied the deputy.

Junior grabbed Clay by the arm and forced him to sit in the chair to his right. "Plant the other one at the head of the table," he ordered his deputy. Jimbo was led to the other end of the conference room and shoved into a chair. He wiggled to get comfortable in the seat, having to lean forward because his hands were cuffed behind him.

"Okay, let's start with you," gruffed Junior as he flopped in his chair. "You two are the Bennett twins. Ain't that special?"

Neither Jimbo nor Clay responded.

Junior nonchalantly leaned forward in his chair, ostensibly to review his list, but then he swatted Clay across the side of his head. "Wake up, boy! Which one are you?"

"Clay. Clay Bennett."

"Now, there's a start. Okay, Clay Bennett, where have you been for all this time that has allowed you to stay fat, dumb, and happy?"

Clay glanced toward his brother as the ringing in his left ear subsided. He set his jaw and silently returned Junior's gaze.

Junior shook his head. "Deputy, smack the other side of his face to see if you can shake his memory," ordered Junior.

Before Clay could react, the deputy hit his other ear, causing him to nearly fall out of his chair before he caught his balance.

"Stop!" yelled Jimbo.

"Well, glory be," said Junior. "This one speaks, but unfortunately, it's not his turn yet." Junior raised his arm to provide Clay another whack.

Clay rolled his neck to alleviate the tension and then responded, "We went to Nashville to watch the Cowboys on TV with some friends. We heard the town was back to normal, so we came home."

"How'd ya hear?" asked Junior.

"Huh?"

"How'd ya hear that things were back to *normal*?" Junior pressed the issue, putting a sarcastic emphasis on the word *normal*.

Clay glanced at Jimbo again and thought fast to provide a plausible answer. "We were at a FEMA food distribution location and were told by one of the soldiers that the mayor and the sheriff were arrested."

"And you considered that a good thing? Good enough to return home? Back to normal?"

Clay became nervous and fidgety. He demurred. "Well, I mean, we were going to head home anyway."

"Here you are. Both of you, in fact. Now, where is Carey's real kid?" Junior asked as he thumbed through his list. "Beau Carey."

Jimbo answered for his brother. "He's back too. We're all back," he said defiantly.

Junior stood and punched Clay across the face, knocking him to the floor. "Not your turn, twinkie! When it's your turn, you'll know it. Now, I'm gonna keep bustin' on your brother until, A, he answers or, B, you shut up!"

Clay managed to get onto his knees as blood dripped out of his mouth. "We don't know anything. We just got back a few days ago, I swear."

"Get him up!" ordered Junior. "Stand him up!"

Clay stood up, allowing the blood to flow freely onto the front of his jersey.

Jimbo attempted to stand and shouted, "No!"

In a flash, Junior pulled his revolver and cocked the hammer. He pointed it first at Jimbo, who immediately sat back in his chair, and then at Clay.

"This next answer better be a good one," started Junior, pushing the revolver closer to Clay's chest. "Who would be wearing a Hardin County Maroon sweatshirt with the number one on it?"

Clay answered, spitting blood onto the conference table and Junior's list, "We all have one because we're winners. We're all number one."

CHAPTER 11

3:00 p.m., November 23
Savannah

Coach Carey jimmied the locks on the back side of the State Farm offices and popped the door open. He waved for Beau, who was hiding between a hedgerow and a block wall, to join him. For over an hour, the Careys patiently waited to gain access to the small office building less than one hundred feet to the southeast of the Detention Center. From this vantage point, they could choose any number of windows to gain an unobstructed view of the jail's intake location.

First, Coach Carey and Beau cleared the building and made sure that they couldn't be seen by anyone from the outside. They located an attic storage space where they could hide if Junior sent anyone after them. Coach Carey was satisfied, so they settled in to watch the activity going in and out of the jail.

"Dad, I don't know what's worse, the devil you know or the devil you don't."

"I agree, Beau," said Coach Carey. "Ma and Junior aren't the brightest bulbs, they're the meanest ones, however. They have no regard for human life. They proved that over and over again."

"Should we have executed them?" asked Beau, who offered a sip of his bottled water to his dad.

"I've thought about that every day since we caught them," his dad replied. "Honestly, as it turns out, we're better off that we technically did the right thing by turning them over to the federal government. If we had summarily executed them, I don't think Rollie would've been as professional as he was. There probably would've been a slaughter yesterday."

Beau left the window for a moment and pulled up a couple of chairs stacked in the corner. The men settled in for the long haul.

"Whadya think is goin' on in there?" asked Beau.

"I don't know, but they've locked up half the town. I suspect Clay and Jimbo are in there too."

"Did you get a good enough look at that body last night to determine if it was one of the guys?"

Coach Carey stretched a little closer to the window to get a look at an approaching vehicle off Water Street. "It was hard to tell in the low light, but I think the body they were dragging was taller and thinner than either of our boys. Whoever it was looked pretty dead from my view."

The low rumble of a diesel motor grew louder as two M35 troop carriers came into their view. They slowed as they drove through the unattended security gate, entering the Detention Center compound. The trucks passed intake and drove to the rear parking lot before circling around next to the roll-up doors.

"They're not too tall to fit in the building," said Beau as both intently watched the activity.

"Might be more soldiers," muttered Coach Carey. "Great, just great."

However, only the two drivers exited the vehicles. They lazily walked to the rear and pulled open their canvas coverings.

"They're not bringing anyone in," started Coach Carey. "Maybe they plan to transport some out."

"To where?" asked Beau. "Why not let them go?"

Coach Carey stood and made his way to the hallway. "C'mon, we can get a better look from the storage room."

Beau hustled to catch up with his dad and they arrived at the last window in the building just in time to see the prisoners being escorted out of the jail and toward the rear of the trucks. They all wore chains around their waists and then were tied together by a long chain. There were ten per group.

Several guards escorted them to the rear of the trucks and then brusquely forced them to climb into the back. One woman slipped and fell, busting open her chin on the grated steel steps. She received an additional kick in the ribs for her mistake.

"Dad, look! The last one in line. That's Jimbo!" Beau exclaimed.

"Thank God he's okay," said Coach Carey. "Wait, is that …" His voice trailed off as Clay led a second group into the truck parked to the rear. His jersey was covered in blood and his face was battered.

"They beat him up!" shouted Beau, whose raised voice momentarily caught the attention of a guard. The guard stared in the direction of the building and accompanying parking lot before turning to the task at hand.

"I know, son," said Coach Carey. "I saw, but he's alive. Your brothers are tough boys. Besides, it isn't the first time Clay's had a busted mouth."

"Are you talkin' about that big fight we got into with Memphis Carver last year?"

"Yep, that's the one." Coach Carey chuckled. "Clay learned that if you're gonna fight on the football field, keep your helmet on. It wasn't two seconds after he threw his helmet down that one of their players sucker punched him in the mouth."

"I remember," said Beau. "Clay's bloodied up, but he looks okay. He probably gave them the *what for* and it earned him a couple of shots."

The trucks were filled with four sets of ten chained prisoners before they departed toward the north. Coach Carey surmised that they were being taken to Jackson and the FEMA camps. Based on their surveillance, none of the prisoners had been released to go home. It was possible that Rollie intended to move everyone to Jackson, where he could control them better. There were a lot of hungry mouths in that jail, and a lot of the food had been taken out to be used for the Thanksgiving Day dinner.

"Should we get in the car and go after them?" asked Beau.

"Son, we wouldn't make it a hundred yards. I believe everyone in town is locked in that jail or hiding under their house. If we drove anywhere, they'd probably shoot first and ask questions later. We need to regroup at the house and try to raise Colton and Alex on the radio. I'm sure they'll help us get Jimbo and Clay back."

Chapter 12

Evening, November 23
Hardin County Airfield
Savannah

Stubby leaned over the folding table and studied the aerial maps unfurled by Gunther. He quickly got his bearings and identified Shiloh Ranch, which was split in half by Lick's Creek. There just wasn't an area flat enough to land these airplanes. The ground was undulating and trees dotted the landscape, providing the cows a place to cool off.

He then focused his attention on the area surrounding Childer's Hill. Colton and Jake should be making arrangements to bug-out to the Wolvens' at this point, so landing farther south and west made sense.

"There!" he exclaimed, pointing to a large green space on the map. "This is Johnson's Sod Farm, which is about four miles southeast of the Wolven Place. They supply turf grass to golf courses all over the area. The ground will be solid and flat. Heck, you could land a 747 there."

"*Sehr gut,*" said Horst, pleased with the choice. "We'll fly out early tomorrow morning just as the sun begins to rise."

Stubby continued to analyze the aerial photograph. "It's likely that FEMA has set up a roadblock here, to our southwest. Can we start out flying toward the east and make a wide circle over the dam?"

"*Ja,*" replied Horst. "The route you have chosen will only take up a quarter of our fuel capacity. We can return, if necessary, or travel elsewhere."

"The FEMA soldiers might hear us initially, but they won't be able to place us anywhere near Shiloh or Childer's," added Alex.

Stubby nodded. He glanced again at the proximity of the Pickwick Dam to their flight path. Thus far, the troops stationed on the dam by the Army Corps of Engineers had shown no interest in venturing out into the countryside. Jake and Colton had estimated a dozen men encamped on the structure, blocking traffic and monitoring the dam's functionality.

"Horst and I will prepare the planes," said Gunther. "We need you to bring us any gear that will be traveling with us. The Spartan is a three-seater that can handle more weight. There is a scale in the hangar for our calculations. If there is too much, we cannot risk being unable to take off."

"I understand," said Stubby. "Alex, we'll take care of weighing the essentials and then hiding the rest around Clayton's. For now, we'll leave their food supply behind. We can either pick it up later or use it in case we have to mount another operation from here. Having a weapons and food cache on this side of the river sounds like a pretty good idea."

Horst and Gunther, who wore matching blue jean overalls, practically skipped through the doors into the hangar. If the brothers were wearing white gloves and matching hats, one might think their names were Mario and Luigi.

Alex retrieved the two-way radio from her backpack and sat behind the desk in the front office. Periodically throughout the last twenty-four hours, she scanned the channels, listening for chatter from the Tiger Tails. She never picked up a single communication, which caused her to worry about Beau.

"Let's start at the top, shall we?" Alex mumbled to herself. Normally, she'd start with channel 1 and then work her way up. Subconsciously, she'd become discouraged midway through the channel cycle and moved through the bottom half of the spectrum too quickly.

After several minutes, her heart leapt out of her chest. *"Tiger Tails, red right. Tiger Tails, red right. Return. Red right return."*

"Stubby, I've got the right channel," shouted an excited Alex. "What should I say?"

He rolled up the maps and tied a rubber band around them. Stubby twirled them like a baton through his fingers as he joined Alex in the office.

"Say something that either Beau or Coach Carey would recognize so that there's no doubt it's you," suggested Stubby.

"Tiger Tails, Tiger Tails, QB1. First Date. QB1. First Date. Over."

There were several seconds of silence, which seemed like an eternity to Alex. Did they not hear her? Should she repeat it?

"*Roger, First Date. Status? Over,*" asked a voice that sounded like Coach Carey.

"Clean break. Headed home. You?" replied Alex.

"*QB1 and I are safe. Two of our brothers are in custody. Transported with many others northbound. Need assist. Over.*"

"Stand by," replied Alex. She turned to Stubby, who frowned.

"I thought FEMA intended to round people up," started Stubby. "They must have transported them to Jackson. Do you know who the two brothers are?"

Alex rubbed her face and fought back tears. She was glad Beau was safe, but the Bennetts were not. Returning to Savannah briefly crossed her mind, but she blocked it out.

"He's referring to Jimbo and Clay. They've been taken to the FEMA camp!"

Stubby saw that Alex was distressed and he squeezed her hand. "Don't worry, we'll get them back, but first things first. Tell them to meet us at Croft Dairies on Sunday noon. Can you do that in code?"

Alex nodded and keyed the microphone. "Roger that. We'll be milking the cows after church on Sunday. Beware of the keepers of the south."

"*Roger. Tiger Tails out.*"

Alex tossed the radio on the desk. "Stubby, I should've shot Ma between the eyes. It would've been so easy because I was really mad."

"You don't think I haven't second-guessed my decision? I could have killed Junior and left him in the Hornet's Nest to rot away. We can't dwell on it anymore. Let's fight one fire at a time and then we'll tackle the Durhams later. Deal?"

"Deal."

CHAPTER 13

Dawn, November 24
Hardin County Airfield
Savannah

Most of the weapons and ammunition were able to be loaded onto the two biplanes. Stubby was provided some mechanic's overalls and goggles to make the ride a little more pleasurable. Alex was given a sheepskin-lined, B-3 leather bomber jacket with a scarf. Along with the pair of Ray-Ban sunglasses she'd found while foraging Thursday night, Alex resembled Kelly McGillis in *Top Gun*.

The two vintage aircraft did not enjoy the modern conveniences of starter motors. Alex watched the Splinter brothers go through their final checklists and then Horst, along with Stubby, got settled into the lead aircraft.

Gunther took his position in front of the single propeller and grabbed it with both arms. He stretched up on his toes as high as he could and, with a quick pull downward, gave the propeller a spin. The thought of standing that close to a moving airplane propeller gave Alex the heebie-jeebies. She immediately visualized how Indiana Jones killed his assailant in the *Raiders of The Lost Ark* movie. Propeller blades were a brutal way to die.

But both pilot and propper were old hands at this. The Spartan fired up and leveled off at a steady idle. Gunther quickly settled himself into the cockpit in front of Alex and gave her a quick smile. Alex was nervous about the prospect of flying around in an airplane that was nearly a century old, but she embraced the experience as one more adventure in the apocalypse.

The engine fired immediately and they were ready to pull out of the hangar. The sun was just peeking over the eastern horizon as they taxied onto the runway. The temperature was around forty degrees, and in the open-air cockpit, the wind chill would be below freezing.

"Today, we fly!" shouted Gunther as he followed his brother down the runway and into the sky.

The first thing that Alex realized was that she couldn't see very much. Looking straight ahead, she mainly saw the face of the wooden instrument panel. A glass windscreen approximately six inches tall shielded Gunther, but clear sky was the extent of Alex's visibility.

Gunther muscled the center stick and turned the plane toward the south. This gave Alex her first view of the horizon. She instinctively gripped the seat with both hands as the feeling of falling out of the open-air cockpit grasped her psyche for a moment. Then Gunther completed the turn and leveled out toward the south.

The rising sun hit Alex's face and immediately warmed her body. She began to relax and enjoy the ride. Flying in the open air like this was surreal. She took in the scenery as the clear skies provided her many miles of visibility. Up here, she thought, the world seemed too beautiful and peaceful. Only God should have a view like this.

Gunther banked slightly to the left and then corrected back to the right. This maneuver enabled him to fly side by side with his brother. Alex waved to Stubby, who was only a hundred yards away. He didn't wave back, simply shaking his head. Alex chuckled as she realized Stubby was none too happy about this plane trip.

As they passed to the east of Pickwick Dam, Alex noticed that the soldiers were no longer patrolling the top. In fact, there were only two vehicles, one on each end of the facility, with a couple of guards assigned to each. This was a big change from what her dad had seen.

Another thing she noticed was the incredibly high water levels. During the heavy rains several weeks ago, the water rose rapidly on the banks of Shiloh Ranch. Lick Creek had flooded and Stubby became concerned about the safety of the cows. The dam was not overflowing per se, but the water was lapping up against the top of the spillway.

Gunther turned them toward the right, giving Alex an up-close-

and-personal view of the water. The devastating flooding had taken its toll on South Hardin County. Mobile homes and vehicles were stacked into piles on the north bank of the Tennessee River. Erosion had toppled large trees, exposing their roots. The river had persistently carved its way into the landscape. Alex craned her neck to view the Tennessee as it wound its way from the east. She wondered just how powerful it might become if the rain swelled it beyond Pickwick Dam's control.

They continued westerly now and then Gunther once again performed a series of maneuvers to follow his brother. The population was sparse in the area where they were flying. From the maps they'd studied, Alex immediately recognized Johnson's Sod Farm when they glided past it to their right.

"My brother wants to do a flyby," shouted Gunther.

"By what?" asked Alex, but in a voice that Gunther couldn't hear.

The plane began to circle a hill next to a creek. Several people ran out of a house and shielded their eyes as they looked up at the spectacle of two antique airplanes flying overhead. That was when Alex recognized her parents below. She began waving wildly and smiling. She shouted to the group below, who had no hope of hearing her. Alex realized how glad she was to see her parents.

After doing a complete three-hundred-and-sixty-degree loop around Childer's Hill, the biplanes began their descent toward Johnson's Sod Farm. Gunther reduced the speed to what seemed like a crawl. Alex saw a tab located on the wing flutter as the needle dropped from ninety to eighty miles per hour. She sat up in her seat and looked to see if the plane had a speedometer. She stared back at the device on the wing. It read fifty miles per hour. *This is the speedometer?*

Alex tried to look forward to watch their landing. Once again, only blue skies were within her field of vision. Then she noticed that Gunther, who was shorter than she, couldn't see either. Alex gripped the seat with both sweaty palms. *How does he see to land?*

Gunther then stretched up out of his seat and looked over the side of the airplane. He continued to steer with one hand as he dangled his left arm over the side, craning his neck to look at the ground.

The mile-per-hour needle fell into the red zone. Alex looked over the side too. She could see the ground. The gap between flying and landing was closing. The plane slowed and then the wheels touched down.

Hop—hop—hop.

Gunther gently touched the wheels to the turf a couple of times before pulling back on the throttle. It was a smooth, successful landing, allowing Alex to loosen her death grip on the seat.

As he taxied to a stop next to his brother, Gunther turned around and faced Alex with a grin that showed all the wrinkles of age.

"*Sehr gut, ja?*" he asked.

"*Ja!*" exclaimed Alex, who immediately burst into uncontrollable, sense-of-relief laughter. "*Ja! Ja! Ja! Sehr gut!*"

Chapter 14

Afternoon, November 24
Main House
Shiloh Ranch

Madison comforted Emily as she cried quietly on the front porch overlooking the cows grazing on the hay being dispersed by the ranch hands. Emily did her best to be excited for Stubby and Alex's return, but the lack of news about Chase immediately set her mind to considering the worst-case scenarios.

She had argued with Jake that morning about the decision to leave Chase behind. Jake did his best to remind her that if Chase had been caught by the FEMA soldiers, they would have been as well. Chase was a resilient young man, he'd reminded her, and therefore would find a way to survive until he returned home. If need be, he promised, they'd mount a rescue to bring him back to Shiloh Ranch.

"Emily," Madison whispered in her friend's ear, "they want us to come back inside. Some decisions have to be made and they'll involve Chase. Are you okay to talk?"

Emily nodded her head and wiped the tears from her cheeks. "This world is horrible," she said to Madison. "He's my son, Madison. I love him like nothing else in the world. When Jake was away all the time, it was just me and Chase, you know?"

"Yes, honey, I do," replied Madison. "We're gonna find Chase and bring him home safe."

"I feel like something's wrong," continued Emily. "He's been hurt or worse. I just know."

Madison wiped the tears off Emily's face and kneeled on the deck in front of her. "Emily, Alex has this saying. Whenever one of us is thinking negatively, she uses a golf analogy that goes *don't hook it in the rough*."

Emily laughed. "Golf?"

"Yeah, it's actually brilliant when you think about it. Alex explains it this way. When you're standing on the tee, awaiting your turn to tee off, if you stare at that rough down the left side of the fairway, worrying about hitting a bad shot that might land you in trouble, invariably you will. The more you think about hooking into the rough, the more likely it is that you will."

Emily thought for a moment and then added, "The more you dwell on the negative, the more likely it is that the negative will come about."

"That's exactly right, Emily," added Madison. "Now, I prefer to pray and put it in God's hands and the energy He provides us, but Alex also has a way of thinking that makes sense."

Emily took Madison's hands and rose out of the chair. She gave her friend a hug and whispered thank you in her ear. The two walked into the house, arm in arm, with a new sense of purpose.

*****

Stubby conducted the meeting and laid out the *State of the Union*, as he called it. Based upon his conversations with Colton and Javy, they could have the most valuable supplies moved out of Shiloh Ranch and down to Childer's Hill in two days. The Mennonites were already packed and ready to go, and Javy's men were gathering up all of the supplies in their buried survival caches around the ranch.

Once everyone arrived at Childer's Hill, it would be an inconvenience for everyone for a few days while they got settled. Without hesitation, they were on board to invite the Splinter brothers into the group. Despite their age, the Germans had a tenacity about them that would help the group in the event they had to fight again.

"I know there's a lot of uncertainty concerning FEMA's

intentions," started Stubby. "All I needed to hear was the name Roland Durham and that's when I knew a confrontation was inevitable."

"They'll definitely come to the ranch," said Colton. "Now, whether they'll act professionally or in the mold of Junior is anyone's guess. But I, for one, am glad that we bugged-out to Childer's Hill. We'll be closer together and the terrain makes it more defendable if it comes to that."

Stubby nodded and pulled out a map of West Tennessee, which included Jackson. "Okay, here's the next order of business. We've learned that the Bennett brothers, the adopted sons of Coach Carey, are in FEMA custody. They've been transferred to Jackson at one of three FEMA camps. We need to help Coach Carey find them and remove them from the camp."

Emily stood and voiced her opinion. "Shouldn't we be finding my son too?"

"Emily, we will find Chase, but we don't know where to start," replied Stubby. "The Bennett boys may have some information for us, but besides that, Coach Carey and the Tiger Tails will be preoccupied with retrieving them from Jackson. Without Carey's help, we'll never find Chase, much less rescue him from custody, if that's where he is."

Emily fell back onto the couch and slumped next to Madison.

Madison whispered to her, "Don't hook it in the rough, honey. Trust the guys. They've got this."

"Based upon conversations I had with people during Thanksgiving, it appears that FEMA has established three different facilities," said Stubby, who turned the map on the coffee table so everyone could see.

He continued. "The first one, where Junior and Ma were delivered that day, is located at the Jackson County Fairgrounds. From what Colton and Alex observed, this appears to be an administrative facility as well as a vehicle and supply depot. There were no tents or temporary housing."

"It was the start of a dog and pony show," interjected Alex. "It was designed to suck people into their charade."

"Agreed," said Stubby. "The second location appears to be here at Union University. We believe the FEMA troops are stationed and housed here. From what I was told during conversations with some of the locals after Thanksgiving dinner, there are no refugees or prisoners of any type at this location."

"Where are they?" asked Madison.

"They're located on the east side of town at the Jackson State Community College," replied Stubby. He traced his finger around the location on the map so the group could get their bearings straight. "The campus contains a dozen buildings and a lot of green space, which has been enclosed within a tall chain-link fence. The top has been encircled with razor wire and there are armed guards roaming the perimeter."

"This sounds very risky," said Jake. "Maybe we better opt out of this one."

The close-knit group grew silent as they pondered the suggestion. Some looked down, as they didn't want to be the first to speak.

"I mean, haven't we taken enough risks for one lifetime?" asked Madison. "Surely we can find Chase first. The Bennetts, if they are in custody at Jackson State, are safe and sound. Chase, however, may need our help now."

"Mom, we can't do that," stated Alex firmly. "These guys have saved my, no, our lives more than once. We owe it to the Bennetts and Coach Carey to help. Chase may be there, or he might be walking home as we speak. Either way, I have confidence that he'll be fine while we reciprocate and help break out Jimbo and Clay."

"Anybody else have any thoughts or opinions?" asked Stubby.

Nobody spoke up and Stubby rolled up the maps. "Tomorrow, Alex and I will ride over to Croft Dairies to meet with Coach Carey at noon. He is most familiar with Jackson and can give us an idea of how to get into the Jackson State facility."

"Who do you plan on taking to Jackson to mount this rescue?" asked Madison.

"I'm going," answered Alex immediately.

"Me too," said Colton.

"Yeah, of course you two volunteered," Madison grumbled.

Chapter 15

11:30 a.m., November 25
Croft Dairies
Nixon

Alex bolted out of the skiff and ran up the hill to an awaiting Beau. He was grinning ear to ear as he knelt down to scoop her up in his arms. The two embraced and shared a kiss as tears of delight streamed down Alex's face.

"Hey, lovebirds!" shouted Stubby. "I could use a hand down here." The aluminum boat was rocking back and forth, as the wind had picked up, causing a ripple of whitecaps on the river that morning. Stubby attempted to hold the dock with one hand while tying off with the other, and he wasn't succeeding.

"Oh, sorry, Stubby!" shouted Alex as she led Beau by the hand back down to the dock. They tied him off and then helped him out of the boat.

"My drill sergeant used to tell me that every soldier should learn survival on land, sea, and air," grumbled Stubby, the former Army Ranger who preferred fighting on terra firma. "I've had my fill of the sea and air part."

Coach Carey made his way down the hill to join the visitors. "We got here early. The roadblock was set up at the south end of town just like you suggested, so we had to improvise."

He and Stubby shook hands and the two walked a few paces ahead of the teens. "Glad to see you're in one piece, Coach," said Stubby. "I'm sorry to hear about your boys. Let's talk about where we are and then formulate a plan."

"Thanks, Stubby, and I have an update as well. Miss Rhoda made us some lunch and sweet tea. We'll fill our bellies while we figure out a plan to rescue the boys and Chase."

"Chase too?" asked Stubby.

"Yeah," replied Coach Carey. "C'mon and I'll tell you what we've learned."

The group joined Rhoda and several of the Feisty Fifteen in the dining room. The girls chattered with Alex as they exchanged stories on how they'd escaped the FEMA soldiers. Six of the girls were still missing, but the Tiger Tails were monitoring all parts of the town to find them.

"Okay," started Coach Carey. "Let me tell you about Chase first. After Beau and I pulled out of the adjacent building to gather the Tiger Tails together, we reassigned one young man to continue surveillance. Early this morning, a Red Cross truck arrived and removed four injured prisoners, including one on a stretcher. Based on the description, I'm pretty sure it was Chase."

"Oh no," gasped Alex.

"During the melee, I gathered the Tiger Tails in the far end zone away from the woods," said Coach Carey. "I saw three men dragging an unresponsive body across the adjacent gravel lot. The person was tall and lanky, unlike the build of Jimbo or Clay. Our recon person described the body on the stretcher as tall and lanky, but also described Chase's face."

"Do you think they took him to the hospital?" asked Alex. "Dr. Fulcher will help him."

Coach Carey took a seat at the table and broke off a piece of bread. "No, our team there didn't report any activity. Later, I learned that the Red Cross truck headed west out of town."

"West?" questioned Stubby.

"Yes, the bridge has been cleared and all the military traffic goes west down Highway 64, presumably before they travel to Jackson on U.S. 45."

"Won't that make our trip to Jackson more difficult?" asked Alex.

Coach Carey munched on the bread and chased it with some sweet tea. "Back roads are always the best bet, and based upon what

I've heard, and Stubby correct me if I'm wrong, it's most likely the boys are being held at the Jackson State FEMA Camp."

"I agree, Coach," said Stubby. "We'll take an easterly route. Are you guys familiar with Jackson State?"

Coach Carey and Beau shook their heads.

One of the girls staying with Miss Rhoda spoke up. "I am. I played on the Lady Tigers basketball team. We played in the State Regional Championships there last school year. They gave us a room in the dorms and we stayed on campus pretty much the whole time."

Stubby smiled. "Do you think you could draw us a map, you know, with a layout of the buildings, et cetera?"

"Yes, sir. No problem."

Miss Rhoda escorted the young woman and one of her friends who was also on the team into the kitchen, where they created a detailed map of the Jackson State campus. The conversation then turned to Chase and whether they should tell the Allens.

"On the one hand," said Coach Carey, "I was glad to know the boys were alive. On the other hand, I'm out-of-my-mind pissed off that they're in custody in the first place. But if they were injured, and Clay has been, I would be in a frenzy to help them. Trust me, it's all I can do to sit here and wait to implement a plan."

"Should we lie to Jake and Emily about Chase's condition?" asked Alex.

"I hate to say it, but that's an option," replied Stubby. "We can tell them that he's in custody and that we're going to get him back, but omit the part about his being hurt."

The group remained silent for a moment while they pondered their options. It was Miss Rhoda who made the suggestion.

"You can't hide this from the young man's folks. They're worried sick as it is, I imagine. You'll give them sufficient hope, Stubby. I know that you can."

Stubby nodded and smiled at Miss Rhoda. He appreciated the confidence she had in his abilities. He wasn't as confident as she was.

"Okay," said Beau. "When do we get started?"

"No time like the present," said Alex. "Why can't we start today?"

"We have our gear," replied Beau. "Dad and I are anxious to get my brothers back."

The girls emerged from the kitchen and presented the map written on the back of a cardboard box.

Stubby studied the layout. "The gymnasium on the west side of the campus would be a good location for a holding facility, as would this classroom building in the middle of the complex."

One of the young women grabbed a green sharpie and added to the map. "There are homes and businesses on three sides of Jackson State, as well as major streets. However, from the southeast corner, there are trees and a few lakes. It could give you some cover."

"Plus, the administration building is on the opposite side of this area, which is probably where most of the guards are, right?" asked the other member of the Feisty Fifteen.

Stubby looked to the young woman and then to Alex. These young women were warriors.

"Good intel," replied Stubby. "We'll have to get ready tonight and travel just before dawn. Once we arrive, we'll test the fences and see what we're dealing with."

"Does that mean that we're comin' with y'all to Shiloh Ranch?" asked Beau.

"Heck yeah, Beau," replied Alex. "I can't wait to show you around."

Chapter 16

5:30 a.m., November 26
Shiloh Ranch

"There ain't no way that I'm not goin' to save my boy," protested Jake as Stubby made one last-ditch effort to encourage him to stay and watch over things. After they became reassured that Chase was alive, Jake and Emily insisted that Jake go along. Stubby tried to explain to Jake that he was too emotional and that, frankly, his weight and lack of athleticism might slow them down. Stubby's arguments fell on deaf ears and Jake was officially on the rescue team, along with Stubby, Alex, Colton, Coach Carey and Beau.

Stubby acquiesced in part because they were going to need two vehicles anyway, so an extra passenger, and a good shooter, would be of help. Also, he had confidence in Javy and the women to vacate Shiloh Ranch while they were gone. Stubby didn't know what to expect in Jackson. The trip could take a day, or several, depending on what they faced upon arrival.

"Let's go. Saddle up," urged Jake as the rest of the group loaded up the vehicles. Jake stood on the floorboard of a 1972 Chevrolet Kingswood Estate station wagon. The blue color had faded and the white top was worn from the weather, but the machine ran like a top. This was one of four vehicles Stubby and Jake had commandeered from Savannah as part of the spoils of victory. Because of the scarcity of gas, they were only to be used for emergencies, like this rescue mission. Otherwise, the horses were still the preferred method of transportation.

Coach Carey and Beau settled into a four-door Chevy Malibu while Colton slid into the front seat next to Jake in the station wagon.

Alex was the last to load up and she sheepishly looked to her dad for approval. Colton could read her mind and encouraged her to ride with the Careys.

Stubby pecked Bessie on the cheek and finished loading the provisions in the trunk. Because of the uncertainty as to the length of the rescue, Stubby had Bessie retrieve enough MREs from their prepper pantry to last three days. After the collapse, they'd agreed to exhaust all of their other food resources before they dug into the MREs, which they saved for a last-minute bugout or a road trip.

All of the roadblocks put into place for the battle with Junior remained, so the group took a less direct route northbound. At this early hour, they hoped to avoid any confrontations, but every passenger stayed on the ready as they traveled the back roads littered with fallen trees and stalled cars. Every encounter posed a potential threat. Colton and Alex knew this well. They had been there and done that on the trip from Nashville.

The sun was beginning to rise when they approached the intersection of Highway 100 at Jack's Creek. Jake slowed and allowed Stubby and Colton a minute to analyze the surroundings.

"What do y'all think?" asked Jake. "Looks pretty quiet."

"Yeah," replied Colton. "Ironically, I recognize this intersection. After I tried to get through Jackson on my trip back from Dallas, I was turned away by their local law enforcement. I continued my journey and came right by here."

"Well, the sign over there says the barbeque joint is now open on Mondays." Stubby chuckled. "Maybe we should stop and see what they have to offer?"

"Ha-ha. Very funny," replied Jake as Coach Carey eased the Malibu up to their side.

"What's the plan?" asked Beau.

"We're gonna bust through the intersection," said Jake. "After that, we'll turn towards Jackson. The next small town is called Beech Bluff."

First Jake and then Coach Carey roared through the Highway 100 interchange. Perhaps they were being overcautious, but they didn't want to expend time or ammo fighting off some locals who were trying to ambush passersby.

Mile after mile, they took in the countryside and the complete lack of human activity. Ninety days into the collapse, the population was either dying off or finding shelter in larger metropolitan areas under the care of the government. If there were survivors in this area, it was doubtful that they knew of the troubles in Savannah, just forty miles to their south. Towns like Jack's Creek and Beech Bluff became the center of their universe unless they permitted themselves to become the charges of the government.

The skies were dark and overcast as they approached the outer limits of Jackson. Several people were seen walking toward town, but the group was surprised that there were no roadblocks thus far.

"Looks like they've rolled out the welcome mat," opined Colton.

"I guess there are too many roads into town to block them all," added Jake as he carefully turned north past an abandoned warehouse.

They drove another half mile when Stubby told Jake to slow down. "Look at that!" he exclaimed.

On the left-hand side of the road, a half-dozen people had broken through a chain-link fence into a distribution facility for Pinnacle Foods. They were using crowbars and sledgehammers to break into the back of the semitrailers parked to the rear. Boxes of toilet paper and cleaning supplies were being discarded on the ground as the desperate looters searched for food.

"Dang fools! That toilet paper is worth its weight in gold," muttered Jake.

Suddenly a siren could be heard, causing everyone to look in all directions. They continued forward to get away from the looters and the police, who were probably headed their way.

"This distraction might actually help us," said Stubby. "Jackson State is just around the curve. Keep going another few hundred yards. Easy now. There! There it is!" The excitement in Stubby's voice elevated the intensity in the car.

"Left here?" asked Jake.

"Yes, through the trees," replied Stubby, pointing as he spoke. "The map and the layout by the girls is perfect. Let's find a place to ditch the cars and we'll cut through the trees on foot to get a better look."

Chapter 17

Noon, November 26
FEMA Camp #3
Jackson

The five guys and Alex opened up the hatch of the Chevy station wagon and began to unload their gear. Each person had a black or camo backpack, which included a water hydration pack called a CamelBak, their knives, a flashlight, extra magazines filled with ammunition, a notepad with pencils, a two-way radio, and binoculars. Everybody also wore a watch. The rest of the gear was locked in the trunk of the Malibu to avoid being noticed. On Colton's suggestion, they left the windows down and the doors unlocked so that no one would break in to the vehicles. If they wanted to rummage through the glove boxes, they could have at it.

They split off into teams. Stubby and Alex would circle around to the front of the camp near the north entrance. Coach Carey and Beau were to handle the south side of the fenced area overlooking the open space. Jake and Colton would recon the east fence, which was a much smaller section because of the camp's rectangular shape. They'd be closest to the vehicles in case the group had to beat a hasty retreat.

"Take my mom's phone; it's fully charged," said Alex as she handed Beau the device. "We kept them in Faraday cages the night the solar storm hit, so they still work. Use it to take pictures and videos of what you see."

Beau took the phone from Alex and shook his head. "You guys thought of everything."

"Not really, we had to learn fast and pick up things as we went," replied Alex. "Most of it was common sense, actually. The cell phone thing in the Faraday cage was something my mom read in a prepper book about EMPs."

"I'm glad you thought of this, Alex," said Stubby. "Everybody double-check your watches. Make sure they're fully wound up too. These old-school timepieces are worth their weight in gold."

Jake laughed as he stuck out his arm to show off his Rolex. "Mine probably is. Emily gave it to me as a present when we got engaged. It's a windup and never missed a beat as a result of the storm. I haven't worn it until today because, well, time didn't matter until now."

"Speakin' of time, we need to get rollin'," said Stubby. "Let's meet back here at five o'clock to compare notes. It's too late and there is a lot to learn before we can make a move. While you're in your designated sections, look for a place where we can hunker down for the night. Any questions?"

"Nope, let's roll," said Jake as he and Colton headed toward the eastern fence line of FEMA Camp #3. Coach and Beau followed them before splitting off to the left. The four men disappeared into the trees without making a sound.

Alex turned to Stubby. "I'm ready, General."

"Yeah, right. General, no thanks. Too much politics to get there and even worse to stay at that level. I like my rank just fine, thank you."

"No prob," said Alex as she adjusted her backpack and shouldered her AR-15. "How do you wanna do this?"

Stubby studied the map from the girls and then looked back toward Whitehall Street. "We're gonna have to make a wide loop around the intersection back there. It's impossible to cut across to the north without being seen. Let's cut back through the woods, cross where we drove in, and then muddle our way through it."

"Lead the way, Ranger Stubby." Alex laughed, staring at Stubby with her thumbs hooked through her backpack straps.

The two trudged through the underbrush until they found an opening near the parking lot of Aldersgate United Methodist Church.

After observing the road for several minutes, they dashed across the street one at a time, prepared to lay down cover fire if they got surprised.

Stubby was breathing hard after the forty-yard dash to Alex's position. He crouched down on one knee and glanced in all directions to make sure they'd made the crossing unseen.

"You gonna make it?" Alex chuckled as she looked through her scope toward their next destination, the Exxon across the intersection.

"Yes, young lady, I'll make it just fine," said Stubby. "I'm not used to all this running. Unlike you, who spent your last couple of years chasing around a little white ball with a stick, I was managing fat, slow-moving cows. I'm a little out of shape."

"Golf is exercise!" Alex protested.

"Sure it is." Stubby laughed. "Listen, I'm better on short spurts rather than long runs. I can hold my own within ten to fifteen feet."

Alex burst out laughing. "Good to know."

"Seriously," continued Stubby as he rationalized his getting out of shape as the years passed. "Some athletes are built for speed and others are made for the grunt work in the trenches. I'm more of a trench kinda guy, hence the nickname Stubby."

"What is your real name?" asked Alex, out of nowhere.

Stubby shook his head and chuckled. "Clarence. Clarence Crump."

Alex couldn't contain herself. She busted out laughing, so hard in fact, that she fell on her backside. "I'm sorry," she started, attempting to regain her composure. "It's just that, you know, you don't look like a *Clarence*."

"That's why I didn't protest when they started calling me Stubby in high school," he replied. "At five foot eight, it was easy to make fun of my height. But when I started packing on the muscle around sixteen, they shut their mouths after I busted a couple of them. One day, one of the bullies attempted to apologize for hanging me with the nickname Stubby. He called me Clarence instead. I busted him in the mouth for that too."

Alex continued laughing as she stood and adjusted her backpack. She returned to the seriousness of their mission but dryly added, "Stubby is better."

After analyzing the open intersection near the gas station, they decided to move farther north and cross where the woods covered both sides of the road. They found a number of trails used by local kids to cross from one neighborhood to another. Dotting the leafy floor were opened canned goods and cereal boxes. Alex surmised that people were foraging in the surrounding areas and used the woods for cover while they consumed the food. With the FEMA camp three hundred yards away, people apparently avoided entry as long as they could.

Using the same cover-and-run method used earlier, they made it to the north side of the FEMA camp. Alex spotted a trail and began to make her way towards the entrance of the woods when Stubby stopped her.

"Look down there," he said, pointing to the sign of an auto salvage company. "On the way back, let's see if there's anything useful."

"Roger." Alex chuckled.

They raced through the well-worn path in the woods and around the back side of a looted Jehovah's Witness Church. They were directly across from the entrance to the camp. The two carefully slipped around the building and crawled on their bellies to a hedgerow that gave them a perfect concealed location to observe the majority of the northern perimeter of the former junior college.

Stubby pulled out an MRE energy bar and bit off a hunk. He handed the rest to Alex. She wolfed it down and then took a long draw of water out of her CamelBak. She powered up her cell phone and checked the time. It was almost one o'clock.

"That took nearly an hour," she muttered to Stubby.

He pulled out his binoculars and studied the entire length of the Jackson State Community College. He began to describe what he saw.

"The chain-link fencing appears to be ten feet high and topped with concertina wire."

Alex interrupted him. "What kind of wire?"

"Concertina wire, or razor wire," he replied. "It comes in large coils and the military uses it to create barriers. In a prison, it's mounted to the top of fencing sometimes. This place has been fortified like a high-security prison."

Stubby continued his assessment. "In order to save resources, the fencing is stretched from building corner to building corner. The parking lot in front of the administration offices is open."

He reached into his backpack and retrieved the map drawn by the girls at Croft Dairies. He unfolded the cardboard material. He studied the names and locations of the buildings before he returned to observing the camp through his binoculars.

"To the right of the large parking area, there is a long stretch of fencing connecting the administration building to the basketball auditorium. It encloses a baseball field and a large grassy space. Alex, there are hundreds, if not thousands of people milling around. A lot of them are wearing orange jumpsuits like you'd get in a county jail."

"Do you see any guards?" asked Alex.

"Not from this vantage point. Let me have your camera."

Stubby took the iPhone and inched his way between the shrubbery so that his shoulders were protruding through the other side. He began snapping pictures from the left to the right. Then he activated the video function and filmed the entire stretch of fencing. Using his elbows, he slid back through the partially leafed plants.

"There is a long section of woods directly across from where the refugees are milling about," said Stubby. "Let's cut through the woods and get a better look."

They quickly found their way behind the church and then ran through an open field until they reached cover. There weren't any trails in this section of the woods, so they had to push their way through a lot of underbrush. Eventually they found a small side street that formed an intersection directly across from the baseball field where the residents of FEMA Camp #3 were gathered.

Within minutes, they were once again in a well-hidden location with a wide field of vision to assess the camp's defenses. First, Stubby used the camera to take additional pictures and more video footage. They got settled in and began their observations, periodically pointing out changes in activity.

Alex grew restless and commented, "It's another boring day at Camp Fema. The guards don't move from their perches on top of the buildings. I haven't seen any vehicles come and go. The people just wander around, but they don't talk much. It's a real snoozefest."

"Just the way we want it," said Stubby. "My guess is that nothing much happens here, so both guards and refugees have grown complacent. I don't know what the mood is on the inside. These people look like prisoners. Are they happy and well fed? Does this facility contain both refugees and those taken into custody like the Bennett boys?"

"There is no hospital here," added Alex. "How do we know for sure that Chase is here also?"

Stubby thought for a moment. "There's only one way to know for sure. We need someone on the inside."

"Oh yeah, sure." Alex chuckled as she continued to stare at the camp through her binoculars. "You first, okay."

"Okay," Stubby mumbled.

"Wait, no way, Stubby. You can't be serious? You can't go in there."

Stubby slipped off his backpack and stowed his binoculars. He handed Alex back her phone as he sat with his elbows propped up on his knees.

"Someone has to and I'm the logical choice," replied Stubby. "Look at me. I haven't shaved in nearly two weeks. Don't I look like a straggler in from the road?"

"Maybe, but that's not the point," argued Alex. "We're not a hundred percent certain that the guys are in there. If you get stuck in the camp, then we have two rescues to deal with. Plus, it's just not safe. What if Junior has some stupid APB or wanted poster hanging on the wall with your picture on it?"

Stubby laughed and rose to one knee as he noticed the refugees were leaving the fence area. He glanced at his watch and noticed it was a few minutes before three o'clock.

Ignoring Alex's protestations, he said, "They're going inside. Three o'clock sharp. They must be allowed some form of recreation time and then they're locked up again."

"Okay, but you're avoiding the point," grumbled Alex.

"No, I'm not," said Stubby. "It's something to consider. Let's meet up with the rest of the group and look at all of our options. C'mon."

Stubby, wanting to avoid further discussion with Alex because he knew she was probably right, hustled toward the woods to trace back their route. Entering the FEMA facility was risky, but not because of wanted posters or any kind of all-points bulletin. There was the realistic possibility that they couldn't break him out. Getting stuck in a FEMA camp was not in the plans.

Alex and Stubby continued the trek back to the five o'clock meet-up with the rest of the team. As they walked, Stubby expressed his additional concerns about how they could create a distraction worthy of the attention of the half-dozen FEMA security guards posted around the recreation area.

He was thinking of various options when they prepared to cross the highway near the auto salvage yard. He stopped and stared in that direction for a moment when something compelled him to look at the U.S. 70 Auto Salvage for answers.

"Follow me," he said to Alex, leading the way along the shoulder of the road. He broke into a jog in order to avoid their time exposed to any vehicles on the highway despite the fact they hadn't seen one all day except for a lone military Humvee, which had pulled into the parking lot an hour ago.

Alex picked up the pace to catch up, periodically turning around to check their six, as Stubby had taught her.

"What are you thinking?" she asked as she caught up to his right shoulder.

"We need a distraction. Maybe there's something up here that'll help. Just a hunch."

CHAPTER 18

Late Afternoon, November 26
FEMA Camp #3
Jackson

Darkness had set in as everyone gathered back at the vehicles stowed in the woods. It was colder too as the sun's warmth, the source of life on Earth, as well as death, disappeared for the evening.

"Do we dare build a fire?" asked Jake as he tucked his hands into his hunting overalls. Jake wasn't built for recon work and didn't have clothes for the task either. He did, however, have a full-sized pair of camo overalls for hunting. They were meant to be used in the winter and did a great job to ward off the nighttime chill.

"I don't think we'll be here that long," said Stubby. "This land yacht is big enough to fit all of us if we wanna stay warm while we discuss our options."

"Okay," said Alex. "Beau and I will crawl in the back and you guys can have the front seats. Here's my phone, Daddy." Colton took Alex's phone and then shot Beau a *Daddy's-watching-his-daughter* look. Beau nodded, indicating that he was going to respect the boundaries that Colton expected.

Once the group was in the car and their body heat warmed the interior, the windows began to fog up, causing all of them to complain about the heat. Windows were quickly cracked open on all sides of the Chevy.

"Coach, tell me about the southern perimeter of the camp while I study your pictures and video," said Stubby.

"I guess I would describe it as a mirror image of the north side," started Coach Carey. "The several buildings to the east were interconnected by the chain-link fencing and razor wire. Then there's a maintenance building before a long stretch of open ground, including a softball field. The fence contains this large open area until it attaches to the corner of the gym on the western edge of the campus."

"Were there people outside during the time you were watching?" asked Colton.

"Yes, but only in the area of the ball field," replied Coach Carey. "There are a dozen large white tents set up along the fence perimeter. At three o'clock, when the buzzer sounded, everyone moved towards the classrooms or into the tents. It must be overflow housing."

"Buzzer?" asked Stubby.

"At around five 'til three, a buzzer sounded and the refugees began moving toward their housing units. Those in civilian clothes went into the tents and those in orange were entering the classroom building, which must be converted to some type of dormitory-style housing."

Stubby handed the camera back to Colton, who in turn passed it back to Alex. She and Beau swiped through the still shots on her camera, as well as the one he used.

"How many guards did you see?" asked Alex.

"One on the rooftop of the maintenance building and two stationed behind the classroom, um, dorm building, answered Beau.

"What about foot patrols?" asked Stubby.

"None on foot," answered Coach Carey, and then he continued. "But we did see an old John Deere six-wheeler with a guard plus a maintenance man riding around."

"Could you establish any kind of pattern for their activity?" asked Stubby.

"Nope."

The group sat silently for a moment as Stubby contemplated this information. Colton turned sideways in the backseat and rested against the passenger door. He pointed toward a bottled water and Alex handed it to him from the back.

"Thank you, Allie-Cat," said Colton.

Beau snickered.

"Shut up," Alex teasingly admonished him under her breath.

"Well, the good news is—" Stubby broke the silence. "The good news is that they appear to be undermanned to protect a facility of this size. Either the people inside aren't dangerous, or FEMA doesn't care if they get out. Regardless, I do think there is a way to pull this off."

"Tell us," said Colton.

Stubby folded up the campus map he'd been carrying for more than half an hour and put it on the dashboard. "I'm not gonna light up this map with a flashlight, but all of us have the visual in our minds. The south side has several spots hidden from the view of the guards on the roof. When they set up their security, they probably didn't envision the dozen or more large white tents used to house temporary or new refugees. I suspect that these folks are still in street clothes because they're the newest."

"Makes sense," said Jake. "If that is true, then the boys may be sleeping in these tents."

Stubby sighed. "I've got to get inside, locate the boys, and be ready to bolt out of there when the time is right."

Stubby was prepared for the onslaught of protests, but he held his ground. He and the rest of the group knew this was a necessity. After the discussion subsided, Stubby laid out the rest of the plan.

"Alex and I have identified the weakest part of their perimeter fence adjacent to the baseball field. There are two fence posts that are leaning toward the road because they were planted in a ground swale. Every time it rains, water puddles around the bases of these posts, causing their foundations to be weak in the wet soil. If we could pull the fence down in those two sections, it would direct the attention of guards and refugees alike to the gaping hole."

"Will you guys run out the front with the rest of the crowd?" asked Jake.

Stubby shook his head. "Too risky. We don't know how these guards will react. There's a reason that they patrol the grounds from the rooftops and not near the refugees on the ground. If something goes haywire, they may have shoot-to-kill authority. We don't want to be in a middle of a stampede turned killing field."

"How will you and the boys get out?" asked Coach Carey.

Stubby sat up in his seat and looked them in the eye. "We'll sneak out the back door. The guards will either react by joining the fight at the front of the facility, or they'll hold their position but be distracted by the chaos. We'll slip to the rear of the tents and stay out of their line of sight. Your team will cut us an opening through the fence. While the crowd rushes through the front, we'll escape to the rear."

"Sounds workable," said Colton. "Let's get started."

Stubby held up his hand to slow their enthusiasm. "Hang on, there's bad news. I'm going to get in there tonight, but there's no guarantee that I can find the boys by tomorrow. We can't pull this off until we're ready. We have to wait until the day after tomorrow to execute the plan. I can get a lay of the land and test the fences, so to speak."

"We have to wait two days?" asked Alex.

"Yup, preparation for something like this assures the successful execution when the time comes," replied Stubby.

"I don't like it, but only because I'm anxious to get the boys back and we don't know what's happening back home," said Jake. "However, Stubby's right. We'll get our ducks in a row, bust you guys out, and get the heck out of Dodge."

Chapter 19

Evening, November 26
FEMA Camp #3
Jackson

Colton wheeled the Kingswood Estate into the parking lot of the salvage yard. The ambient light from the moon allowed them to traverse the back roads away from the camp, without headlights. Once they arrived, Colton, Jake and Alex hugged their friend and wished him well.

"I'm gonna go on foot from here," said Stubby. "The walk will give me some time to get into character. I want these guys to look at me like a refugee. We can't afford any delays."

"All right," said Jake, who pointed over his shoulder to an early-seventies model wrecker. "I'll see if I can get this thing runnin'. We've got a couple of days to make it happen."

Alex spoke next. "Stubby, I'm gonna do recon again. You never know if things might change. If you are able to find the guys tomorrow and can make your way near the fence, it'll help us a lot to know your status."

"Good idea, Alex, I'll do my best," said Stubby, who then turned to Colton. "You and Alex have to lay down cover fire to get Jake out of there. If for some reason you can't get the wrecker running, then use the station wagon and come up with some type of quick release on the tow chain. I don't like that option because it's risky as all get out."

"Don't worry about this wrecker, ole hoss," interjected Jake. "It looks like a GMC, which means there are a ton of parts lying around here for it. It'll run. You just go in there and find our boys."

Colton patted Stubby on the shoulder and smiled. "We've got this, my friend. You be safe, find the boys, and let's take it to the house."

Stubby hugged everyone and slipped off into the night. Alex watched him the longest, as she was concerned about his ability to get inside without getting hurt. These FEMA people seemed to have a crappy attitude toward the people they were supposed to support and protect.

*****

Stubby jogged across the road and nonchalantly walked up to the double glass doors that marked the entry to the administration building. As much as he thought about his approach to gaining entry, it really boiled down to figurin' it out on the fly. He took a deep breath, put on his game face, and pulled the handles to enter.

The doors were locked.

He tried them again to make sure. Same result. *Really?*

Stubby pushed his face up against the doors and cupped his eyes with his hands so he could see inside. It was dark except for a glow of light emanating from a closed door at the back of the open entry.

He tried knocking, politely at first.

Nothing. Stubby began to get aggravated. *What kind of operation is this? It's not that late at night.*

His mind raced as he reconsidered the entire plan. If the people in charge of this camp were this inattentive to the front door, maybe there was another way to extract the boys. Heck, he could come back tomorrow and simply ask if they'd turn them over to him, no questions asked.

He knocked again, and when there wasn't a response, he pounded the door. Befuddled, Stubby stomped a foot and rested his hands on his hips. Then he came up with an idea. Growing up as a kid, they used to joke that the quickest way to go to jail was to throw a brick through a post office window. As a U.S. government facility, it would guarantee you a federal jail cell.

Stubby shrugged and looked around the landscaped beds for a

brick. He found a river rock and decided that would do. He gave the door-knocking approach one more try to no avail before he heaved the heavy rock through the plate-glass door, shattering it from top to bottom.

The rock was still skipping along the tiled floor when it rested at the foot of a National Guardsman with his rifle pointed at Stubby. Suddenly, two side doors opened in the hallway as partially dressed soldiers emerged with their weapons drawn.

Stubby stepped into the foyer, avoiding the broken glass, and approached the men. "Greetings, gentlemen," he announced sarcastically. "I knocked, but nobody answered. I'd like to check in and get a room, please."

The guards closed the gap quickly and Stubby considered running but decided to take his licks. He knew what was coming.

"It doesn't work like that, you moron," shouted one guard, who wore nothing but boxer shorts.

The other guard swung his rifle around and struck Stubby on the side of the head, knocking him to the floor. He tried to get up, and cut his left hand with glass in the process before the other guard kicked him in the ribs. He was about to receive another kick when a voice from the end of the hallway shouted at the guards.

"That's enough! I guess we'll give this idiot what he wants. Cuff him and take him to the infirmary. Also, find the orderlies and tell them to clean this mess up."

The officer giving the orders immediately turned around and returned to his room and slammed the door behind him. Stubby thought he could hear the sound of a woman giggling in the background although the ringing in his ears distorted everything at this point.

One of the guards kicked him in the thigh and ordered Stubby to get on his feet. He quickly obliged. He pulled a shard of glass out of his left palm and wiped the blood off his face with his sleeve before his arms were twisted behind him to be cuffed.

One of the guards summoned two orderlies via their two-way radio system and another guard arrived to watch the front entry.

Devil's Homecoming

Stubby was led away, hopping on his good leg. He had been given a serious charley horse and it hurt to put any weight on it.

Stubby did his best to act incoherent and troublesome for the guards, although not overplaying it. He was keenly aware of his surroundings and made mental notes of everything he saw. From the sounds and smells emanating from the closed doors, he gathered the administration building had been converted to the guards' barracks.

As they continued pulling him toward the east end of the building, he glanced down another hallway and saw two guards smoking cigarettes just outside the door.

They reached the end and pushed the handle on a glass door, opening it into a courtyard between three large buildings. A fence connected the corners of these buildings, which prevented refugee access. There were no guards necessary for this area. They stood him upright and pushed him forward.

"Don't run off, short stuff," growled the heavyset taller guard.

The guard laughed. "This bum ain't goin' anywhere. He's probably gonna enjoy the best meals of his life in here."

"Yeah, especially the ALPO served on crackers." The taller guard laughed. "These people in here are so dang stupid."

They continued across the courtyard and reached a building marked the Jim Moss Center for Nursing. Blood dripped down Stubby's face and blocked his vision somewhat. At least the ringing in his ears had subsided.

The infirmary seemed clean and it was well lit. A smallish woman who had been reading a paperback book walked from around a desk in the center of the large entry and studied Stubby's face.

"Here ya go, Annie Wilkes." The taller guard laughed. "This one busted through the front door a few minutes ago, literally. He cut his hand and bumped his head in the process. He was talkin' trash too. Ya might wanna keep him in cuffs."

"Thank you, gentlemen," said Nurse Annie Wilkes as she cupped Stubby's bearded chin and looked into his eyes. "You ain't gonna give me any trouble, are ya?"

Stubby shook his head from side to side. "No, ma'am," he replied politely. He had to be careful because he wasn't sure which side of the fence the nurse belonged to.

"Okay, gentlemen, we'll take it from here," the nurse said as she led Stubby to an examination room. She cut loose the zip-tie restraints, which were beginning to cut into Stubby's wrists. He rubbed his wrists to relieve the pressure, drawing a wince because of his lacerated hand.

"Well, mister, you're all busted up, ain't ya?" observed the nurse.

"Yes, ma'am," Stubby replied. "I guess I kinda had it comin'. I knocked on the front door to come in and nobody answered. I gotta little impatient and threw a big rock through the glass door. Your friends there didn't appreciate my improvised doorbell."

She took Stubby's injured hand in hers and chuckled. "Oh, sweetie, they ain't my friends, trust me. I don't wanna be here anymore than the rest of these folks. It's just that my husband and I ran out of options and they promised us our own private quarters plus the good meals they feed the guards. At our age, we decided that's the best we could do under the circumstances."

"Well, thank you for taking care of me, Nurse Wilkes," said Stubby. "My name is Clarence."

"Pleasure to meet you, Clarence, but my name isn't Annie Wilkes. They call me that because I like to read and take care of patients. My real name is Donna Sheridan. My husband and I are retired physician's assistants. Fred handles the day shift and I take the night shift. You'll see him in the morning."

Stubby wiped his face off with his sleeve and Nurse Donna quickly grabbed some gauze to begin cleaning him up. She retrieved an orange jumpsuit from a cabinet and encouraged Stubby to get out of his blood-soaked clothes. At first Stubby hesitated, but then he thought it would be a good idea to mix in with the crowd.

While she politely turned her back, he stripped down to his skivvies and changed into the jumpsuit. It hung on him like a sack of potatoes, but it was comfortable nonetheless.

"Clarence," the nurse said, "I'll have an orderly wash these up for you. We have some folks here like Fred and I who volunteer to do chores for the guards in exchange for better food. Trust me, if you broke in here for three hots and a cot, you've come to the wrong place. Folks are sleeping on the floor. The meals they serve refugees don't resemble real food. We don't have near enough medication to keep the elderly alive. Heck, we probably lose two or three a day to malnutrition."

Stubby sat quietly while Nurse Donna washed out the cut on his hand and bandaged it up. He wiggled his fingers and clenched his fist, pleased that he maintained his mobility. After she had Stubby hold a compress to his head wound, the bleeding subsided and she put a large butterfly bandage over the gash.

"You're probably gonna have a scar there, but it will heal up fairly quickly," she said. "I've seen them bring in a lot worse, you know."

Stubby sensed an opening. "Ma'am, my friend's son went missing a couple of days ago. A neighbor claims he was beaten and dragged into a truck or something like that. The boy's in his late teens, thin and lanky. His name is Chase. Have you seen him?"

"Well, I'll be dogged. What a small world," she replied. "They did bring him in here. Badly beaten, that one was. Fred and I fixed him up with some fluids and Advil. Young people can bounce back faster than folks like me and you, I'll tell you that."

Stubby tried not to jump out of his orange jumpsuit with excitement. "Where is he now?"

"He's down the hallway in a recovery room," she said. "Fred was gonna look in on him in the morning, and if he slept well, he was gonna be transferred into the GenPop."

"GenPop?" asked Stubby.

"General population," she replied. "That's what the FEMA folks call the refugees. If they've committed a dangerous crime, then we fix them up and they're locked in the hole."

"The hole?" Stubby's curiosity accompanied his desire to learn more about his surroundings.

"Oh, honey. You don't ever wanna go near the hole. You can trust me on that one."

Stubby nodded and contemplated what happened in the hole.

Then he got back to business.

"May I visit with the young man, Chase? I mean if you don't mind."

Nurse Donna helped Stubby off the treatment table and he got steady on his feet. The charley horse needed to be worked out, but he had time to do that. He wanted to lay eyes on Chase.

"Come on with me, Clarence," she replied. "I'll do you one better than that. There's another bed in his room. You guys can hang out together until Fred comes in to check on you. Okay?"

"Okay," said Stubby, smiling. *Just what the doctor ordered.*

Chapter 20

Evening, November 26
FEMA Camp #3
Jackson

The group split up into two teams and began their preparations. Coach Carey and Beau spent the evening on the south side of FEMA Camp #3, studying and exploring the fence line, looking for vulnerabilities they might have missed on their earlier recon assignment. Jake, Colton, and Alex were huddled under the hood of the old wrecker, staring down into the abyss of an engine that hadn't started in years.

"This thing is supposed to be our secret weapon?" asked Alex snarkily.

"I've seen better," replied Jake. He pulled on some plug wires and fumbled through the engine parts to squeeze the hoses. "Believe it or not, it's not in bad shape. We're fixin' to find out if it'll run."

Jake put his most valuable post-apocalyptic talent to work and made his way under the dash of the old wrecker. The rusted-out vehicle would be strong enough to serve their purpose, which was to provide a gaping hole for the refugees and prisoners of the camp to come streaming out. If they couldn't get the wrecker to run, then their other option was to use the Chevy station wagon. The car's engine had more than enough power with its four-hundred-and-fifty-four-cubic-inch engine, but the tires were balding. It was likely the lightweight rear end would spin, unable to rip the fence down.

The wrecker's weight was sufficient to get traction to the four rear wheels. The right front tire was flat, so they'd have to find and mount a replacement. It didn't have to match perfectly. Old Hoss, as Jake dubbed the nearly fifty-year-old machine, just needed to pull the fence twenty feet. That would git 'er done.

Jake prepared the ignition wires and touched them together.

TICK—TICK—TICK.

Jake grunted as he slid out from under the steering wheel. He came back around and joined the two heads staring inside the engine compartment of the wrecker.

"Battery's dead. We've got to find another one that's got top posts like this one." Jake tapped the end of his flashlight on the old Eveready.

"Alex, you stand watch at the entrance. Jake and I will rustle up a battery. There are some newer model cars parked at the rear of the Exxon down the street. I'm thinkin' that any batteries around the junkyard will be worthless."

"Okay, Daddy," said Alex.

Jake started toward the road and hollered back at Colton, "Grab that tire iron. We might need to bust in the windows to get to the hood latch."

"I love you, honey," said Colton as he gave his daughter a peck on the cheek. "Keep your eyes open."

"I love you too, Daddy. I will."

Colton jogged off into the darkness, attempting to catch Jake, who'd strutted off with a purpose. He'd picked up his pace considerably with Chase at risk. Alex hoped that after Chase was rescued, it might mark a new beginning for him and his dad.

Alex walked around to the front of the auto salvage's offices and sat on a mesh lawn chair. She looked around at the property. Now everybody's car was junk except for the ones that had avoided the fate of the Highway 70 Auto Salvage in years past.

Other than an occasional barking dog in the distance, the night was quiet and still. Alex's mind wandered as she thought about the events of the last month. She'd seen more drama than most kids see in a lifetime. But she no longer considered herself a kid. Before the solar storm, she was somewhat defined by her age—what grade she was in or whether she could drive a car. Within a few years, she'd be able to vote, serve in the military, or drink alcohol. In a normal world, all of these things were defined by her legal age.

Now age didn't matter. You were defined by your ability to survive. It didn't matter whether you were fifteen or fifty. All that mattered was whether you could provide for yourself and the ones you loved, with the priorities being shelter, water, food, and security.

Alex's birthday, her sweet sixteenth, was coming up in just a couple of weeks. For a young woman, this was once considered a rite of passage and an event to be celebrated. Alex wondered if her parents would remember. Personally, she didn't care if it was considered a day when she would be considered to have come of age.

She'd come of age the day she killed Jimmy Holder's stepfather. Unlike most people who would probably have a mental breakdown of some kind after taking another's life, she did not. She was glad to be alive and would do it again to protect herself.

After that fateful moment, killing took on a whole new purpose. Sure, it was necessary to defend herself and the ones she loved. Shooting to kill now took on another justification—eliminating threats.

The day she'd joined Charlie Koch in their sniper hides, she didn't see Junior's men as human beings. They were menaces, bad actors who intended to do her harm. She'd shot and killed without compunction.

She would never admit this to her folks, but Alex had changed in the moment she killed Mr. Holder. Sitting quietly in her room that afternoon, she'd turned to the Bible, seeking answers. She'd found the Gospel of Matthew and read it repeatedly. Eventually, she'd twisted the words of Jesus in the Sermon on the Mount to read *do unto others before they do unto you.*

Kill, or be killed.

*****

Coach Carey and Beau entered the UPS offices through a broken glass door. With their weapons at the ready, they slowly crossed over the pieces of shattered glass and tried to allow their eyes to adjust to the complete darkness.

Beau bumped into the back of his dad and they dropped to one knee to assess the situation.

"Dad, it's pitch black in here. If we turn on a flashlight, anybody hiding will be all over us."

"I agree, son, but we can't find the things we need this way. We gotta take a chance."

Beau reached into his backpack and took out a small tactical flashlight that he'd packed. His other one was affixed to the rail mount on his AR-15.

"Dad, let's make our way into the package-sorting area in the back. We'll stop and listen; then I'll turn this light on and slide it across the floor. If anybody's hiding in there, it might flush them out."

"Good idea," his dad replied. Coach Carey felt his way through the entrance and around the back of the customer service counters. Debris was everywhere, as the facility appeared to have been looted early and often.

He slowly pushed open the lightweight steel swinging doors and was greeted with a rush of stale, humid air. Without electricity, the rear of the building had no ventilation and the hundreds of cardboard boxes raised humidity levels within the building considerably.

Beau joined his father's side. The ambient light coming through the skylight helped their visibility as their eyes adjusted.

"Doesn't look like we'll need the flashlight," quipped Beau. "Besides, there isn't any floor to slide it down anyway."

In addition to the big brown trucks parked throughout the space, hundreds of packages had been ripped open and their contents were strewn about. Scavengers had torn open every available box, looking for food or other useful items. The only way to walk through the debris was to shuffle their feet to move things out of the way.

They stopped to listen for a moment, but the silence continued. "Okay," started Coach Carey, once again dropping to one knee while keeping his gun at the ready. "Let's spread apart and work our way through all of this. Chances are, the things of value to us didn't attract the attention of the folks who came before we did."

"Sounds good," said Beau. "I'm gonna make my way over to that tool room. I might find our bolt cutters there."

For the better part of the evening, the Careys worked their way through the warehouse area before settling into a makeshift bed of two dozen Tommy Bahama beach towels found in one of the torn-open boxes. They alternated sleeping for a few hours while the other stood watch and continued to plow through the debris. As the light of dawn began to appear through the large wall fan at the east end of the building, Coach Carey woke up his son and they started their day.

"The bolt cutters were a huge score," said Coach Carey.

"Yeah, we found a lot of things that will help," added Beau. "But, Dad, what's with the stuffed tiger."

His dad began laughing as he twirled the tiger by the tail. "You'll see."

Chapter 21

**Morning, November 27
FEMA Camp #3
Jackson**

After a brief conversation in which Chase told Stubby that he couldn't recall much after the beating took place and that he had very little to offer in the way of information about the camp, the two agreed to get a good night's sleep in preparation for the next day. Once released into the general population of FEMA Camp #3, they would have to be sharp mentally. Time was of the essence, as they had to find the Bennetts and make sure Stubby's plan was doable.

"Rise and shine, gentlemen," said a guard as he flung open the door to their recovery room. "It's chow time!"

The guard flipped the lights on and an orderly rolled a cart containing trays of food into the room. "Hey, nobody told me we had a new guy," the older man protested as he distributed the trays to Stubby and Chase.

"Just feed 'em and keep your mouth shut," snarled the guard. "If we run out, we run out. It's not our problem."

Neither Stubby nor Chase made eye contact with the guard, something Chase did suggest when they'd discussed his experiences at the camp so far. After the guard and orderly exited, Stubby opened up the lid of his tray and found runny oatmeal, a packet of sugar, and an apple.

"Looks like slop," complained Chase.

"Better than nothing, I suppose," said Stubby.

"Sadly, that's the way most of the refugees feel." A woman's voice startled Stubby. He didn't realize that they'd been overheard by

Nurse Sheridan, who had approached the door with a man dressed in scrubs.

"Sorry to interrupt, guys, but I'm gonna turn you over to my husband, Fred. He's gonna give you both a look over and decide if you can move into the rest of the facility. FEMA likes to keep these rooms available, just in case."

The guys set their trays aside and gave the Sheridans their full attention. Chase planned on playing down the pain that he was still enduring in order to be released to GenPop with Stubby. He was anxious to check out of Club FEMA permanently.

"Here are your clothes," said Donna. She handed them to Stubby and then added, "You're in very capable hands now." She paused to kiss her husband before exiting.

"Well, Clarence, I understand you made quite an impression on the boys at the front door last night." Fred chuckled. "They've actually labeled you on their intake form as *hostile*."

"Well, um, I guess impatient would have been a better characterization of what I did," Stubby said, smiling. "Really, I knocked first, but no one answered. So I knocked a little too hard the next time."

Fred set down his clipboard and picked up Stubby's left hand. "This wound wasn't too deep and the bleeding is definitely under control. Let's take a look at the side of your head."

He peeled back the bandages and saw that the gash was healing. Then he pulled out his penlight and looked into Stubby's eyes.

"Good, good. The knot on the side of your head will begin to subside over the next few days. I'm gonna put you on the approved list for ibuprofen, eight hundred milligrams. It's just a stronger dose of Advil. This afternoon, when they come around your tent for count at four o'clock, a member of our staff will administer medications."

Stubby sat a little higher on the edge of his bed. "Does that mean I'll be released from medical today?"

"Yes, sir," replied Fred. "Right after they serve the meals, the guards will come around and assign you to a cot in a temporary tent. Unfortunately, that's the best there is to offer right now because of the overcrowding. You'll be settled in by ten o'clock count."

"Count? What's that?"

Fred moved on to look at Chase's head wounds. He examined the bruises and also conducted the penlight test. He made a few notes on Chase's chart and then responded, "Several times during a twenty-four-hour period, the guards will go around and count everyone to see if anyone has escaped or is hiding somewhere. Plus, to see if anybody has died. During the daytime, the counts occur at ten in the morning and then again at four in the afternoon. In between, they allow recreation time outside."

"Sir, will I be released today?" asked Chase. "I like you guys and all, but it gets really boring in here."

"You know what, Chase? You've healed up remarkably well. I'm going to prescribe the same medications for you and let you go today."

"Awesome!" exclaimed Chase, laying it on thick.

"But, young man, let me caution you that you took quite a beating," said Fred. "The first signs of dizziness and blurred vision, I want you to put in a request to see me. Got it?"

"Sir, yes, sir!"

Fred replaced his pen in his pocket. "Fellas, finish up your breakfast and the guards will come get you. Let me add one thing, gentlemen. Watch your tongue and mind your p's and q's. These guys are short-handed and equally short-fused. Don't push your luck, especially you, Clarence."

Stubby stood and shook Fred's hand. "Thank you for tending to us. You and your wife are good people. Compassion like yours is probably in short supply around here."

"Well, thank you. Just be mindful. Watch yourselves."

Within seconds of Fred exiting the room, Stubby quickly closed the door and gave Chase a high five. Being released right away meant they could set their plan in motion. They talked further about what was happening outside of the fences until a guard burst into the room.

"You lovebirds ready to go?" he asked.

"Yes, sir," said Chase politely.

"All right then, let's go. I want you to listen carefully as we find your bunk assignments."

The guard pushed his way past an orderly and leaned backwards as he pushed the exit bar on the security door. The three emerged into another hallway that led to the Walter L. Nelms Classroom Building according to the campus map on the wall.

Both Stubby and Chase quickly studied the map and made mental notes. Stubby smiled slightly as he considered how accurate the makeshift map was that he and the group had to work with. Creating a memory usually came from paying attention. The young ladies at Croft Dairies had mastered that art.

"This building was converted to dormitories after the Disaster Declaration by the President. In the last month, as it got colder, more and more people began to show up and it got overcrowded."

He pushed another security door open and they were hit with a gust of cold, refreshing air. Then, the warmth of the sun hit Stubby's body immediately. The combination invigorated him and he found himself walking with a little pep in his step.

The guard continued in his monotone voice. "You two will be assigned to these temporary facilities. The tents are not heated, and we will issue extra blankets if you're cold at night. If beds open up in the dormitory for some reason, they're assigned on a first-in basis. I wouldn't look forward to getting a bed anytime soon."

Stubby quickly realized that nobody left and the only way beds *came available* was through the death of their occupants. His mind considered the best-case scenario and then he vowed that they would only spend one night here. Tomorrow was going to be their release day.

Chapter 22

Noon, November 27
FEMA Camp #3
Jackson

"How in the heck are we gonna find them in this crowd of people?" asked Chase as he and Stubby surveyed the two baseball fields full of refugees. From the outside, Stubby estimated a few hundred. Now that he was in the middle of the camp, his number rose to a thousand or more.

"This is way more than I imagined," replied Stubby. He stared into the throngs of orange-suited refugees and newly admitted people, who still wore their civvies. He thought about the fact that Nurse Donna was kind enough to clean his clothes until he considered an alternative purpose. "They segment us."

"What?" asked Chase.

"They can't keep up with who's who, so they divide us by sleeping quarters and clothing. If you sleep in a tent, you wear the clothes you came in with. The people who arrived early are given the better housing and the orange jumpsuits to set them apart."

Chase laughed and then grimaced as he instantly hugged his ribs, which were likely bruised rather than fractured. "It'll be like playing the Where's Waldo game. Ignore everything you see in orange and focus on the street clothes."

"Exactly, think for a minute. The guys were playing a scrimmage. Which uniform were the Bennetts wearing?"

"White. I'm sure of it," replied Chase.

For the next thirty minutes, Stubby moved around the outskirts of the crowd. He and Chase began to focus their attention on anyone wearing white. Jimbo and Clay would stick together, they agreed, which made the task easier. As they walked through a group of orange-clad people, they emerged onto the softball field.

"Look, up there," said Chase, pointing to the bleachers. "They're sitting alone on the top row. Do you see them?"

"Dang straight! Way to go, Chase! C'mon."

Stubby and Chase pushed their way through the masses and onto the infield. After navigating through the dugout, they nonchalantly walked up the bleacher steps.

"Hey! What the …?" Clay stood and shouted toward them. Stubby quickly motioned with his hands, instructing Clay to calm down and sit.

"Guys, play it cool," Stubby responded as he sat down on the back row next to them. "Act like we just met."

"Yeah, okay," said Jimbo. "Chase, what happened to you?"

"When everything broke loose, I helped my parents get away by distracting the soldiers," Chase replied. "I was doing fine until I got clotheslined by a tree limb. That let them catch up to me, and, well, you see the end result. How about you, Clay? Look at your jersey."

"Junior smacked me around a little," said Clay, looking down at his bloodstained jersey.

Stubby shielded his eyes from the sun and surveyed the yard. The refugees were lethargic, barely moving and interacting. He contemplated whether they were drugged and then he noticed their clothing. They were definitely malnourished. *Does FEMA not have enough to feed these folks? Or are the food rations being reassigned to more important mouths?*

"Listen up," said Stubby. The three boys leaned forward and huddled together. "Based upon the plan I laid out with Coach Carey, Jake and Colton, the plan is to break out of here through the fenced area behind the tents. It will happen sometime during tomorrow's eleven to three rec period."

"What can we do on this side of the fence?" asked Jimbo.

"Nothing really, but for now, it would be a good idea to get as close to the north fence line as possible so that Alex can see that we're together."

"Alex? How do you know she's out there?" asked Clay.

"I guarantee she's been hiding in the woods, watching, since we walked out of those tents," replied Stubby. "Let's make our way over there. Chase and I will go first and you guys catch up in a few minutes."

The guys worked their way through the crowd, looking up at the guards positioned on the rooftops from time to time. They were alone and armed with automatic weapons. Stubby didn't see any guards on the ground level or working the perimeter fencing. He realized that the minimal amount of security might be because Rollie had pulled too many of the National Guardsmen to Savannah.

When the Bennett twins arrived, the four guys stepped away from the crowd and toward the fence. They spread apart slightly and stood facing the street fronting the camp. Although Stubby couldn't see Alex, he knew she was there. He tried to signal her with his hands. He held up one finger and then provided a thumbs-up. Stubby repeated the signal. Since it was well past one, Alex would know that the one finger would represent tomorrow, as they'd agreed upon before they'd parted ways.

"Let's make our way back towards the tents," instructed Stubby. "I need to sneak around the back side and try to make contact with Coach Carey and Beau."

"You have to be careful because that part of the camp is considered out of bounds," said Jimbo. "We heard a story about someone wandering too close to the tent and they were badly beaten. Then they were taken to the hole, whatever that is."

"Jimbo's right," added Clay. "The guy never came back, they said."

Stubby continued walking in that direction and the three teens laid back a little. Suddenly, Stubby stopped and looked at the rooftops. He was determining where the blind spots were. If he could identify them from the inside, hopefully Coach Carey had done the same from the outside.

After a moment, he decided the second and third tents from the end were ideal. He instructed the boys to stay put while he walked between the tents. If he got caught, he would explain that he was new and didn't know where the latrine was. He'd pretend he was taking a leak. This might draw a rebuke, but it wouldn't land him in the hole, hopefully.

After one final glance, Stubby made his way between the two tents and peered around the corners to make sure that there were no perimeter patrols. He was relieved, and surprised, to find that there weren't any.

He stood there for a moment, peering into the woods, looking for a sign. Nervously, he walked behind the tent so that his silhouette showed against the white background.

Several minutes passed and he was about to leave when he heard the faint sound of limbs being moved and leaves crunching underfoot. He resisted the urge to bolt back to the tents.

Stubby focused on the underbrush and focused on the spot where the sounds came from. There was a twenty-foot cleared space between the fence and the woods, so he knew that Coach Carey couldn't show himself. Then, without warning, an object flew towards the fence from his right. It landed on the ground and rolled up against the fence within ten feet of him.

Stubby chuckled as he looked at the projectile. It was a stuffed tiger. The Tiger Tails had found him. He signaled the Careys with one finger and a thumbs-up. He repeated the signal and then grinned.

Tomorrow at one o'clock. He and the boys would be ready. Tiger Tails out.

CHAPTER 23

Noon, November 28
FEMA Camp #3
Jackson

The skies were becoming overcast and the wind was picking up as everyone took up their positions near the entry to the camp. Alex positioned herself directly across from the intrusion point where Beau would hook up the chain to the wrecker. During the evening, Jake successfully got the vehicle running after an hours-long search for a replacement for the cracked distributor cap. When he successfully got Old Hoss started, it immediately backfired with a blast that sounded like a high-powered rifle. He quickly shut down the motor and knew exactly where to look. Age was not kind to the important plastic part of the truck's ignition system, and they searched high and low for a replacement.

Also during the night, Colton and Beau swapped places. It was agreed that Beau would be best suited to affix the chain to the fence without detection. He was faster and better capable of dodging gunfire if it came to that.

While Colton and Coach Carey got into position to extract Stubby and the teens from the south side of the camp, Alex and Beau got everything ready to pull down the fence as a distraction.

It was almost time to find out if their preparations would pay off. Jake parked the Chevy station wagon behind the Jehovah's Witness Church immediately across from the entrance of the camp. All five members of the extraction team now waited for one o'clock to arrive.

*****

Precisely at one o'clock, Beau fired up the wrecker, which was tucked into a side street a hundred yards to Alex's right. As Jake promised, there was no backfire this time. Through her scope, Alex moved from rooftop to rooftop to gauge a response from the guards. They were distracted by the mob within the fence. A thousand people confined in an open area still made a lot of noise from their conversations and milling about.

Beau eased out onto the street and drove until he was in position. He abruptly steered onto the grass directly in front of Alex's hidden spot in the woods. Slowly, he exited the vehicle and walked around to the front of the truck, pretending to look for a mechanical problem. He raised the hood under the pretense of making a repair.

Beau did a great job of parking directly over the top of the tow chain's hook. After looking under the hood and keeping the wrecker between him and the guards, whose attention he'd now grabbed, Beau slid under the wrecker and hooked the chain to the bumper's tow hooks.

Alex moved her rifle from rooftop to rooftop, quickly finding her marks and analyzing the guards' reactions. The two shooters closest to Beau began talking into their radios.

Something else was happening. The refugees, who had become accustomed to the humdrum, uneventful life in Camp FEMA, immediately became curious about Beau's actions. In unison, they began to work their way towards the front fence to get a better look.

Alex saw two guards running down the fence from her right. "Come on, Beau. We've gotta go!" she muttered aloud.

Beau was on the same page as he hustled to close the hood of the truck and jumped inside. He fired up Old Hoss and put the wrecker into gear with a clank. Slowly at first, he pulled the slack out of the chain. The tension popped the heavy-duty chain out of the tall grass and it was now fully visible to the guards.

Without warning, they opened fire on the wrecker, tearing up the dirt around it. Beau pulled harder and then gave it gas. The wheels spun initially and then they found traction. *Let the festivities begin!*

SNAP—SNAP—SNAP!

The steel ties that attached the chain-link fence to its posts began to snap, causing the refugees to scream. The wrecker pulled one section after another loose as a gaping hole opened up in the secured fencing.

More gunshots rang out as the rooftop shooters found their mark. Bullets ricocheted off the rear deck and the tow truck's boom. Beau pressed on as the fencing got stuck in between the trees. The tires began to spin as the truck was being held back. Beau was a hundred yards short of where he was supposed to run the truck into a ditch and dart across the street to the church.

He stopped and then gave it gas again. Bullets were penetrating the fenders and the passenger's door. Alex watched as he gave it one more try and then the tow truck stopped running.

"Crap!" she exclaimed as she took off down the trail to her second observation point. When she arrived, Beau was exiting the truck as bullets flew over his head. She quickly debated whether to return fire. The plan was to avoid a shoot-out. Everyone agreed that the guards would spend their time dealing with the jail break if there weren't guns blazing all around. Hopefully, this tactic would allow them to get out of Jackson without being pursued.

Alex studied her target options through her scope. The rooftop guards were partially obstructed by leafless oaks. The pursuing guard's line of fire was blocked by the refugees running through the gap in the fence. There was no activity at the entrance to the camp.

"Over here!" she yelled to Beau, who quickly responded.

He raced across the street and made his way down the grassy shoulder on the other side. Bullets penetrated the asphalt behind him, but never came close to his zigzagging course. Within fifteen seconds, he leapt over a hedgerow and ran across the parking lot. Beau arrived at the rendezvous point before Alex did.

"Way to go, QB1!" she shouted as she ran into his arms. "You did it!"

Beau was heaving, trying to catch his breath. All he could do was hold her and gasp for air.

"Quick, get in!" shouted Jake as he fired up the Chevy. The teens jumped into the backseat and Jake spun the tires as he drove down a gravel road that connected the church to a small set of duplexes to the rear.

Alex turned in her seat and watched for any signs of pursuit. Jake wheeled the vehicle through the intersection nearest the camp and took a hard left, throwing Alex off balance and into the side of Beau, who held her close.

"Nice driving, Jake," Beau said laughingly. "You make a good wheelman and an even better wingman."

*****

"Here we go!" exclaimed Stubby as the uproar consumed the recreation yard. "Walk slowly toward the tents so you don't attract any attention. There's only one guard assigned to watch this area and I'm sure he's focused on the other side of the compound."

The three teens crouched to lower their visibility and followed Stubby. An hour ago, Stubby confirmed that the fence had been opened up for their escape. Coach Carey had torn the tail off the stuffed tiger and attached it to the chain-link fence near the ground. His precision cut in the galvanized steel was barely discernible to the guards unless they stumbled upon it.

"Quickly," urged Coach Carey in a hushed voice from his hiding place in the underbrush. "The guard is holding his position, but he's not looking this way right now."

Stubby squeezed through the fencing, followed by the boys. Jimbo, the last in line, grabbed the tiger tail and stuffed it in his pocket.

Coach Carey and Colton held up some tree branches for the foursome to duck under.

"Everybody good?" asked Colton as he handed out weapons to Stubby and Chase.

"Yeah," replied Stubby.

Within a minute, they were free and running toward the industrial buildings that bordered the perimeter of Camp FEMA. The faint retort of gunfire could be heard from the other side of the camp, which drew concerned glances from Colton and Stubby.

"Do you think we need to circle around and help them?" asked Colton.

Stubby looked to Coach Carey. "Have you guys maintained radio contact?"

"Jake and I checked in at 12:30," Coach Carey responded. "He said he'd radio us if they needed backup or when they were headed south. Nothing so far."

"Let's get to the car and be ready," said Stubby as he gave FEMA Camp #3 one last look.

Coach Carey stopped at the edge of the clearing before they crossed the road. Overcome with emotion, he turned to his two adopted sons and hugged them both. The widowed father had tears in his eyes as he held them both tight around the neck.

"Are you boys all right?" he asked.

Clay, the more emotional of the twins, nodded and wiped the tears from his cheeks. Since the death of their parents, the Bennett boys had become a part of the Carey family. The four guys shared many bonds, especially the love of football, but in this moment, the only thing that mattered was being together.

"Yes, sir," said Clay, pulling his bloody jersey away from his chest for everyone to see. "Junior beat the snot out of me."

"Literally," chimed in Jimbo, who was also becoming emotional.

"Shut up, Jimbo." Clay laughed through the tears. "One time Junior smacked me 'cause Jimbo ran his mouth."

"That's 'cause you sat there with that dumb look on your face." Jimbo was egging him on.

"You get the same look, carbon copy," shot back Clay. Calling his brother carbon copy was a reminder that for every sibling insult he hurled at Clay, it also applied to Jimbo, his identical twin.

Coach Carey laughed and looked at Colton. "So much for our moment of brotherly love."

Chapter 24

Late Afternoon, November 28
Childer's Hill

Colton drove in silence as he followed Stubby winding his way through the back roads of Hardin County. Coach Carey said very little after the two groups reunited just outside of Jackson. The Bennett brothers had relayed a lot of information to the group during that short respite while they regrouped for the trip to Childer's Hill, their temporary home away from home.

It was a lot of information to digest and he wasn't sure how Madison was going to react. The families who'd come together at Shiloh Ranch had grown accustomed to news that was beyond their comprehension. The concept of living in a world without power was not on the forefront of anyone's mind. The threats and atrocities of their fellow man dominated their thoughts.

Colton followed Stubby as he drove up the hill to the Wolven place. The vehicles were greeted by the friendly waves of Javy's men, who stood guard every hundred yards. For Colton, it was a relief to see their smiling faces. The men never complained about the tasks they were given and had fought fearlessly alongside Stubby at Shiloh Church.

They parked the cars and were barely able to open the doors before they were greeted by Madison, Emily, and Bessie. The Wolvens stood on the front porch, arms around each other's waists, watching the tearful, but happy reunion. Coach Carey and his teens stood awkwardly to the side for a moment while the families reunited, and then they were properly greeted with hugs as well. The extended family just became even larger.

"Y'all come on inside this house where it's warm," shouted Char. "We've fixed up a mess of chili that could feed an army. By my head count, we've got one!"

The dozen members of the Allen, Ryman, Crump, and Carey families walked across the front lawn and made their way inside. The fire was roaring in the oversized stone fireplace at the end of the Wolvens' open home. The group greeted the Splinter brothers, who were helping the Wolvens in the kitchen. The men, jovial as always, cracked jokes in their German accents to the delight of everyone. Colton was glad the men eased the tension, at least during dinner.

Reminiscent of a soup kitchen, Char doled out the chili and crackers to everyone. A few folks, Jake included, added Char's homemade habanero hot sauce. It made the big man's tears flow and nose run with every bite.

The group chattered throughout the meal as the spoons clanked the bottom of the bowls. Of course, accolades were heaped upon Char for her culinary talents, and Jake especially sang the praises of the hot sauce. The man liked to torture his intestines, Colton thought to himself.

"What kind of news did you learn in Jackson?" asked Bessie.

"Jimbo, you wanna relay what you've learned?" asked Coach Carey.

"Yes, sir," replied Jimbo. "Well, the first thing that we learned is that the rest of the country is a mess too. The big cities like Memphis, Nashville, St. Louis, and Atlanta are all war zones. Gangs have formed and they are better armed and organized than the military. We met refugees from all over the place and the story was the same. The cities are burning."

"What about Washington, D.C.? Aren't they doing something?" asked Emily.

"It's hard to tell because nobody knows for sure," replied Jimbo. "Telephones are still not working. I didn't hear of any location where the power has been restored. It's just plain chaos everywhere."

"Except in the small towns, like ours," added Clay. "Places like Savannah helped each other."

Jimbo interrupted his brother. "But not all of those stories are hunky-dory. We were told by a lot of refugees that the towns weren't always very nice to newcomers. They took care of their own, but not necessarily outsiders. There are just too many mouths to feed."

Stubby summarized the boys' intel for the group. "It's like we always suspected. The metropolitan areas rage out of control. The small towns circle the wagons around their own in order to survive. Savannah and our surrounding communities could have done the same successfully had it not been for the Durhams."

"Stubby, we better bring you up to speed about what's happened down this way," said Madison, who took on a serious tone that Colton hadn't seen from her in a while.

"Sure, what've you learned?" asked Stubby.

Madison took the floor. "Well, we felt like Javy and the boys had the hill protected, so we sent the Mennonite men out on horses to see what was happening elsewhere. The first day, they traveled as far north as the Wyatt farm and reported that there was no activity. But yesterday they rode all the way to the bridge and saw military trucks full of men returning from the north."

"You mean from Jackson?" asked Colton.

"No, from along the river," replied Madison. "Our people found a man with his two young daughters hiding in the woods along the trail. They were shivering and scared out of their wits."

"What happened?" asked Stubby.

"They managed to sneak across the river in a canoe," answered Emily. "Without exaggeration, the entire town of Savannah has either been arrested or people have evacuated. The man said Junior was, quote, *cleaning house*."

"Everybody?" asked Coach Carey.

"Pretty much, according to this man," replied Madison. Everyone began to mumble between themselves, especially the Bennett brothers and Beau. They were obviously concerned about their friends in the Tiger Tails.

Madison continued. "Wait, there's more. The FEMA soldiers are commandeering farms on the north side. The Mennonites learned from another group of people fleeing toward the west that FEMA is posting the martial law declaration on every door and removing anything of value. They were even hooking up their big military trucks to the ranchers' cattle trailers and forcing the owners to load the cattle up."

Stubby stood and paced back and forth in front of the fireplace. He furrowed his brow and spoke. "They're taking everything in the name of martial law. The declaration gives Rollie the authority to do pretty much anything he wants on behalf of the government."

"Or for his own benefit," said Colton.

"How can they get away with this?" asked Emily.

"Well, for one, as we learned in Nashville," Colton began to answer, "there isn't anybody to stop them. We saw so much corruption in those early days, imagine what someone like Rollie could do working in conjunction with his demented family. We've seen the work of Ma and Junior already. Now, couple that with the military power of the government. This is not good."

Madison reached for Colton's hand and gave it a squeeze. Their family had been through so much. Colton had thought they could make a life for themselves at Shiloh Ranch with the Allens and the Crumps. Here they sat, displaced once again, while the Durhams misused the power of the government to run roughshod over people who were just trying to survive.

"Do we make a stand again?" asked Colton.

Nobody responded immediately, and Stubby, contemplating their options, sat down at the hearth next to Alex. He decided to voice his opinion first.

"It's just a matter of time before they make their way to Shiloh Ranch and beyond. It's possible they might give up the hunt for us unless Junior presses the issue. But as long as Rollie and FEMA have a presence in Hardin County, we'll be living in fear."

"Do we push farther west and relocate again?" asked Madison. "Or maybe we'll move into Mississippi. We have a lot to offer a large farming operation. I'm sure we can make some kind of arrangement."

Coach Carey spoke next. "I can speak for the boys in saying that we're tired of hiding. Since the solar storm hit, we've been living in the shadows in our hometown. We thought those days were over. Our vote is that we end it so that we can live our lives as freedom-loving Americans. There is no room for tyranny in Savannah."

"Well said, Coach," said Jake. "Emily and I feel the same way. Chase too."

"I believe the root of all evil is the abuse of power by our government, small and large," started Stubby. "We'll never be free as long as our homes and lives are threatened. We need to end this once and for all."

"Agreed."

"Us too."

"Without hesitation."

Colton made a point to look everyone in the eyes as they voiced their opinion. The group had to gear up for another fight and he wanted to make sure everyone was committed. They would be fighting trained, heavily armed soldiers now. These were not Junior's band of misfit deputies.

Colton continued to look around the room, when a cold chill ran up his spine as he realized that somebody in this room was likely to die in the coming days.

Chapter 25

Late Afternoon, November 28
Cherry Mansion
Savannah

Junior felt like it was déjà vu all over again except this time the roadblock in his way was his brother instead of that fool Bill Cherry. His town had been running just like he wanted it until the day those people from Nashville showed up. They'd been a thorn in his side ever since. Junior thought it was way past time to round 'em up and bury them in the woods with them old Indians.

"Junior, it don't matter what you want. I've gotta go back to Jackson and take most of my men with me," said Rollie as he joined Ma and Junior on the porch. Ma's Brumby Rocker was fully repaired and in high gear as she listened to her sons bicker.

"Dang it, Rollie, you promised that I'd get my vengeance against the disdants. They humiliated both me and Ma. We deserve to get our due!"

Rollie stomped a cigarette out in the lawn. He walked up to Junior and blew smoke in the shorter man's face. "Look here, Junior. That colonel who rang me up today don't give a dang about your *disdants*. Somebody busted into one of my camps and tried to let everyone out. Do you hear me? Twenty-three hundred people had a big old invitation to hit the dusty road and it happened on my watch! Except I wasn't watchin'. I was down here fixin' your dang mess!"

Junior bowed up and looked up to his brother's chin. "You gave us your word. Just tell your men to fix the fence. How hard is that?"

Rollie pushed Junior away with one hand. Junior, caught off guard by the physical gesture, stumbled backwards. But he caught his balance and charged his brother.

BANG! BANG!

Ma pulled a small Ruger .380 from an ankle holster and shot two rounds into the air. Both boys grabbed for their weapons before Ma got their attention.

"Shut up! Both of you. Neither one of you boys are old enough or bad enough to keep me from jerkin' a knot in your tail."

"Yes, Ma," said an apologetic Junior.

Rollie, who had been away from home long enough to know that Ma didn't have any real power over him, simply scowled and ignored Junior.

"Look here, Rollie," said Ma. "Have they fixed the fence up there?"

"Yes."

"Okay, how many people did you lose? You know, how many refugees got away that you've gotta go round up?"

"Actually, not that many," replied Rollie. "Here's the thang. They got no place to go. Most of them are there voluntarily. We give 'em enough food to keep them alive and that's it. Truth be known, they could leave anytime they wanted if they'd just ask. We discourage it because part of my pay is based on the population of the camps."

"What pay?" growled Junior, still sore about Rollie's lack of cooperation. "Money ain't worth nothin' now."

"It's accruin'," Rollie snapped back. "We're told the government's gonna change the greenback to be like the old days. You know, the gold standard."

"They gonna pay y'all in gold?" asked Junior.

"No, but the money is gonna be worth its value in gold or something like that," replied Rollie. "I don't know, Junior. But it don't make a difference. I gotta job to do. If I don't, they'll find somebody that will."

Here we go again, Junior thought to himself. "How 'bout the job you committed to doing down here for your family? Huh? You gonna just kick us to the curb. I've got no men for security. Heck, they cleaned out the arsenal, which means all those guns are out there, pointing at me and Ma."

"Rollie, Junior's got a point," interjected Ma. "Sit down with me, boys. Both of you, please."

The guys put away their differences for a moment and sat down on the stoop next to their mother. Regardless of age and stature, your mother always deserved your respect, if only to hear her out.

"Our first order of business was to clean out the bad apples from our town," Ma began as she holstered her pistol and snapped the clasp shut on the leather strap. She adjusted her dress to hide the weapon she'd carried for years. "Rollie moved them to the camps in Jackson. Junior, even you agreed that some of the men allowed to stay were trainable, right?"

"Yes, ma'am," he replied.

"Okay, so you pick 'em and train 'em to run security around town," said Ma. "This will free up more of Rollie's men. Now, Rollie, how many men did you use when you took over the list of farms I gave you on the northwest side of the county?"

"About sixteen to take over the farms and another eight to move the livestock to the slaughterhouse in Jackson."

"Did you meet a lot of resistance during the process?" asked Ma.

"Yeah, but my boys took care of it. If they didn't respond to a proper beat down, then we just put 'em in the ground. They're gonna die anyway after we cleaned them out."

"Well deserved, in my opinion," said Junior. All three of the Durhams chuckled.

Ma continued rocking as the sun began to set over the ridge. The days were getting shorter and fall was rapidly turning into winter.

"I was prepared to send them south beginning tomorrow," said Rollie. "But the colonel's breathing down my neck and I gotta make an appearance."

Ma was in deep thought and Junior's wheels were spinning in his head. In just a few days' time, Rollie could steamroll Stubby and those folks from Nashville. The job could be easier if he whipped up a bunch of *Wanted Dead or Alive* posters like in the old days. He could offer a reward of that worthless money he'd found in the TBI's safe.

"How about this, Rollie," started Ma. "Send your crew down south tomorrow like you said. Let them have a couple of days to get the lay of the land, and then add more men from Savannah if you need them. Junior, you recruit as many new deputies as you can tomorrow to guard the checkpoints and the major supply stores like Lowe's, Kroger's, and Walmart."

"But, Ma, what about Jackson?" asked Rollie.

"Go up there and spend a couple of days," she replied. "Make sure everyone sees you and call that colonel every dang hour if you have to. Let him know that you're on top of it and then get back here to finish the job we started. Once we've cleaned them all out, you can return to Jackson and run FEMA."

Both men looked at each other and conducted internal debates. This worked for Junior because the sooner he got rid of Rollie, the better. He wanted to run things his way again, and if it meant a few days' delay in getting even, it was worth it.

"Sounds like a plan," said Rollie.

"Yup. I'll do my part," added Junior.

Chapter 26

**Early Morning, November 29
Shiloh Ranch**

The great cattle drives began in the mid-nineteenth century because ranchers of the Midwest had a product the folks back east wanted—beef. From the conclusion of the Civil War through the end of the century, nearly twenty million cattle were herded from points in Texas and Arkansas to the railheads of Kansas City. The mighty locomotives carried the beef in cattle cars to the stockyards of Chicago and elsewhere east of the Mississippi.

Drivin' cattle was no easy task and it became even more complicated by the invention of barbed wire. For decades, the great cattlemen of the eighteen hundreds like Jesse Chisholm could cross from one ranch to another unimpeded until barb-wire fencing came into use to identify boundaries. The construction of railroads led to more stockyards like the one in Fort Worth, and the epic cattle drives seen in Western movies became a thing of the past.

When Stubby suggested they take the morning and attempt to remove the cattle from Shiloh Ranch to the protection of a small farm near Childer's Hill, Jake and Colton laughed themselves silly. Both men had Texas roots and immediately had visions of Billy Crystal and friends in the *City Slickers* movie.

After their initial guffawing abated and they realized Stubby was serious, they began to weigh the merits. It was a given that Rollie and Junior intended to direct their FEMA troops in the direction of Shiloh Ranch. Stubby and the rest of the group were surprised it hadn't happened already.

The dairy cows at Shiloh Ranch were one of their most valuable resources. Plus, there was an additional problem—they had to be milked. These cows had been producing large quantities of milk daily through the efforts of Javy's men. If the cows were milked a few hours late, it could be painful. Cows had been known to squall, stomp their feet, and carry on to express their discomfort. In some of the worst cases, they could get mastitis, an infection of the udder, which could kill them.

They agreed that they needed to move the herd and it would be all hands on deck to hand-milk them. It was worth the risk of losing a few cows along the way, or even a stampede, to keep the animals out of the hands of FEMA.

"Guys, I have no illusions of our ability to succeed at this," said Stubby. "The purpose of a cattle drive is universal, regardless of the type of animal you're moving. We move them from point A to point B without losing the herd in whole or in part."

"Does anybody have experience at this?" asked Colton.

"Normally, you've got expert wranglers and excellent horsemen to chase down stragglers while keeping the herd on the move," replied Stubby. "Depending on how cooperative they are, we may have to stop to drink fresh water and graze. Two of Javy's men worked as *vaqueros* before they came to America. They'll act as our wranglers."

After more conversations about logistics, they picked their helpers. Chase was ready to saddle up, over the protests of his mother. Alex thought Snowflake would enjoy the adventure. Coach Carey and his boys stayed behind to work security because a lot of Javy's men, who were excellent horsemen, were needed on the drive.

They identified a route that was entirely on the back roads between Shiloh Ranch and Childer's Hill. The abandoned farm had a cross-fenced field near the sod farm that would work for the herd temporarily.

"Saddle up!" shouted Jake as he adjusted his cowboy hat and started down the driveway. Colton and Alex followed close behind. Stubby, Chase, and Javy brought up the rear as the sixteen riders headed back to Shiloh Ranch.

After they arrived, the ranch hands quickly milked the forty-six head they managed to corral easily. Everyone else went through the house, giving one last look for any valuables left behind from packing. Virtually all the food, weapons, and supplies had been moved to Childer's Hill. The main house looked like it had just been abandoned by a bunch of rowdy vacationers.

"If they do take the ranch," said Stubby, "they won't get much with it. Hopefully they'll move on to greener pastures, pardon the pun."

"Yeah, I hope so," said Jake as he ran his hands down the hand-carved banister. He had retrieved a blanket that Emily asked for.

Javy entered the house and announced that they were ready. As the group mounted their horses, Stubby reviewed some of the tips that he'd garnered from Javy's two *vaqueros*.

"As we get moving, don't try to look at this as a herd of cattle, but rather forty-six individual head. It only takes a second for one cow to make a run for it and then all of them will follow the leader. Be on guard and focus on keeping them together."

"What are some of the things we should avoid?" asked Alex.

"Remember to keep this low stress," answered Stubby. "There is no need to yell or shout at the cows. If you need to encourage them to move along, ride up on their hip. They'll instinctively pick up the pace."

Colton asked from the rear as the herd began to move toward the front gate, "Speaking of pace, how fast should we push them?"

"Let them decide, but keep 'em moving," replied Stubby. "If you push them too fast, they'll overreact and scatter. We'll be chasing them down through the woods for hours."

The herd began moving at a methodical pace and the ranch hands began to squeeze them together so they would fit through the gate. Everyone was instructed to walk their horses along the shoulders of the narrow country roads with the herd walking down the center line.

It was five miles from Shiloh Ranch to the sod farm, a long way for an inexperienced bunch of buckaroos. They slowly made their way without incident. Stubby slipped to the rear to join Chase, Colton, and Alex.

Over the sounds of the cows' voicing complaint at having to walk on asphalt and the chatter of the ranch hands encouraging the herd along, Colton heard the roar of trucks.

"Did you guys hear that?" asked Colton.

All four riders stopped in the middle of the road. The rumble of the diesel engines grew louder.

"Vehicles are coming towards us," said Alex.

"We'll lose the herd if we don't stop them," said Stubby. "Colton, ride ahead and tell Jake to keep movin'. I'm gonna take Alex and Chase to see what's going on."

"I'm on it," said Colton. "I love you, Allie-Cat. Be careful!"

"Of course, Daddy!"

Chase led the way because he knew this area on horseback better than anyone. "Follow me," he said. "We'll cut across the fields and head them off at the entrance to the ranch."

Chapter 27

Late Afternoon, November 29
Shiloh Ranch

Chase positioned Stubby and Alex on the outside perimeter of the ranch behind stacks of cut firewood. The cords of wood provided excellent cover for them, leaving them close enough to the barn to provide fire support in the event Chase was seen racing across the field.

The trio waited for the military vehicles to drive past the entry to Shiloh Ranch and continue down Federal Road in the direction of the cattle drive. When the three Humvees turned into the long driveway and blasted through the locked gate, Chase and his companions were relieved, but concerned about the fate of the ranch.

It was getting dark as Chase suggested that he slip into the barn. As a kid, he had developed a number of hiding places within the barn and the areas surrounding the main house. His plan was to get as close to the soldiers as possible to determine their intentions. After he was safely in the barn, Stubby and Alex would rejoin the group at Childer's Hill and prepare to defend their new home.

Stubby instructed Chase to be vigilant, but not to risk getting caught, or worse. If it appeared that FEMA was heading south in their direction, Chase assured Stubby that he had trails through the woods and fields that could easily beat the convoy to Childer's Hill. If it appeared that the soldiers planned to set out daily on an established search grid, Chase would monitor their activity and report back to Stubby as he could.

Chase crossed the two-hundred-yard clearing in less than a minute, using piles of hay provided for the cows as cover. When he reached the barn, he gave Alex and Stubby a final wave and slipped inside unnoticed. After an uneventful few hours of watching and stalking the perimeter of the main house, he settled in the hayloft and fell asleep.

*****

A rooster, which was left behind during the evacuation, announced that it was just about daybreak. Chase jolted himself out of a heavy sleep and quickly gathered his wits. He grabbed his weapon and descended the ladder leading to the loft. Just as he reached the window facing the house, he heard voices.

Two of the FEMA soldiers came out of the house to urinate in the front yard. Bessie would've beat them with a broom as they did, Chase thought to himself. He considered shooting them right then and there while their hands were full, but knew that he'd have to deal with the four men inside. Remaining disciplined, he waited and listened.

"Man, I'm tellin' ya," said a short, stocky soldier wearing only his britches and a white tee shirt despite the chilly temperatures. "That was the best night's sleep I've had in weeks."

"You ain't kiddin', brother," said his lanky, rail-thin partner. "I can live like this forever. But where's the food? I thought these rich farmers had stockpiles of food."

"Maybe they've been looted? The place was picked dry."

"It looked to me like they left in a hurry," stocky replied. The two finished up their business and wandered through the yard toward their Humvees. They opened the rear hatch of one and removed a case of MREs.

They loitered for a moment, which allowed Chase to hear them more clearly.

The stocky soldier spoke first. "The CO wants us to do sweeps of all the homes in the area, lookin' for these people the sheriff's got his panties in a wad over. Between you and me, I don't give a crap about his manhunt. I'm kinda lookin' for a place to settle down. You know, find a wifey and hunker down for the long haul."

"I get it," added lanky. "The government is paying us in IOUs. What the heck are we supposed to buy with that? Also, the food we're getting now is nothing but these crap MREs. They promised us hot meals, meat and taters and all. I'm sick of this Vietnam War tastin' crap. Listen, I'll take a place like this one, plant some crops, marry me a farmer's daughter …"

His partner began laughing. "Yeah, if you can find one."

The lanky soldier replied, "Oh, I'll find me one, don't you worry about that. This is what I wanted to talk with you about. I don't care about this wild-goose chase either. I say that while we're on our patrol, let's start gathering food, supplies, and farmer's daughters. I think it's high time that we start looking out for us two *numero unos*."

"Agreed," replied stocky. "Guys are defecting right and left. This new CO handpicked us without having a clue what we're capable of. He promised the sweet spoils of victory, but so far, all I've seen is cattle getting loaded on trucks and headed for Jackson. That ain't gonna fill my belly down here."

The lanky soldier slammed the door shut and took one of the cases of MREs toward the house. "So what's the plan for today?"

"We're supposed to head west with each of us taking a handful of roads and houses to search. Tomorrow we work our way south."

"Ain't we supposed to get some home help?" asked lanky.

"Yup, another half-dozen men will be here tomorrow as we push south. The CO needs to get this over with. By the way, did you hear about the new rules of engagement?"

"Nah," lanky stumbled over a tree root as he approached the porch. "What are they?"

"Let 'er rip. Don't waste time asking questions."

"Sweet."

Chapter 28

Early Morning, November 30
Childer's Hill

Both Chase and his horse were out of breath as he finished his ride up the long winding driveway to the Wolven home on Childer's Hill. Jake, Colton, and Stubby greeted him with a hot cup of coffee.

"How're ya doin', son," asked Jake as he pulled straw out of Chase's jacket collar and pockets. "What've ya got for us?"

Chase took a long sip of the strong, black brew and allowed it to soak in. It was getting colder and the clouds building above portended rain.

"Okay, first off, they're not coming here today, but they will be coming down this way tomorrow with a force twice as large as we watched roll into the ranch yesterday. They have three two-man teams, who will divide up the area west of Shiloh Ranch and continue the *manhunt* as they call it. Tomorrow, they're expecting another six men and plan on moving south."

"That's not good," said Jake.

Chase finished his coffee and wiped his mouth with his sleeve. The group made their way inside, where the fire immediately warmed their bones. Emily greeted Chase with a hug and helped remove his jacket. Bessie emerged from Char's kitchen with the campfire coffee pot and refilled his mug.

"There's more, kinda on the bright side, I guess," said Chase.

"Go ahead," said Stubby as he motioned for the men to join him at the dining table. Chase grabbed a corn pone out of the basket and wolfed it down.

"I was able to listen in on a long conversation between two of the men," Chase continued. "These guys don't have their heart in it. They talked about defections in their ranks. They complained about the money they're being paid as worthless with no purchasing power. In my opinion, their goal is to find an abandoned home and move into it. And, find a wife, of course."

"Really?" Jake laughed. "A wife? Do they think women are sitting around on their front porch swings, looking for a soldier to swoop them off their feet?"

"I guess, Dad. Specifically, they want to find a farmer's daughter."

Stubby finished off his mug of coffee and shook his head. "We might be able to use this to our advantage."

"How so, Stubby?" asked Colton.

"Well, we need to act quickly, but we can pull it off," he began. "We know the area and now we know their plans for the day. What if we break into groups and isolate each of the three search teams. We can neutralize them and hide their gear. We'll make it look like they defected. If we miss a team, one of our own will be waiting at Shiloh Ranch and take them out."

"Stubby, this is ambitious," said Colton. "By *neutralizing* and *taking out*, I'm assuming we'll kill them and hide the bodies, right?"

"That's what they have planned for us," interrupted Chase in reply. "They said their rules of engagement have changed."

"What are they?" asked Stubby.

Chase looked around the room to determine if anyone else was listening. He leaned forward and replied in a whisper, looking around to make sure nobody overheard the conversation. "The soldier said *let 'er rip* and *don't waste time asking questions.*"

Everyone sat in silence for a moment as they contemplated what Chase reported. FEMA, an organization designed to protect and care for American citizens in a time of crisis, had become militarized with a primary focus on enforcing the President's martial law order. Furthermore, individual soldiers were looking out for themselves first, regardless of the pain and damage they inflicted upon civilians.

In Jackson, they'd witnessed the squalor and sordid conditions that the refugees lived under. Chase had received a beat down from FEMA's men during the Thanksgiving Day raid. Now, soldiers under the authority of the United States were planning on using their resources to loot and commandeer private property, not to mention killing U.S. citizens in the process.

"The depravity of man," mumbled Colton, reminding himself of his grandfather's words. He did not intend to add to the conversation, but the words had a profound effect on the group at the dining room table.

"We don't have a choice," said Stubby. "If we don't strike first, they'll double their numbers by tomorrow and then we'll have to fight them as a cohesive military force. Honestly, I don't like our odds if that happens."

Jake leaned back in his dining chair until the wood back creaked. He clasped his fingers together and rested them on his belly. He smiled and spoke to Stubby. "We know the risks, old friend. Just tell us what to do."

Stubby rose and walked across the room to grab his roll of maps. He fumbled through them until he found the one that included the area west of the river.

"If they're going to search west of Shiloh Ranch today, that means they'll probably divide the area up like this." Stubby used utensils left on the table and created boxes to define roads that meandered through the west part of the county. Then he grabbed a couple of knitting needles out of Char's craft bag, which sat in a chair by the window. He made a straight line along the county road bordering the area.

"My guess is that they went to the farthest point first and will work their way back to the ranch," Stubby began, using a third knitting needle as a pointer. "At this hour, I'd imagine they're already on their way. If we act fast, we can slip in behind them, catch them by surprise, and cut off their return."

"Doable," said Jake.

"We'll break off into four groups of four—" started Stubby before Jake interrupted.

"But there are only three of their teams to *neutralize*, as you say."

Stubby nodded and sat back down. "Yeah, we'll have three in the field and one back at the ranch, waiting for anyone who gets past us. No matter what, by the time the day ends, all six of these disgraces to an American uniform will be considered AWOL or MIA."

Colton expressed his concerns. "Stubby, that means we'll be pulling sixteen of our own away from Childer's Hill. That leaves us really vulnerable."

"I know, and I don't like it. But trust me, we don't want to face a dozen or more heavily armed, trained soldiers tomorrow. It's a risk we've gotta take. Unfortunately, risk taking is the new normal."

Chapter 29

Noon, November 30
West of Shiloh Ranch

The skies opened up with a heavy downpour as the four teams set out on their assignments. The period from Thanksgiving through early January was typically the wettest for this part of West Tennessee. Heavy, sustained rains were the norm and the gusts of wind whipping the treetops were a reminder that they were located in Dixie Alley, one of the deadliest regions in the country for tornadic activity.

Coach Carey, Beau, and the Bennett brothers took the Chevy station wagon because they had the farthest to travel. Two of Javy's men who had performed admirably at the battle against Junior at the Hornet's Nest rode in the rear. None of the guys in Carey's squad were trained marksmen, so the ranch hands picked up the slack. They also knew the surrounding area.

The teams assigned to the FEMA search squads included a foursome comprised of Colton and Jake with two ranch hands, plus Javy and Chase with two more of Javy's men. Alex and Stubby were assigned to lie in wait for the stragglers who attempted to return to Shiloh Ranch.

Stubby outfitted everyone with the communications gear that had given them a huge assist during the battle against Junior. He would continue to spearhead the activities of everyone as his group of inexperienced fighters set out to take down members of the U.S. military.

The more Stubby thought about it, the more his stomach was sickened at the way things had turned out. These guys were opportunists abusing their power, no different from Ma and Junior. With Rollie's orders, he couldn't take the chance with the lives of so many people weighing on his shoulders.

Putting the three teams in place was a matter of traveling via backroads and identifying known choke points. When they'd set up the overall perimeter defenses of Shiloh Ranch weeks ago, they'd put into place road barriers designed to prevent access to their driveway. The Humvees were capable of driving around the blockades of debris they'd used.

However, with the heavy rains, Stubby and his teams were blessed with an ally that General Patton once infamously called upon during World War Two—the Good Lord. Patton asked his chief chaplain to pray for clear weather so his Third Army could advance upon German positions in France. The chief chaplain wrote the prayer and then distributed it to the quarter million soldiers of Patton's army. The weather cleared, Patton's tank rolled forward, and the Third Army punched through the German assault line at Bastogne, France, leading to the Allied victory at the Battle of the Bulge.

On this day, Stubby hadn't prayed for rain. Whereas the night before he'd prayed for guidance, this morning he prayed for strength and protection for his extended family, none of whom had military experience, against a foe that should be a friend.

"It could be worse," said Alex, interrupting Stubby's thoughts. "It could be snowing."

"What? Oh, yeah," said Stubby. "This part of West Tennessee is like the Nashville area in that respect. We're right on the edge of *not cold enough for snow* most of the time. What we get here is just damp, wet bone chill."

The two dismounted near Lick Creek and tied off their horses under a large fully-leafed magnolia tree that would provide them cover from the rain. They got their gear together and began the trek through the woods along the driveway's fence line.

Stubby and Alex needed to confirm that all of the FEMA units had left the ranch and were on patrol. Then they would take up positions on both sides of the driveway to create a cross-fire ambush.

It was possible that the soldiers had been alerted to the surprise attacks being put into place. By the time they got back to the ranch, they would be on their toes.

Stubby performed a final radio check. "Bravo, Charlie, Delta, this is Alpha. Radio check. Over."

"*Alpha, this is Charlie, five by five. Over.*"

"*Alpha, this is Delta, loud and clear.*"

Bravo team, which was Coach Carey's squad, didn't respond. Stubby confirmed the broadcast back to Colton, who was Charlie team, and Chase, who was Delta team.

"Roger, Charlie and Delta. Alpha out."

Stubby waited a moment and then repeated the call to Coach Carey, "Bravo, this is Alpha. Radio check. Over."

This time Beau responded, "*Alpha, this is Bravo. Say again. Over.*" Static accompanied his response and Stubby was about to key the mic when a heavy gust of wind snapped a dead tree limb in the woods behind him.

"Stubby, this is miserable," Alex said. "Those guys may not stay out there all day."

"Bravo, this is Alpha. Do you copy?"

Nothing.

Stubby immediately began to be concerned about his plan. The heavy rain and wind might turn out to be a blessing as well as a curse. If the FEMA troops called it a day, the three intercept teams might not be in position in time. All three FEMA squads could return to Shiloh Ranch and descend upon their position.

"Alex, listen up," started Stubby. "If our guys aren't in place to cut off their retreat, we may have to deal with all of them."

Alex pulled her cap down over her eyes to shield them from the rain. "We'll handle it." With that, she climbed over the fence and sloshed across the driveway before disappearing into the underbrush. Stubby strained to follow her movements and then he caught a glimpse of her settling in behind two large rocks next to the fence. She had a perfect line of sight down the driveway and excellent protective cover.

The rain was coming down steadily with the occasional wind squall forcing the moisture to blow sideways. Through the brutal weather, Stubby heard the sounds of gunfire, but he was unable to discern from which location. At this point, it was best to maintain radio silence to keep from distracting his teams.

The waiting was excruciating. He wanted to hear a report—a confirmation that each team was safe and their mission accomplished. Stubby pulled his radio several times from his belt, only to tuck it away. *Patience.*

Then the steady roar of wind and rain was broken by static.

"*Alpha, this is Delta. Over.*"

"Roger, Delta. Go."

"*Two kills. Vehicle intact.*"

"Well done, Delta. Hold position. Over."

"*Roger, Alpha. Out.*"

Stubby glanced back toward Alex, who stuck her hand, with a thumbs-up, above the lowest fence rail, acknowledging that she'd heard the news.

Two to go.

Chapter 30

Afternoon, November 30
Shiloh Ranch

Alex remained prone on the rain-soaked ground and tried to avoid shivering. Before they left Childer's Hill, she'd tried to dress warmly but found that her mobility was constrained. Against Stubby's suggestion, she'd peeled off the heavy hunting jacket that restricted her arm movement in favor of a lightweight, parka-style coat that repelled water, but did little to provide warmth. If something happened that required a lot of movement, she didn't want to be hampered by a big winter coat.

The logic of the morning gave way to reality as the cold and wet began to soak into her body. Alex tried to block her discomfort from her mind by praising herself for her perseverance. *You never know how strong you are until being strong is the only choice you have.*

The sounds of weapons discharging echoed through the woods, capturing her attention. These shots were coming from where her dad's roadblock was. More shots were fired as a gun battle ensued.

Alex rose from her position to get Stubby's attention. Just as she was about to speak, she heard the crackle of the radio and her dad's voice. "*Alpha, this is Charlie. Over.*"

"Roger, Charlie. Sitrep." Stubby was yelling to be heard through the noise created by the heavy rain.

"*They got around our blockade. We lost a man. Their driver is wounded. Headed toward you.*"

"Roger that, Charlie. Locate Bravo team and assist. Alpha out."

Alex was standing now and listened as Stubby repeated the conversation. "Get ready, Alex! They're coming!"

The skies were dark now and their visibility had been reduced considerably. Alex doubted she could get off an accurate shot, so her plan was to spray the vehicle with fire. If she could force them to stop by shooting out the Humvee's tires, then Stubby, who was slightly behind her position, would have a clean shot.

Alex heard the faint sound of a vehicle approaching. The roar grew louder as the headlights of the military truck came into view. The driver nearly lost control as he took the final turn toward the gate too quickly. Alex saw this as an opportunity to catch them off guard.

CRACK—CRACK—CRACK!

She fired off three quick rounds at the driver's window. Two of the bullets shot out one of the headlights, but the third skipped off the hood before finding its mark. The Humvee's windshield shattered and the driver lost control, causing the rear end to spin around. The Humvee was now pointing back toward Federal Road.

Stubby fired several shots into the rear of the truck, tearing through the canvas cover. The vehicle sat still, idling in the road for thirty seconds. Alex wasn't sure what to do although she didn't like the fact the truck was pointing away.

Alex left the protection of the large rocks and moved her way down a narrow path created by the cows walking the fence line. She kept her weapon pointed at the passenger side of the truck. She glanced over and saw that Stubby was doing the same thing on his side.

Suddenly, the driver's side door burst open and a body was thrown onto the crushed gravel shoulder. Stubby began firing toward the open door in an attempt to stop the driver from getting away.

At the same time, Alex broke into a full sprint as she ignored the soggy footing. Stubby fired off several more rounds, but the Humvee lurched forward and headed away from them.

Alex reached a slight clearing and then began shooting at the rear tires. Her sixth round found its mark and the big thirty-seven-inch rear tire exploded, causing the back end to drop. The driver tried to continue, but the shredded tire wrapped itself around the axle. Once again, the vehicle was at a standstill.

Cautiously, Alex and Stubby moved in unison toward the truck. They were now a hundred feet away. Stubby got closer and then shouted to the driver, "Come out of the truck and we won't hurt you!"

The driver revved the engine and threw it into reverse. Alex immediately took a knee and fired into the rear canvas cover of the Humvee. She unloaded nearly ten shots before she stopped.

The truck rolled a few feet and then came to an abrupt halt. The brake lights were illuminated. *The driver's still alive.*

Stubby noticed the same thing and immediately dropped to a knee. Alex, who was exposed in the open area, ran forward to a cluster of trees just fifty feet from the rear bumper. She never took her eyes off the doors of the Humvee and awaited Stubby's signal.

That was when another truck came speeding around the corner toward them. Alex had completely lost sight of the fact that only one of the FEMA squads had been taken out. The other one, along with Coach Carey's Bravo team, was unaccounted for. She suddenly was very afraid for Beau, but she snapped herself back to the task at hand.

If the driver of the disabled Humvee was still alive, she and Stubby were now outnumbered. Stubby moved alongside the parked truck and quickly emptied four rounds into its driver's side window. Following his lead, Alex shot out the passenger windows. The brake light went off.

The other vehicle was upon them and the passenger was firing wildly out of his window. Alex then realized that the driver was going too fast. He'd never be able to stop without crashing into the stalled truck.

She slipped deeper into the woods, looking for cover. The driver was going full throttle as he approached the disabled truck with only one faint headlight. There was going to be a collision, but at the last moment the driver veered to the left toward the open space. Crashing through the fence, the Humvee dipped down into a ditch and then careened up the other side until it was stuck in the soggy turf.

The driver spun the tires to extract himself, but he dug himself in deeper. Alex wasn't going to wait for them to free themselves from the muck. When the driver's door flung open and a leg appeared, she emptied the magazine, riddling the body with bullets. The lifeless body fell out of the Humvee and landed face-first in the mud.

Stubby ran across the street to join her. They had to deal with the passenger.

"I'll go around the back; you take the front," instructed Stubby in a whisper.

Alex obliged and dropped her empty magazine into her wet, wrinkled hands. She methodically jammed another thirty-round mag into her weapon and pulled the charging handle.

Slowly, she walked towards the front of the truck in a low crouch, using the oak trees as cover. She was just about in position to see into the cab of the Humvee when the fate of the passenger revealed itself. His bloody head was stuck in the shattered windshield with a hunk of glass jammed into his eye socket. He must've died instantly when the vehicle bounced through the drainage ditch.

She approached the body of the driver and kicked his leg, waiting for a reaction. Then, just as Stubby had taught her, and without emotion, she put another round through the man's chest.

After Thanksgiving, Alex and Stubby had made a promise to each other—*always make sure the bad guy is dead.*

Chapter 31

Late Evening, November 30
Shiloh Ranch

The rain couldn't dampen the spirits of the group as they cleaned up the mess created by Alex and Stubby during the assault on the two FEMA patrols. Coach Carey and the boys arrived, frustrated by the fact that they were unable to contribute earlier and that their comms had prevented them from relaying their situation to Stubby.

Jimbo and Clay buried the bodies of the dead soldiers in the woods and covered their graves with pine needles. Using the third Humvee, which was fully operational following Chase's precision shooting on behalf of Delta team, they repaired the rear tire of the disabled Humvee and pulled the other one out of the soggy sod.

"Will they all run?" shouted Stubby through the pouring rain.

"Yes, sir," replied Chase. "The front end got knocked out of alignment on this one, but it'll get back to Childer's Hill."

"What about weapons?" asked Stubby.

"Big score there, General Stubby!" Colton laughed as he presented him with two fully automatic M4s.

"Nice!" said Stubby. "How many?"

"We gathered six plus ammo and magazines," replied Colton. "We also have half a dozen forty-five-cal sidearms with backup mags."

"Body armor?" asked Stubby.

"Nope, just their kits, or what's left of them," replied Colton. "They all had knives and leg sheaths, like this one." Colton handed him a black leather sheath with the knife handle sticking out.

"Hmmm," mumbled Stubby to himself. He moved closer to

Colton and saw that they were all the same. He mumbled to himself, "Ka-Bar straight edge. Probably all Marine issue."

Stubby handed the knives back to Colton and motioned for Javy to join him. He led him to the back of the Humvee full of the soldiers' weapons. "Javy, get these guns wiped down and oiled as soon as you get back. We don't want any rust."

Jake emerged from behind one of the trucks with a laundry basket full of liquor. "Of all the things these guys could rustle up, apparently booze was high on the list."

Stubby thought for a moment. Several times during the last few hours, this FEMA squad had been hailed on their radios by their CO in Savannah. Stubby feigned a reply, effectively using the weather and fake static to satisfy their calls. However, if the weather cleared in the morning, the proverbial jig would be up when they didn't get a real response.

He needed to create a working theory for Rollie and his subordinates for when they arrived tomorrow and found their comrades missing. The liquor gave him an idea.

"Okay, listen up!" he shouted. "Load up these two damaged Humvees and take them back to Childer's Hill. Chase, take a moment to tend to your horse and then meet me at the main house. Alex, come with me. I've got an idea."

The rest of the group shared duties of returning on horseback with another in tow or riding in the blood-soaked Humvees. Despite the torrential downpour, most of the group begged for horseback.

Stubby took the liquor from Jake and pushed the basket into the backseat. As they drove to the house, Chase waved them down and he jumped in the backseat.

"Hey, hey!" He laughed. "Are we gonna party?"

"No," replied Stubby. "But they are."

Stubby pulled up to the front door and the three of them piled out. The ground sloshed around their feet and a gust of wind caught Alex's hat, sending it off into the darkness.

"Whatever," she said with a slight tone of disgust.

As the group entered the house, they saw that the soldiers had made a mess of the place. But they also found more things of value. These men were undisciplined, as evidenced by their lack of a standing guard over their temporary headquarters and the way they'd acted in the field. The lackadaisical approach ultimately got them killed.

Alex illuminated the room with the flashlight attached to the rail of her AR-15. "Should we clear the house?"

"I don't think it's necessary," replied Stubby. "Chase's intel was on the money."

Stubby found a couple of Coleman lanterns in the dark and lit up the great room. "The generator is off. These fools probably didn't try to fire it up."

"Look at these!" exclaimed Chase, holding up two shotguns. "They don't look like my Remington."

Stubby took one of the weapons from Chase and examined it under the lantern. "This is a Benelli M4 Tactical. Again, Marine issue."

Chase lifted two heavy ammo cans and dropped them on the dining table.

"Easy there, muscles," said Stubby. "Bessie and your momma will slap you silly if you scratch their table. Do me a favor? Chase, go fire up the generator so we can see. We'll turn it off before we leave tonight."

Stubby relocated the weapons onto the sofa and then he rustled through the kitchen, gathering up the MREs. Within minutes, the power was on and the house was lit up.

Alex joined him and then caught a glimpse of herself in the mirror. "Yep, I look like a wet rat." After setting her rifle on the kitchen island, she fumbled with her hair and then reached into her backpack to pull out a boonie-style hat. She frowned, as the olive drab color didn't suit her.

Chase emerged through the kitchen side door and shook off the rain. "Do you reckon Noah's Ark will sail down the Tennessee anytime soon?"

"Yeah, no kidding," replied Alex. She turned her attention to

Stubby. "I'm gonna see what's upstairs."

Before he replied, she bounded up the stairs. Stubby then laid out the plan for Chase. "Go outside and empty the liquor bottles in the yard. Leave a couple of them partially full. We're gonna make it look like these guys partied hearty."

"I'm on it," said Chase as he gathered up the basket and headed toward the front porch.

"Gross!" shouted Alex from upstairs.

Chase set down the basket and started up the stairs with his weapon drawn when Alex leaned over the rail.

"Men are disgusting animals!" She groaned as she revealed the source of her displeasure. She held up three issues of smut magazines for Chase to see.

"Oh, I thought it was something bad." He laughed.

"This is gross, Chase." She tossed them down the stairs at him.

Stubby emerged from the kitchen and started laughing. "Actually, they're perfect. Alex, I need you to see if any of Emily's unmentionables are still in their chest of drawers upstairs."

"What? No, I won't," said Alex adamantly.

"C'mon, Alex," Stubby continued. "We need them as props."

Alex glared at Stubby and Chase at the bottom of the stairs before turning into the Allens' bedroom.

Stubby and Chase returned to the task at hand. Stubby placed glasses around the great room and kitchen. He then prominently displayed the girlie magazines on the couch and tables. When Chase returned, the two of them partially filled the glasses and dropped the empty liquor bottles throughout the downstairs.

Alex quietly found her way down and immediately covered her mouth with her free hand. "It reeks down here!"

"Exactly," said Stubby as he respectfully took Emily's undergarments from Alex. He displayed them provocatively throughout the room.

"Dude, this looks like an episode of *Girls Gone Wild* or an all-night frat party," said Chase. "I'm sorry I missed it."

Alex gave him *the look* and shook her head in disgust. Stubby stood in the center of the room and examined his work.

"That's exactly the impression I was hoping for."

Chapter 32

Late afternoon, December 1
Savannah

Roland Durham was the son of a rapist, and he would never forget that. He was also given the name Buford Pusser II before he was adopted by his stepfather, the late Leroy Durham. The resentment he held inside surrounding his birth and his later adoption, where his name was changed based upon his stepfather's favorite cigarette, ate at him every time he came in contact with his mother and brother.

As the boys grew up, Rollie always considered himself a Pusser. He emulated his famous namesake, the grandfather he never knew. He was tough and feared throughout elementary and high school. More than that, he was competitive. His physicality, something his younger brother didn't possess, enabled him to excel in any sport.

Yet he harbored a shortcoming that he was never able to shake, even in adulthood. His brother was the apple of his mother's eye. Perhaps she couldn't forget the memory of Rollie's conception, or maybe it was because at one time, she really loved Leroy Durham. Either way, when her husband gave their son together his name, Rollie immediately became jealous and Junior became the beloved son.

Despite his potential, Rollie acted out, resulting in his sexual assault upon a young girl in his senior year of high school. Ma had scolded and belittled him, claiming that such activity was in his genes. Either way, he was yoked up out of bed one morning and hauled down to the Marine recruitment office, where he volunteered.

Sometimes in life, you looked back at seminal events that, at the time, seemed dreadful. But as time passed and your life changed for the better, you realized that you became a better person for it.

The Marine Corps turned Rollie into a man. He never looked back and he never returned home, until now. For a fleeting moment, he thought that he could enjoy small-town living again. However, the more the aggravations piled up, the more he was ready to get the heck out of there.

Besides, there was the issue of Junior, whom he inwardly had no respect for. Junior was weak. He didn't have the Pusser machismo and swagger. The sibling rivalry between the brothers had resulted in a competition for the attention of their mother. Junior had won the first round when Rollie was turned over to the Marines to be raised.

While away from this dysfunctional family dynamic, Rollie realized that every relationship was fundamentally a power struggle and the individual in power was whoever liked the other person less. Rollie had come to despise Junior and he was going to make one last effort to gain his mother's favor at his brother's expense.

If he failed, then it was *adios muchachos*. He'd be outta there.

The afternoon meeting with Ma typically took place about an hour before sunset. She wanted to talk about the day's events, give her marching orders for the next day, and then enjoy her sunset. Today, in this foul weather, there would be no sunset. And Rollie, who'd arrived early, decided to make his move without Junior being present.

"Hey, Ma," said Rollie with a hint of peaches and cream. "I've got somethin' I need to talk with you about in private."

"You mean without Junior?"

"Yes, ma'am. It's about my job."

Ma gestured for Rollie to sit next to her in the parlor. The room was a showplace of antiques and Civil War memorabilia. The red velvet loveseat upon which Ma was sitting looked straight out of *Gone With The Wind*.

"What's on your mind, son?"

Rollie adjusted his belt and slid his sidearm out of the way so he could get settled in a chair. "My arrival in Jackson was a stroke of luck for you and Junior," started Rollie, getting right to the point. "You were scheduled for transportation to Atlanta to stand trial. I'm gonna tell ya, there ain't much to these trials. They look at the affidavits and then they find you guilty. You get locked up in a federal penitentiary forever."

"Yes, I know. I'm very glad you protected us from that." Ma studied Rollie's face, attempting to probe his mind to see his intentions. He had to play it cool. She had a knack for seeing inside people.

"I risked a lot with my superiors to come down here and clean up Junior's mess," he continued. "I wasn't looking for anything in return at the time, but after more than a week now, I've got to make a decision."

Ma stretched her fingers then balled up her fists. Rollie knew her mannerisms. This was not an angry response, but rather one of concentration. She wanted to know what he was thinking.

"What decision would that be?"

"I'm catching a lot of heat from my commanding officer about the use of my team and the unit's resources down here," Rollie replied. "For the first few days, I was left alone. But last night, I got my butt reamed over *the occupation of a dinky little town in West Tennessee*, as he put it."

"Is he gonna make you pull out?" Ma asked.

"Maybe, but maybe I won't," replied Rollie. He knew he was being too cryptic, so he best get to the point. "The attack on the refugee camp didn't help, but I got that patched up. But now, I've lost a squad of six men hunting down Junior's problem."

Ma sat upright in her chair and began to probe further. "You lost six men? Were they killed?"

"No, they went missing, or AWOL," he replied. "When they didn't respond on the radio this morning, I sent another squad to find them. They were gone, together with their vehicles and gear. The place they were staying, the Allen place that Junior suggested, looked like a wild party had taken place. You know, booze and broads."

"So you're pulling out because of that?" she asked.

"No, well, maybe. You see, if I have one more problem like this, I'm gonna get reassigned, probably demoted or worse."

Devil's Homecoming

"Son, what can I do to help?" Ma asked sincerely.

"I guess what I'm saying is," started Rollie before pausing, "I'm risking my career down here for Junior's debacle. I want to make sure that I have something at the end for me when I succeed."

Ma was trying to coax the purpose of this conversation out of him. "C'mon, son. Spill it. What are you saying?"

"If I make a push into the south part of Hardin County and find these folks that Junior desperately wants to bring to justice, then in return I want to run things. Specifically, I want to move back to Savannah and be the sheriff, mayor, you know, the whole ball of wax."

Junior was eavesdropping in the foyer and began laughing. "You do, do ya? The whole ball of wax? Is that all? You want the whole enchilada too? What else can we adorn you with, King Rollie? Screw you, brother! You gotta lotta cajones comin' here like this—making demands. For years, Ma and I've been holding down the fort. You wanna waltz in here with your fancy title and uniform, thinkin' you're gonna run things. Ma, I call bull—"

"That's enough, Junior!" Ma exclaimed, interrupting her youngest son's tirade. "Rollie came to me to voice his genuine concerns for his career because, yes, he is cleaning up your mess."

"But, Ma, I've got it under control now," Junior plead his case.

"Maybe so, but it was your brother that made it happen," she shot back. "Rollie pulled us out of that FEMA jail cell and gave us a second chance. We owe him for that. And, as requested, he rounded up all of the folks who opposed us and shipped them off to Jackson. He gave you a clean slate to work with."

Rollie sat silently and listened as Ma dressed down his brother. Junior's tirade would have earned him a beat down when they were young boys. Now, Rollie bit his tongue and allowed Ma to fight his battle. Besides, there would come an opportune time to shut his little brother's mouth.

"I know and I've righted the ship. Just today, we put on eight new deputies to help cover the checkpoints. That freed up eight of his precious soldiers."

"They're Marines," Rollie gruffed. "Don't call them soldiers."

"Whatever. Anyway, you can have them back," said Junior. He turned his attention back to Ma. "I have everything going in the right direction. I can take over security now. Rollie can leave anytime he wants. I just need him to finish what he promised, which is to find the people responsible for all of this—Stubby Crump, the girl, and her parents."

Rollie began to speak and Ma held her hand up to stop him. She contemplated for a moment before rendering her verdict.

"You're both my boys and I'm not gonna choose between you. Here's what I want you to do. Junior, put your folks in place and don't mess up. Rollie, pull your men out of town and do whatever it takes to flush those vermin out of their holes. When can you do it?"

"I can make the arrangements for day after tomorrow. But then what?" Rollie never got an answer to his original demands.

"I will make no promises on where we go from here," answered Ma. "I do have options that could work for both of you if you can manage to get along as brothers."

A bright light flashed in the window and then the crack of thunder shook the old home. Ma and Junior instinctively jumped at the sudden noise, but not Rollie.

Lightning doesn't make a sound until it strikes. *I am lightning.*

Chapter 33

Morning, December 2
Pickwick Landing Dam

The 249th Engineer Battalion stationed at Fort Belvoir, Virginia, deployed teams across the United States in a time of crisis. After 9/11, elements of the 249th had been instrumental in restoring power to Wall Street, enabling the world's leading financial center to resume operations within a week. As part of Joint Task Force Katrina, Prime Power, as the battalion was known, had swiftly created the infrastructure necessary to rebuild New Orleans.

Before the massive solar storm knocked out the power grid across the country, units had been deployed to assist in the operation of the most critical of the nearly eighty-one hundred major dams across the country.

Like so many of its counterparts along the Tennessee River maintained by the Tennessee Valley Authority, the Pickwick Dam was a massive generator of hydroelectric power and its functionality was self-contained. The dam's performance was dependent upon hands-on operations, not remote via the Internet like so many other utilities. The Pickwick Landing Dam had also been built in the 1930s as America attempted to pull itself out of the Great Depression. Its electronics were antiquated and in many cases were not hardened against the effect of a massive electromagnetic pulse like the one that had devastated the nation months prior.

The small platoon assigned to the Pickwick Dam could only monitor its function, but couldn't control its spillways. Their role was to prevent traffic from crossing the dam and to notify their superiors when they thought a breach might occur.

When the solar storm had hit, all of the generating units in the powerhouses shut down. The closure of the gates caused water to be diverted to the north and south of the dam's spillways. These embankments began to overflow, sending water across the top and eroding the land below the dam.

When the water levels rose several weeks ago, alarm bells were not raised although the businesses and residents at the foot of the dam would have appreciated notice of the water overflowing. Without the functioning spillways, the massive volume of water found its way to the lowest point, around the sides.

The heavy rains that beset the Tennessee River valley over the last three days now threatened to create massive flooding for the land downstream, eroding the river's banks and flooding land in low-lying areas.

In essence, the Tennessee River was roaring unchecked around the dam, breaching the embankment and compromising the dam abutments. Although the embankment's core material was sound, it was not designed to accommodate the flow of water being experienced today. It was eroding the earthen structure, which allowed water to seep into the dam's concrete base.

Several days earlier, Major Tracie Lashley of the 249th learned of the situation and began to conduct a series of inspections of the nine dams and locks that turned the Tennessee River into a nearly seven-hundred-mile river highway. Together with a team of engineers, they traveled by helicopter along the TVA dam system and determined that the ever-rising water levels were steadily accumulating as the final dams in the system were reached.

Wilson Dam, located fifty miles upstream from Pickwick, but over a hundred feet higher in elevation, had begun to fail two days ago. Massive flooding had occurred throughout Northern Alabama as a result. The dispersal of the river's volume of water was not going to protect the integrity of Pickwick Dam, Major Lashley's report concluded.

The Pickwick Landing Dam would fail, the report stated, and the results for those downriver might be catastrophic. The small platoon manning the facility received word to evacuate the area for their own safety. Their route to the north was already washed out and they had relocated their encampment to the south side of Pickwick in Mississippi.

The platoon commander, weary of the deployment and tired of being away from his family in Birmingham, weighed his options. Warning residents downstream would involve the platoon traveling the backroads of Northern Mississippi and into the area west of the river in Tennessee. Logistically, this was a nightmare, as the water had already washed away the roads near the base of the dam.

For twenty-four hours, he calculated the rise of the water downstream to only be a foot per day. In his mind, this slow rise would give anyone with a little common sense notice that flooding was a real possibility. *It is raining cats and dogs, after all*, he thought to himself.

So he made the call and ordered his men to go give the locals notice that the dam might fail, if they wanted to. It was their choice. He was packing up to go home to his wife and kids, far away from the Tennessee River.

CHAPTER 34

Late Morning, December 2
Childer's Hill

Water is life. Even under normal conditions, a human being can die in three days without it. In rural America, the weather is discussed often, not as a means to make conversation, but because of its importance in growing crops and hydrating livestock. Many farms don't have city water, as folks call the vast system of underground pipes that traverse a metropolitan area. They must rely upon their wells for liquid nourishment. Conversations often center around the phrase *we need the rain.*

There is a point, however, where Mother Nature can provide too much of a good thing. In many Americans' continuous quest to have *a room with a view* in the form of oceanfront or riverfront property, oftentimes large volumes of water resulting from storms cause flooding. Hurricanes wash away homes and rising flood waters in low-lying rural communities render landowners helpless against the power of rivers.

It breaks our heart to see the devastation following a hurricane. Homes are knocked off their pilings and washed away. Folks lose their belongings and look around to anyone for help. But don't you want to ask them—*what were you thinking when you built your home next to the mighty Atlantic Ocean in the first place?*

Stubby stood with his cooling cup of coffee and stared down at Lick Creek from his perch on a limestone outcropping. The water was rising to the point it was lapping over the base of the covered bridge entering the Wolven property.

Drops of water dripped off his boonie cap, plopping one by one into his coffee, when he heard the faint sound of a boat motor. The high-pitched whine got closer. He pulled his binoculars out of his kit and studied the creek one hundred feet below him.

He recognized the boat as being from Croft Dairies. It was Chase. The skiff slowed as it reached the bridge and Chase struggled to grab the wood railing that supported the structure. One of the ranch hands must've recognized Chase because they ran to his aid and tied the boat off on both ends. The gusty winds threatened to tear it loose from its knots. But apparently Chase was satisfied because he began to run up the driveway, rifle in hand.

Stubby met him midway up the hill and took his rifle so that Chase could catch his breath. The young man had come a long way since those reckless forays with Alex. Chase, whose mental errors had put Alex's life in danger twice, had redeemed himself many times over and was now a trusted member of the group.

"They've regrouped and are working their way south," said Chase in between gasps for air.

"Take your time, Chase," said Stubby. He put his arm around the young man and led him toward the house. He took a moment to tighten the drawstring on his hat as a gust of wind threatened to carry it away and then Stubby chuckled. "We ain't in Kansas anymore, Toto."

Chase began to laugh and shook the water out of his shoulder-length hair like a wet pup. "I brought the boat because it was faster than sloshing through the muck with my horse."

Then Chase abruptly stopped in the driveway and said, "I saw him, Stubby."

"Who? Rollie?"

"Yeah. He's a big guy. That night in the jail after they beat me, I was unconscious and never saw him. He makes Junior look like a shrimp."

Stubby laughed. He'd known the boys growing up and Rollie was always looking out for his mouthy, smaller brother. Never one to shy from a fight, Rollie regularly whooped up on anyone who dared cross his sibling. Besides, Stubby had heard, Rollie took to smackin' Junior around on his own from time to time, but considered it to be his prerogative.

"Let's get you inside and you can relay what you've seen to the group," said Stubby.

Coach Carey and Beau greeted them under the porch roof and handed the guys towels to dry off. Everyone's clothes were soaked through and through who were on watch that morning, but the suddenly warmer temperatures eased the discomfort.

Alex, Madison, and Colton were inside with Jake when the group got settled by the fire. Chase enjoyed a mug of strong, black coffee, which helped him calm his nerves as well.

"Give us an update, son," said Jake. Everyone in the house gathered around to hear the latest.

"Okay, well, this morning nine trucks and Humvees arrived all at once. The lead truck had Rollie in it and another officer-looking guy. I don't know anything about ranks, but Rollie would tell him what to do and then he ordered the rest around. Anyway, they went inside for a while and then Rollie came out with his driver and left."

Stubby looked to Jake and Colton, catching the men's eyes to gauge their reaction to this news. Stubby knew what it meant, but he wanted details. "Chase, that left eight trucks. How many men were left behind?"

"I had a hard time counting them because they were milling about, but I'm fairly confident the number was thirty."

The room fell silent. Madison rubbed her husband's shoulders and Alex made eye contact with Stubby. He could tell something was on her mind.

"Coach, during your recon of town, how many men would you say Rollie brought with him?" asked Stubby, returning Alex's stare.

"By our last head count, and keep in mind that was before we all left for Jackson," started Coach Carey, "the last head count was thirty-eight. If we took out six, that would leave thirty-two."

Unintentionally, Stubby gave a slight grin. Alex did as well. He immediately wondered if they were on the same page. *First things first.*

"How are we gonna fight off thirty soldiers?" asked Madison.

"Do we have enough firepower to back them down?" asked Jake.

Stubby moved to calm everyone's concerns. "Okay, I know this sounds bad on the surface, but let me explain to everyone what we have going for us."

Stubby stood and produced a movie poster portraying John Wayne wearing a coonskin cap and a rifle resting on his shoulder. The irony that the poster featured the movie *The Alamo* wasn't lost on anyone. Stubby quickly flipped it over and revealed his rough sketches of Childer's Hill and the surrounding physical features.

"We will station men at all the key points where Rollie's people can advance on us. For days, we've been identifying rock outcroppings, fallen trees, and other areas to provide us cover. Not only will we have the element of surprise, but we'll have plenty of protection when we open fire on them."

"Don't forget about Lick Creek," added Fred Wolven. "We're practically on an island up here, and with the rain we've been havin', that creek can't be crossed except for the bridge."

"It's almost under water," said Chase. "I brought the skiff up from Shiloh Ranch without a problem. No tree stumps or rocks in the creek. The water is up six feet, at least."

It then dawned on Stubby that if Lick Creek had backed up to those levels, it was likely the Tennessee River had risen close to that amount as well. He brought the conversation back to the issue of manpower and weaponry.

"We are a much stronger force than we were two weeks ago. Between Javy and the ranch hands, the people in this room and even the Mennonites, who can handle behind-the-lines communications and watch duties, we almost match them man for man. Throw in the fact that we hold the high ground and have a virtually impenetrable location, we're safer here than we were at Shiloh Ranch."

"I agree," said Colton. "We learned that these FEMA guys don't have their heart in it. Yes, they are trained, but we've seen our share of action too. We have more weapons now and plenty of ammo. We'll be ready for them."

Chapter 35

Evening, December 2
Childer's Hill

For the first time in days, the sun made an appearance as the weather broke and an eerie calm spread across Childer's Hill. The night watch, which consisted of the Mennonite families, took the place of Javy's men around the perimeter of the property. Using the night vision obtained by Alex following the Holder shooting, the night patrols could easily pick up any large-scale threat by FEMA and sound the alarm.

The setting sun cast hues of purple, pink, and red across the clouds, which were moving off to the northeast. The majority of the group stood transfixed on its descent over the horizon, enjoying the spectacle as millions around the world do every day.

Bessie and Char put together a massive meal of chili, cornbread, and shredded cheese. A fire was roaring inside a fenced enclosure by the barn, hiding it from peering eyes and providing warmth for the group as the night set in.

Stubby told Colton and Jake that he expected Rollie's men to discover their position tomorrow based upon the reports he'd received from yesterday's activity. With eight vehicles and thirty men, they were able to cover a lot of ground, especially if they were focused on their target—the people on Childer's Hill.

Colton wandered across the feed pen and located Alex. She had been watching the interaction from afar while sitting with Beau on an upside-down cattle feeder. The two were quiet as he arrived.

"Y'all doin' okay?" asked Colton.

"Yes, Daddy," replied Alex. "We're just takin' it all in. You know, this is how life could be if they'd just leave us alone."

"I know, Alex," said Colton. "Stubby feels certain they'll hit us tomorrow sometime and we'll show them what survival looks like. Pretty soon, folks will stop messin' with us."

"Maybe, but not these people," Alex said. She was not dejected. To the contrary, Alex was incredibly focused on the important events tomorrow might bring. "Daddy, until we deal with the Durhams, we'll always be threatened."

Colton didn't respond.

Alex continued. "Do you know how many times I've kicked myself for not killing Ma that night?" she asked before answering her own question. "Every hour since then."

"I know, Allie-Cat," said Colton. "The whole town understood the ramifications of their decision. Sure, plenty of people wanted to have a trial and execute them. But others couldn't bring themselves to do it, despite the atrocities. I firmly believe that you and Stubby did the right thing by apprehending them in order to be held to account."

"Well, if we'd just killed them, we wouldn't have been run out of Shiloh Ranch. We wouldn't be preparing to fight those Marines or whatever."

Colton responded quickly, "We don't know that, Alex. Killing Ma and Junior might have made it much worse in dealing with Rollie. How do you think he would have reacted? He commands hundreds of troops with more weapons and resources than we could imagine. He might've come down here and wiped the town out instead of just locking people up. So, yeah, I hate the fact that we've got to fight for our lives tomorrow. But at least it's on our terms."

Alex let her dad's words soak in. Of course, he was right, partially. She still saw the problem as residing in Savannah within the confines of Cherry Mansion. Until those three were dealt with, her family and friends, including Beau, would never be safe.

"Listen up, everybody," announced Stubby as he tapped his empty bowl with a spoon.

The murmur of voices died down as people gathered closer to the fire to get warm and listen to Stubby. Once the group had drawn closer, Stubby began.

"We've all come together as a group from different backgrounds and in a variety of ways. The storm that knocked our country to its knees has changed people. There are those who were mean-spirited and selfish but were constrained by a nation of laws, now find themselves free to exert their will upon others. There are others, like ourselves, who've come from all walks of life. We've banded together for a common purpose—survival."

Alex hopped off the feeder and grabbed Beau by the hand. She gave him a smile and nodded for him to come closer to the fire with her. As they approached, Jimbo and Clay stood to the side to give them a front-row spot near Stubby.

"The course of action we've chosen is full of danger, much as life can be anyway. But tomorrow, in all likelihood, we'll be fighting an opponent who doesn't know anything more about us than we know about them. They have orders to kill us from a maniacal leader who is part of an even more psychopathic family.

"We've learned that since the power went out, society collapsed rapidly. The cost of our safety and survival is high, but we will persevere and survive. No matter what, we will not submit or surrender ourselves to the tyranny of the Durhams.

"Tomorrow, we will turn away this threat, not only for our survival, but because we demand freedom to continue our lives without a cloud of danger over our heads. With God's help and your strength, we will succeed."

The group erupted with spontaneous applause. Hugs were shared and high fives were exchanged. Stubby was slapped on the back and afforded praise for providing the uplifting words as the group prepared to fight for their lives.

As the celebration died down, Alex let go of Beau's hand and whispered to him that she would be right back. She walked toward Stubby and took him by the arm.

"We need to talk," she said only loud enough for him to hear. They walked through the crowd and found their way to the barn, where they could be alone.

"Alex, this morning I could tell that something was on your mind," said Stubby.

"I did the math. Stubby, I know you did too."

"I did. Their troop levels on this side of the river tell me that Rollie has thrown everything at the problem. I don't know if I'd say that this is a last-ditch effort, but I do believe that he intends to find us and end it."

Alex looked through the barn door to see if anyone had noticed they were gone. The conversations continued around the fire.

"Yeah, it's more than that," said Alex. "If Rollie sent all of his men over here, how many are left on the other side, in Savannah?"

Stubby shook his head and wandered away, looking to the hayloft for guidance. "Alex, I know what you're thinking and the thought immediately crossed my mind this morning. When I caught your eyes, I saw the dang things light up."

"Then you agree?"

"No, I haven't agreed to anything yet."

Alex started laughing. She picked up a pitchfork and began stabbing a defenseless bale of hay with it. "Yes, Stubby, you have agreed."

Stubby got serious with her. "Do you understand what you're suggesting? We're not assassins. It ain't that easy. My name isn't Jack Reacher and you're not Lara Croft, Tomb Raider, or whatever her name is."

"They're unprotected," Alex shot back. "They'll never expect us to come at them now."

Stubby took the pitchfork away from her and hung it back on the wall. "I should've just killed Junior in the Hornet's Nest," said Stubby as he leaned against the partially closed barn door.

"Yeah, and I should've ended Ma's life too," said Alex. "But things happen for a reason. I don't know what else to do. If we stay here and fight and win, it won't be over. The troops will retreat. They'll bring reinforcements. Heck, Rollie will figure out a way to drop bombs on our heads. I don't think we can count on Horst and

Gunther to fight off Rollie's air attack."

The two stared at each other awkwardly until Alex began to smile.

"Your parents will never approve of this."

"Yes, they will. Besides, it doesn't matter. This has to be done. It's up to you and me. We've got unfinished business and tomorrow is the perfect time to take care of it."

Chapter 36

Late Afternoon, December 2
Near Pickwick Landing Dam
Big Bend Shoals

Steven Popham's home was surrounded by military vehicles and soldiers with their weapons drawn. He and his neighbor, Steven Prince, had survived by fishing and foraging for food in abandoned homes. They had little contact with the outside world anyway and sure didn't care much for the government.

Their two homes built on pilings were unobtrusive in their design and structure. The folks who lived along this stretch of the Tennessee River had only one constant, the massive Pickwick Landing Dam, which hovered over them like a mountain.

When two Humvees and a dozen members of the Tennessee National Guard unloaded at their doorstep, their first inclination was to shoot in order to defend themselves. But they knew they had bigger problems than men with guns.

The spillway of the dam had been closed since the lights went out. Once water had poured over the top like it always did, a steady flow, causing only a ripple of wake along the river.

Not today.

Today, a raging torrent of foam and spray rose high into the air. His view of the sky above the dam was obliterated, as was the massive concrete structure itself. From a mile away, the roar was deafening as tens of millions of gallons of water per minute crashed around, over, and quite possibly through the dam.

The soldiers questioned him and Steve-O, as he called his neighbor. When you had two guys named Steven P, it was easy to get them confused. So he remained Steven, since he lived there first, and his friend became Steve-O.

Steve-O was telling the soldiers about the aircraft they'd heard several days before. He described them as Snoopy and the Red Baron having a dogfight, and then they landed to the west *sommers*. Steve-O was from the country and pronounced the word somewhere as *sommers*.

There's way too much water coming our way, Steven thought to himself as he watched the water overrun the banks below them. In fact, based upon the rapid rise of the river's elevation, he was thinking that they really needed to go. Now.

He thought about the giant lake on the other side of Pickwick. The width and depth of Pickwick Lake dwarfed the Big Bend Shoals turn northward of the Tennessee River. If that water overtook the dam, they'd be washed away.

"Officer or Sergeant or whatever, look here," started Steven. "You see that dam over there? Sumptin's wrong. I've lived here for most of my life and I ain't never seen it throw water like that. Now, y'all are welcome to chat or whatever. But I'm leavin' before the river takes me downstream with it."

The sergeant walked past Steven and stared at the dam for a moment. "Wow," he muttered. "Do you think they've opened the spillway because of the rain? I mean, that's normal, right?"

Steven shook his head. "I ain't never seen it like that. The water's risin' and it looks like it's fixin' to rain even more. I don't want any part of this, you know?"

The sergeant nodded his head. "Let's go, Corporal, it's gettin' late," he ordered before turning his attention back to the two Stevens. "About these airplanes you mentioned. Is there a landing strip or small airport over there? I didn't see one on any of my maps."

"No, there ain't," said Steve-O. "About the only stretch where they could land would be on Johnson's Sod Farm. It's nice and flat over there."

"Hmmm," said the sergeant as he turned on his heels and left.

Steven continued to stare at the dam and asked his friend, "Whadya reckon those folks did to bring the dang Marines down after them?"

"I dunno," Steve-O responded. "I know this. Them boys are mad as hornets about it."

CHAPTER 37

Dawn, December 3
Childer's Hill

Alex came out of the room she shared with her parents, outfitted with her gear. She loaded her backpack with extra ammo and magazines, strapped one of the Ka-Bar knives to her leg, and made sure both her weapons had full mags in them.

"Can I please talk you out of this, Alex?" begged Madison through the tears. "There has to be another way, honey. Please."

Alex didn't respond initially and gave her mom a hug instead. She whispered to her mom and said, "Sometimes the hardest thing and the right thing are the same, Mom. I've made my decision and I'm comfortable with it. Please don't worry about me."

"You're such a big girl now," said Madison. "Of course I'll worry, as a mom. But as a woman, I couldn't be more proud. I will pray for your safety and Stubby's too."

"Pray for our success too. We'll be able to make a life for ourselves when this is over."

Alex broke her mom's embrace. She knew her mother would hold on forever if she didn't. Saying goodbye to her dad would be tougher.

Colton had seen the determination and drive in Alex long before the world got turned upside down. He had raised her to be strong and confident. Early on, he'd impressed upon her that she should never underestimate her strengths, and likewise, she should never overestimate her weaknesses. This concept led her to the *hook it in the rough* axiom that she lived by. As she grew up, her mind-set was always *can-can-can* rather than *can't*.

Although she loved her mom, Madison could never see through Alex's and Colton's eyes when it came to embracing a challenge. There wasn't a difficult task they couldn't overcome.

"Watch your back, Allie-Cat," said Colton. "You guys make a great team, but you never know what might sneak up on you."

"I know, Daddy. Expect the unexpected."

"You've got it," Colton said, laughing. He gave his daughter a tight hug and whispered that he was proud of her.

"Take care of Mom. She's strong too, you know."

"Oh, I know that," said Colton. "She doesn't go looking for fights, but she doesn't shy away from them either. We'll be fine. You just come back to us after you take care of business."

"I will, Daddy. I love you."

Alex walked down the driveway, where Stubby awaited with Chase, Coach Carey, and Beau. Stubby was outfitted similarly to Alex. He carried his AR-10, a .45 holstered in his belt, and one of the Marine-issued Ka-Bar knives strapped in a sheath to his leg.

"Alex, Chase is gonna take us down to the river and then we'll be on our own," said Stubby. "He'll retrieve his horse and hightail it back up here. This will give him a chance to see what's goin' on around Shiloh Ranch."

She turned to Coach Carey and Beau. "Thank you for staying here and protecting everyone."

"You're welcome, Alex," said Coach Carey as he gave her a hug. "We've gone over all of your options to sneak into town and I think you guys know what to do. I'd just get in your way."

Beau moved in for the final goodbye. He and Alex had become extremely close, almost inseparable. When she'd announced her plans to him last night before bed, he protested. The two didn't have an argument in the sense of a couple bickering with each other, but Beau was insistent that he come along to help.

Eventually, Alex had to tell him that she and Stubby were best suited for this. She promised him that they would make it quick and easy. Then it would be over. Beau was better suited to defending Childer's Hill and protecting her parents.

"Beau, promise me that you'll stay by my dad's side and have his back."

"Okay, Alex. I'm not gonna ask you again. Just, please, be careful. If you can't get it done easily, get out of there and come back here. We'll figure it out."

Alex hugged him tighter and gave him a long kiss. She felt in her heart that this wasn't the end. Alex knew that this day would mark the beginning of a great life with Beau and her new family.

"We gotta roll, guys," said Chase, interrupting the embrace. "Daylight's coming and the clouds are building. We don't want to get caught on the water with the skies opening up or Rollie's men around."

Alex and Stubby provided one final set of goodbyes and they marched down the driveway to the boat. Little was said between the three passengers as Chase carefully navigated the swollen creek toward the river. Thunder began to rumble in the distance as they approached Shiloh Ranch. After they crossed Federal Road and entered the property, Chase cut the trolling motor and handed wooden paddles to Alex and Stubby. They rowed the last quarter mile to where Chase's horse was tied off.

They tied the skiff to a tree and climbed out for a moment to ready themselves for the trip across the river. Stubby climbed up the embankment to get a better look at the main house through his binoculars.

"Alex, I don't want to have some mushy goodbyes, okay?"

Alex started laughing. "Were you anglin' to get a kiss or something?"

"No, nothing like that," Chase retreated, slightly embarrassed.

"I'll kiss you if it'll make you feel better." Alex chuckled.

"No, dude, seriously. I was just gonna say that you are amazing. You know, in a real cool sister kinda way. You're not really a girl, right? You're more like a man in a woman's body."

Alex jokingly placed her hand on her pistol and unsnapped the holster. "I'm not sure how I feel about that statement."

Chase backed away and held both hands up. "Nah, I didn't mean anything bad by that. I mean, I'm just sayin' you're braver and stronger and smarter than any girl I've ever met. I have no doubt that you're gonna take those scumbags out."

Alex snapped her holster strap and approached Chase to give him a hug. Her friend had been through a lot, not to mention being ostracized for things that had happened while they were out foraging. She'd never held him responsible, but in hindsight, the events had made him grow up quite a bit.

"You are like my brother, and you're also my partner. When this is over, we'll get back to finding stuff. It was an adventure, right?"

He gave her a hug and patted her on the head. "All of the things we went through out there have prepared you for this moment. You're my partner and always will be. Hurry back so that we can get back to it."

"Deal," said Alex, who gave Chase a kiss on the cheek.

Stubby made his way down the embankment and reported what he'd seen. A loud smack of thunder caused all three of them to duck.

"They're loading up now. Chase, you better get movin' so they won't catch you on the road somewhere. Tell Jake and them that it's time."

"I will. Be careful, Stubby," said Chase.

The thunder clapped, causing everyone to look upward. The rain began to fall again.

Stubby grabbed Chase by the shoulders and said, "I'm proud of you, young man. You're the grandson I never had. Promise me that you'll protect Jake, Emily, and my beloved Bessie. You guys are my family. I don't want any harm to come to any of you."

"Yes, sir," said Chase, who quickly gave Stubby a bro-hug.

The rain began to pour down on them and the winds started pushing the trees around like palm trees in a hurricane. Stubby looked to Alex and nodded.

"Let's go. This is gonna be one heckuva day."

Chapter 38

Late Morning, December 3
Childer's Hill

Colton jogged along the fencerow and reached the opening where the Wolvens' long driveway made its way across the partially flooded bridge. He'd just watched Jakob, one of the young Mennonites charged with perimeter security watch, as he rode across the rain-soaked field before his horse stumbled from a sprained leg. Leaving the limping horse behind, he zigzagged across the remaining five hundred yards, stumbling several times before he found his way to where Colton could provide him assistance navigating the overflowing waters of Lick Creek onto the bridge.

Through the howling winds, radio communications between the line of nearly thirty Childer's Hill refugees was difficult. With Jakob's return, the last of the Mennonites was back on the property and acting as messengers. If the comms were unusable due to the rain, they would create a human chain of messengers to pass along vital information.

"They're coming, sir," Jakob said to Colton. "They're now on the other side of the sod farm. They found the airplanes."

Colton patted the young man on the back. "You did a great job, Jakob. Catch your breath and tell your brother to bring the tractor down here."

While he waited, Colton sloshed through the two-foot-deep water, holding onto the rail to maintain his balance. With the rain, Lick Creek's banks were overflowing significantly, but the current wasn't fast like a creek filled with mountain runoff. It was simply rising, an indicator that the surrounding tributaries, like the Tennessee River, were rising with it.

At eleven feet wide and just under nine feet tall, the covered bridge barely accommodated a large SUV, much less the military vehicles used by the National Guard and FEMA. Nonetheless, Colton wanted to block access to the bridge to any smaller vehicles they might be using.

The old John Deere 7020 tractor powered by a six-cylinder diesel engine rumbled into view and worked its way across the bridge. Colton wondered if its weight would prevent it from becoming buoyant.

The tractor rolled across the bridge, water covering the top of its yellow front rims, but all four wheels remained firmly on the bridge floor. Within a few minutes, the young man deftly maneuvered the tractor in place, wedging it from side to side. With the amount of firepower focused on this only means of access to Childer's Hill, Colton was confident the bridge was well defended.

Colton retreated to his position behind the square baler at the foot of the driveway. Resting his back against the six-foot-wide steel farm implement, he was startled by Beau, who raced down the driveway to join him before dropping to a knee.

"I thought you were covering the east end of the fence line," said Colton.

"I was. Chase and I traded positions. He can use his sniper rifle to pick them off in the field better from over there. Plus, I'm acting on my superior's orders."

"Who, Stubby?"

"No, sir. Your daughter's."

"What did Alex say?"

"That your back needed watching." Beau laughed. "So here I am."

The baler was not big enough to cover three guys, so Colton sent Jakob to Javy's position on the rock outcropping. He and Beau would work together at the foot of the driveway, the closest position to the oncoming attackers.

"Well, Beau, now we wait."

CHAPTER 39

Late Morning, December 3
Savannah

Stubby and Alex circumvented the roadblock manned by Junior's new deputies on the south side of Savannah. Unlike his previous hired mercenaries who took pride in their jobs because of the types of payment they received, this new bunch barely noticed as Stubby carefully maneuvered the white Ford Elite through connected driveways just two hundred yards to their west.

As they traversed the neighborhood streets on the west side of town, they eventually ran into Town Branch, the five-foot-wide creek that Colton had followed on the day they arrived in Savannah. The branch, however, was now five feet deep and nearly fifteen feet wide. The car wouldn't make it through, and driving around it wasn't an option because it took them back to CR 128, the main north-south highway in town.

The rain was coming down again and the situation was not going to get any better. Their best option was to walk around the creek, looking for higher ground. Scurrying from house to house in order to avoid detection, the two made quick time, moving nearly a mile to the east.

"Stubby, look! The cemetery sits on a rise. We can cut through it and make our way towards town again."

Alex led the way as they used the gravestones and massive oak trees for cover. Running from point to point in wet clothes and with sloppy footing, they were both heaving for air. Eventually they found Cherry Street and moved parallel with it toward the electric power substation. They tucked themselves into a lean-to shed to catch their breath and avoid the never-ending supply of rain.

After recovering from the sprint, Stubby said to Alex, "I've only seen flooding like this one time since I've been a child and that was around Christmas of 2015. That year, the waters rose eight to ten feet and the damage to the area was substantial. People tried to drive through the flooded creeks, only to be carried downstream and, in a couple of cases, down the Tennessee River. An eighteen-wheeler toting a Sysco Food trailer jackknifed, sending the trailer into a creek on the west side of the river. It floated a few hundred yards before it got stuck on the bridge abutments."

Alex looked up to the sky and then toward the burgeoning Town Branch in front of them. "And you say this is worse?"

"Without a doubt."

The sound of a vehicle driving toward them caused Stubby and Alex to hide behind some fifty-five-gallon drums in the lean-to.

The truck pulled up to the bridge before crossing the creek and stopped. The unarmed driver stepped out of the pickup and walked through the water, which reached just below his knees. He returned to his vehicle and backed up, seemingly smart enough to turn around and go another way. Then he abruptly stopped, revved the engine and spun the tires as he sped toward the crossing.

As the truck hit the knee-deep water, it immediately decelerated as if hitting a brick wall, thus throwing him forward in his seat. His mouth hit the steering wheel and he spewed blood and teeth all over the dash. The truck's momentum carried across the bridge before coming to a stop twenty feet from the lean-to.

The man fell over in the front bench seat, groaning in pain. Alex shouldered her rifle and reached for her knife when Stubby stopped her.

"Leave him. He's got enough trouble. Come on."

Stubby moved a barrel out of the way and ran past the pickup at a safe distance. He and Alex then walked across the concrete guardrails like they were on a tight rope before landing on firm ground on the other side. Without looking back, they raced through the tall grass to their next point of cover, a small white clapboard house just two hundred yards from the Hardin County Detention Center.

Chapter 40

Noon, December 3
Childer's Hill

Every high school kid learned about that first fateful shot fired at the North Bridge during the battles of Lexington and Concord. Historically known as the *shot heard around the world*, it represented the initial foray by the colonists in their quest for independence and freedom from a repressive government.

Colton doubted that this initial burst from the M4 seized from the FEMA patrols would ever be written about in history books, but to this group of survivors, it was just as meaningful. The shots found their mark and served his primary purpose—disable the lead vehicle of the approaching convoy just as it reached the bridge, thus providing an additional blockade for the only means of ingress.

The vehicles quickly fanned out through the fields and took up positions along the tree line about two hundred yards from Lick Creek. Colton's opening salvo was a signal to all of the brave men and women defending Childer's Hill to open fire, which they did.

The Humvees were accompanied by two MRAPs and an M35 Deuce and a Half. The barrage of gunfire riddled the vehicles with bullets and penetrated the glass windows, wounding several of the soldiers. Caught off guard, the men scrambled for safety by piling out of the side opposite of Childer's Hill.

Colton keyed the mic. "Hold fire. Hold fire." Gradually, the weapons of his friends grew quiet.

The scene was surreal as the line of military vehicles created a crescent-shaped line along the tree row, stretching from below the covered bridge until Lick Creek meandered back across the field at the base of Childer's Hill. For several minutes, the two sides assessed each other, neither wanting to make the next move.

A bullhorn broke the silence.

"My name is Sergeant Nathan McIntosh of the Tennessee National Guard here on behalf of FEMA. I have orders to arrest the occupants of these premises from Major Roland Durham pursuant to the provisions of the Declaration of Martial Law. You are commanded to lay down your weapons and grant us immediate entry."

Colton looked at Beau and shook his head. He resisted the urge to yell *nuts* in response. He remained in control and stayed silent. There was only going to be one end to this story, and that was with the FEMA soldiers leaving or dying.

He set his rifle to the side and removed his jacket. The day was beginning to warm up and his anxiety had raised his body temperature. Colton thought the group was in for a long day, so he decided to get comfortable.

The winds whipped the tops of the trees and a huge gust caused the hay baler to shake slightly. As the rain began to fall again, he wiped the lenses of his binoculars and turned to study their adversaries.

Somebody was going to have to get impatient and make a move; otherwise they'd sit here all day—waiting.

Chapter 41

Afternoon, December 3
Childer's Hill

An hour had passed and not a single shot had been fired. Sergeant McIntosh had repeated his demands precisely every ten minutes until the last attempt, which was followed by the vehicles starting up in unison.

"Are they leaving?" asked Beau.

Colton paused and then replied, "I don't know, but I'm not sure how that helps us. They may leave enough men to keep us trapped up here and wait for the weather to break. Or they might return with more firepower."

Suddenly, the trucks turned toward the woods initially and then moved in reverse toward the creek. The sergeant was positioning them closer to Childer's Hill. Colton caught a glimpse of the soldiers advancing toward them by crouching low and using the vehicles as cover. As a signal to the others, Colton opened fire with the hopes of stalling the advance.

Once again, bullets rained upon the vehicles, causing a wide variety of pings and dings as they ricocheted off the tailgates and fenders. But the trucks moved closer to the creek, undeterred.

One of the massive M35 transports got stuck in the mud and began to spin its tires. The driver rocked the vehicle forward and back, to no avail. The entire convoy stopped to maintain a relatively straight line. As if performing a synchronized swimming move, the trucks maneuvered to park broadside to the creek, providing their men ample cover from which to attack.

Now the FEMA troops were in a position to fight, using their superior skills and firepower to assault the shooters, who had the high ground. Colton studied them through his binoculars.

Without warning, gunshots rang out to Colton's right. One of his groups of shooters had opened fire on the M35, which was still trying to break free of the hole it had dug in the muddy ground. Colton realized the error the shooters made in an instant.

The entire squad of soldiers opened fire on that position. The explosion of automatic fire ripped through the trees and tore up the ground around the two nervous ranch hands with happy trigger fingers. They were cut to ribbons as they panicked and ran up the hill, seeking safety.

"Hold fire! Hold fire!" Colton yelled into the radio.

This was not going to work. They needed to coordinate their efforts; otherwise the soldiers could focus all of their attention on a particular spot. He had to think. He wasn't a soldier and didn't understand the nuances of conquering a field of battle. The men who flanked him on both sides were defending Childer's Hill, not taking the offensive on the men across the creek below them.

The rains and wind suddenly subsided. Colton looked up to the sky for guidance and noticed that it had changed to an odd hue of green. He recalled the beautiful aurora that had filled the sky during the solar storm at Zero Hour. But this—this was different.

"Why did the sky turn green?" Colton mumbled to himself.

Chapter 42

Afternoon, December 3
Savannah

Crossing Main Street was not an easy task. Junior had four fresh, new faces posted at the bridge, which only had one concrete barricade protecting its access. The westbound lane was only blocked with black and white TDOT sawhorses. The military traffic in and out of town was now sent through Adamsville and then northward toward Jackson. As a result, security was beefed up at the bridge.

The decision to cross near the bridge was a difficult one. Stubby hated that they would be exposed as they ran across the four lanes of Main Street, but choosing a crossing point farther east required going past the Detention Center and then yet another highway utilized by Junior's people to travel north and south.

Lightning lit up the sky, followed by a thunderous boom, which rattled the windows of the one-stop oil-change location next to the demolished Hickory Pit BBQ restaurant. Stubby immediately swung his binoculars in the direction of the checkpoint to gauge the reaction of the men manning the barricades.

They all looked miserable standing in the rain in olive drab ponchos with their caps pulled over their eyes to shield them from the storm. Another bright flash of lightning and an immediate thunderclap caused Stubby to jump.

"Wow!" exclaimed Alex. "That was close."

"Yeah, and it also will provide us the perfect cover," said Stubby. "Get ready, Alex. With the next flash of lightning, we need to run across the street to the gas station."

"Together? Don't you want me to cover you?"

"Not this time," replied Stubby. "Those guys are too preoccupied with the lightning. They're distracted enough for us to make our move. Besides, I see the sky clearing to the southwest. We may not get a better chance."

"Okay, it'll be like a track meet," said Alex, who had run track during her freshman and sophomore years at Davidson Academy before she got serious about golf.

The two waited, but the lightning didn't cooperate. They both peered from around the corner of the building. The men at the bridge were getting more comfortable as the raindrops subsided.

"Are you kiddin' me?" said an incredulous Stubby.

Then it happened. The sky brightened as a spiderweb of electric current stretched up the Tennessee River as far as the eye could see.

Neither of them hesitated as they darted across the road, easily clearing the two hundred feet in about fifteen seconds. About the time they hit the yellow stripe down the center of Main Street, the ground shook with the massive explosion of thunder, the biggest thus far. Stubby glanced to his left and saw all of the men cover their heads. *Perfect!*

After they slipped under the gas pump canopy and flattened themselves against the wall out of view, they both released their breath simultaneously. This drew a giggle from Alex, helping to lighten the mood.

"You know, this *Spy versus Spy* stuff is a lot of work," Alex said to Stubby, drawing a chuckle in response.

"I'm too old for this and out of practice too. If I had known this was what life was gonna be like after the crap hit the fan, I would've laid off the cornbread and pecan pie." Stubby pronounced the word *pee-can*, not *pa-can*, like Yankees do.

Alex took one final deep breath and looked around the corner of the gas station to confirm they'd made the crossing undetected. She nodded at Stubby with a determined look on her face.

"It's game time."

Chapter 43

Late Afternoon, December 3
Childer's Hill

Colton tilted his head in wonder at the green hue that slowly was overcome by a foreboding dark gray. He craned his neck above the protection afforded by the hay baler and looked to the south. A black wall cloud was forming, a telltale sign for any Southerner who lived in Dixie Alley, a corridor spanning six states running from Central Louisiana to Nashville.

"Oh no," shouted Colton to Beau. "I think a tornado is forming."

Beau lifted off the ground to see for himself before Colton grabbed him by the belt and pulled him back.

"Careful, Beau. Do you remember those guys across the way?"

"But the wind is dying down," argued Beau. "And the rain has stopped."

Colton looked at the treetops, which remained stoic in the absence of any wind. As a golfer, he'd learned to watch for freak afternoon storms when the atmosphere could become unstable. The weather they'd been having was certainly out of the norm. They'd recently experienced periods of warm days, followed by colder ones, and then weather like today's that approached sixty degrees.

He pulled his binoculars out to assess the FEMA positions. Just as he rose above the hay baler to take a look, he was pelted on the hand, causing him to drop the binoculars in pain.

Tink—tink—tink.

Hail began to fall on the top of the steel piece of machinery.

Bang—bang-bang-bang.

Baseball-size balls of ice had formed and were raining down upon them. Colton knew the telltale signs.

"Everybody! Run! Now! Run for cover in the root cellar."

Colton looked skyward and saw the cloud beginning to rotate. He grabbed Beau by the arm and yelled over the noise, "Jakob and his brother don't have radios. They're near Javy at the rock wall. Run to them and get everybody out of here. I'm gonna lay down cover fire for you guys. Beau, hurry!"

Beau took off to the left and darted through the trees. The soldiers saw the retreat of the men and opened fire. Their high-powered rifles pelted the woods, embedding in trees and dirt. Colton had to give his friends some protection.

He stood up from behind the hay baler and emptied his first magazine into several of the FEMA positions, causing them to back down. He quickly dropped the mag and reloaded.

Bullets accompanied the hail pounding his position. Like an Afghan fighter hiding behind a wall, he raised his M4 and sent a hail of bullets in the general direction of the soldiers.

They returned fire, using the power of a couple of dozen automatic weapons to blister the hay baler. Colton's heart was beating out of his chest. With the retreat to safety by his comrades, he was all that stood between the FEMA platoon and his new family atop Childer's Hill.

Colton closed his eyes and took a deep breath. He was alone, trapped by gunfire flying all around him, and the biggest danger of all was the tornado building to the south.

Chapter 44

**Late Afternoon, December 3
Childer's Hill**

Shots ripped through the underbrush and shredded the bark of pine trees to his left. He heard the sound of footprints snapping twigs and sloshing across the wet forest floor. Colton rose and returned fire, hearing the screams of two men in uniform who'd attempted to move from the cover of one truck to another.

Beau slipped on the wet pine needles as he attempted to slow his momentum, causing him to lose his weapon, which tumbled down the hill and came to a rest in the middle of the driveway. Colton saw that he was considering retrieving it and hollered at him.

"Forget it!" he shouted and then motioned for Beau to come behind their cover position. Colton fired off two short bursts to give Beau the seconds he needed to crawl to safety.

"Thanks," Beau said to Colton as his chest heaved from the sprint through the woods.

"I told you to get to safety," said Colton, looking towards the dark sky above them.

"I know, but I promised Alex."

Colton ducked as bullets ripped up the gravel to their right, leaving a trail of indentations up the driveway.

The rumble he heard next was off in the distance. His first inclination was to look down toward the covered bridge to determine if the trucks were attempting to cross. There was no activity. Then he thought it might have been a helicopter or maybe even two. *So this is how they're breaking the stalemate—with Apache gunships.*

"Colton, it's coming!" exclaimed Beau, pointing at the sky.

The counter-rotation of the clouds created an obviously visible tornado headed in their direction. The rumble became a roar accompanied by a high-pitched swishing sound.

"Now, Beau, run! I'll cover you!"

Beau took off up the hill as Colton opened fire. The winds were whipping the trees, and debris was sailing through the air.

He darted up the hill after Beau and then a searing pain ripped through his shoulder. The impact of what had struck Colton knocked him to the ground. Dazed and confused, he attempted to stand and another projectile ripped into the back of his thigh, knocking him back to the ground. He felt the warm trickle of blood soak the front of his shirt and instinctively felt for the source of the moisture.

Colton's hands were covered in blood. His blood. His eyes glossed over as he fell to the earth. He heard the shouting and then the screams. *Am I entering purgatory?*

He was losing consciousness as he visualized the freight train headed for him, the light on the front shining brightly in his eyes. The sound was deafening and the whoosh of air that passed over his body caused him to shudder.

He could see the passengers, their noses pressed against the window. Alex as a baby. Maddie the day they met. Alex standing proudly with her golf trophy. Maddie flirting with him in a new dress.

Suddenly, the train became black. No loving faces. No light at the end of the tunnel. Only the screams following the train as it streaked by. Agonized moans of the dying permeated the darkness of Colton's mind. Then Colton Ryman blacked out.

Chapter 45

**Late Afternoon, December 3
Cherry Mansion
Savannah**

They'd watched and waited for over an hour as they assessed their options to attack the Durhams. They stalked their prey, moving from position to position around the perimeter of Cherry Mansion, confirming there were no guards but, more importantly, confirming that all three little pigs were ready for slaughter.

For a while, Ma remained upstairs while her sons milled about the first level. Finally, she emerged and entered the kitchen to make some tea. Eventually the three of them settled in the parlor facing the river for their afternoon chat.

Stubby thought the time was right. The rain had stopped and the winds died down. The weather was no longer going to help provide them cover, and time was no longer on their side. He and Alex agreed that entering through the back doors facing the town would provide the Durhams a few additional seconds to react. Their best plan of attack was to burst through the front door, catch them off guard, and finish this nightmare.

With the decision made, they stealthily made their way towards the front of the house. Once in position, they began to move closer by taking turns racing from oak tree to oak tree, one covering the other as they went.

The skies turned an ominous shade of whitish-gray as they found themselves within fifty feet of the front porch. The Tennessee River had risen well above its normal elevation, bringing the water closer and closer to Cherry Mansion.

"Alex, something must've happened to the dam. The river has never been this high in my lifetime."

"I can see the water rising, Stubby. It may reach the house!"

Stubby looked to the rising water levels and saw the debris rapidly floating down the river. Parts of houses and several vehicles bobbed in the river's waves.

"C'mon!" shouted Stubby and they began to jog towards the house. Several cedar trees blocked their view of the front door and the porch steps.

Alex readied her rifle, keeping her eye on both the porch coming into view and the windows, looking for signs of movement. As they rounded the cedar trees, they were both caught off guard by the presence of all three Durhams on the front porch, watching the rising water.

Stubby dropped to one knee and raised his weapon, but a strong gust of wind knocked him off balance. Before he could regain his balance, Alex fired off a burst of rounds, which missed high, tearing into the porch roof.

For a split second, the Durhams were frozen in time. Alex fired again, this time with deadly accuracy. Three rounds tore into Ma Durham's frail body, knocking her backward into a post and then causing her to somersault over the rail into the wet grass.

Rollie's training allowed him to react. He whipped out his sidearm and fired several shots at Alex, the last of which hit the handguard of her AR-15 and twisted it out of her grip. She was spun to the ground and reached for her rifle as more shots embedded in the ground next to her. Rollie attempted to fire again, this time turning his attention to Stubby. Stubby ducked and rolled down the hill to evade the shots. Rollie's magazine was empty.

As he regained his footing, Stubby fired back. His rounds sailed past Rollie and hit Junior in the shoulder, spinning him around to his knees. Junior desperately tried to retrieve his sidearm with his left hand, but three more quick rounds by Stubby obliterated his arm and sank deep into his chest. Junior Durham died instantly while his body was rolling down the front steps of Cherry Mansion to join his mother.

Stubby turned his rifle on Rollie and squeezed the trigger.

Click—click—click.

The M4 he'd taken from Rollie's men jammed. Stubby quickly attempted to clear it.

"I'm gonna drag you to hell with me, Crump!" shouted Rollie as he began to charge.

Stubby reached for his sidearm when the roar of the wind filled the air. Before he could get off a shot, a one-hundred-fifty-year-old oak tree was uprooted from the rain-drenched turf. Its massive arms in the form of branches came crashing to the earth, trapping Alex and Stubby underneath.

Chapter 46

Late Afternoon, December 3
Cherry Mansion
Savannah

Alex had attempted to roll away from the tentacles of the oak tree but was pinned down by its grasp. Pain ripped through her pelvis and right arm as both bore the weight of the top of the tree. Her face had been scratched open by smaller branches, causing blood to flow from her forehead and cheeks.

She shouted for Stubby, who had been fifteen feet to her left. He didn't respond. She tried to wiggle loose, but was trapped by the weight.

"Stubby! Stubby! Are you okay?"

"Yeah," he groaned a reply. "I'm buried under these ..."

"Good," growled Rollie as he stood up in the yard, emerging from the cover of the smaller branches. "It'll save me the trouble of burying ya after I kill ya!"

Alex watched as Rollie tore through the fallen branches and made his way toward Stubby, who was wrestling to free himself. She tried to pull her weapon, but it had fallen out of her holster when the tree pinned her down at the hips.

"Stubby, watch out! He's coming!"

"Shut up!" Rollie snarled, taking a broken branch and heaving it in her direction. "Don't go anywhere; you're next!"

More limbs cracked and Rollie began to stomp on them in an effort to reach Stubby, who was only ten feet away.

Alex wiggled and even dug at the turf to free herself. She frantically attempted to get out from under the tree while also searching for her sidearm.

Whack!

Arrrrggggh!

Rollie was upon Stubby and hit him across the jaw. Stubby found the strength to push the tree branches off his chest and slid underneath them to avoid another blow. It wasn't fast enough to avoid the kick to his ribs, which sent him rolling downhill into another pile of broken branches.

Stubby got to his feet and lunged at Rollie, driving his head into the younger man's stomach. Rollie groaned and gasped for air after he hit the ground with a thud.

Holding his aching ribs, Stubby ran past Rollie's outstretched hands and attempted to get to Alex. She was having some success in moving the tree down her legs, which allowed both hands to be free.

Rollie lunged and jumped on his back, forcing them both into a pile of debris. Like a crazed ape, Rollie delivered blow after blow to the back of Stubby's head.

"Stop! You'll kill him!" shouted Alex.

"You betcha! Then you'll be next, hussy!" Rollie fired back.

He continued to beat Stubby until Rollie lost his balance and slipped, catching his foot under the tree. Stubby had an opening. He attempted to stand and help Alex once again, but Rollie grabbed him by the foot.

Then Rollie pulled Stubby toward him, grabbing his ankles and his pants for leverage. This stopped Stubby's attempt to reach Alex and allowed Rollie to free himself.

That was when Alex saw Rollie reach for Stubby's knife, which was tucked into the sheath around his leg. She had to help. With all of her strength and using the adrenaline that powered her body, Alex heaved the heavy tree branch off her leg.

She found her footing and ran toward the brawling men, but not before Rollie thrust the knife into Stubby's belly. His cackling laugh caused the hair to stand up on her spine.

He hissed into Stubby's ear, "Every man has a devil, and I'm yours, Crump. You're not strong enough to live through this storm."

Alex jumped on Rollie's back and screamed in his ear, "Wrong! I am the storm!" She plunged the knife into Rollie's neck and twisted it, causing blood to spurt all over the men.

Holding his throat, Rollie rolled down the hill. He attempted to gurgle out a laugh through his bloody grin.

Alex pounced on him. *Finish it*, she thought as she jammed the knife into the devil's empty heart.

"Go back to Hell!" she screamed in his face.

After one final twist, she scrambled up the hill to where Stubby lay against the trunk of the fallen oak. He was covered in blood and clutched his stomach where more blood was oozing out.

The floodwaters had risen even more, reaching the root-ball of the tree, causing it to rock back and forth. She helped Stubby to his feet and draped his arm over her shoulder. Using Alex as a crutch, Stubby made his way to the front porch steps before collapsing.

Alex took off her jacket and pressed it against Stubby's wound. She didn't bother to look at it. She knew it was bad.

"Stubby, can you hold on to this? Can you keep pressure on it while I get help?"

Within seconds, her jacket was soaked with blood. Alex looked around frantically, unsure of what to do. She jumped up and ran onto the porch, thinking she might find some medical supplies inside the house.

"Alex, no," Stubby groaned. "It's too late."

"No, it's not," she pleaded. "Stubby, you can survive this. Look what we've been through."

Stubby smiled as Alex returned to his side. "No, Alex, my days are done."

"Bessie! Think about Bessie. She loves you. You fight for your life, for her. For me!"

Stubby touched her bloodied face and nodded.

The water levels crept closer to the house, overtaking the bodies of the dead Durhams. Rollie's corpse was entangled in tree branches and sank below the surface of the river, only to emerge farther downstream. Ma's body began to float, and then it was joined by

Junior's, which rolled over face down in the water.

Out of frustration, Alex stood and grabbed the Brumby Rocker. She heaved it at Betty Jean Durham's gunshot-riddled remains, temporarily sinking it under water before it bounced back to the surface.

"Rot in Hell! All of you!"

Alex began to sob and she rushed back to Stubby's side. "Stubby, please. You can't die. I need you."

She was crying uncontrollably, clutching him close to her chest. "I need you more than you know."

Stubby reached his arm around her neck and pulled her close to his ear. "Alex, a soldier can only die once. I've done my duty. This is my time."

Alex wailed, screaming, "*No, no, no,*" repeatedly. "You have to fight to live. Don't give up!"

The waters rose and the Durhams were carried downriver, one by one, swirling and bobbing until they disappeared into the murky water.

As darkness overtook the day, Stubby pulled Alex's head down and whispered, "Alex, no matter what happens to me, always lead the way."

Epilogue

Five Years Later
Near Lick Creek
Shiloh Ranch

Life is about change. At times, we make choices that lead us in a different direction. Other times, choices are made for us that alter the path we follow forever.

In the 36 hours leading up to the solar storm, Alex sensed that the life she knew, and had become comfortable with, would be gone. She didn't focus on what she had to give up in this new world without power. Instead, she embraced the challenge and adopted a survival mindset.

Alex dismounted from Snowflake, her faithful companion since her arrival at Shiloh Ranch. Despite the fact that the world was rebuilding, and transportation was returning to an extent, Alex still preferred Snowflake to get around. The two were inseparable when she was around the ranch proving that sometimes, your best friend doesn't always have to be a human.

She tied the reigns to the four-year-old apple trees planted atop the Indian Mound overlooking Lick Creek to the south and the fields full of dairy cows to the north. The Tennessee River flowed along nearby, having been returned to the confines of its banks several years ago.

It had been rough-going for the surviving residents of Shiloh Ranch. Despite the removal of evil from their adopted town, the difficulties of healing and rebuilding faced the locals, as well as the families throughout the region.

Full of emotion, Alex walked through the grass which crunched under feet from the first frost. Seeing the gravestones instantly brought tears to her eyes. She knelt between them and laid magnolia tree branches neatly tied with twine on top of each grave.

"Sorry, but flowers are in short supply in December." Alex attempted to mask her grief by making light of the tradition. She wiped away the tears and managed a smile.

Alex learned that people lose people. We are constantly losing things as we grow and adapt to ever-changing conditions in our lives. But, that's what life's about. Over time, Alex decided it's what you gain from that loss that makes life worth living.

"Well," she started. "A lot has happened since I stopped to talk with you guys last. For one thing, Beau proposed to me and we're gonna get married next summer. He wanted to get married right away but I told him it would have to wait until after I get my feet wet on the Governor's new advisory board.

"Which, of course, is the second thing I have to tell you. The Governor has offered me a position on his West Tennessee Rebuilding Commission. My job is to work with local governments on getting reestablished and helping coordinate rebuilding efforts.

"As the power is restored to the small towns and rural counties of West Tennessee, I'll coordinate their local efforts with the state government. Beau will be able to travel with me so we can always be together.

"I miss you both so much. Even though you're gone, you haven't gone away. I feel you walking with me — unseen, unheard, but always near. I'll always love you both. Trust me, I will never give up my feelings for you. Life will go on, but it'll never be the same."

Alex rose from her knees and touched her fingers to her lips, and planted a kiss on the gravestone of *Clarence "Stubby" Crump, beloved husband, Army Ranger and Hero*.

Alex also planted a finger kiss on Bessie's gravestone as well. She'd died months afterwards from pneumonia. But Alex firmly believed that she couldn't bear the loss of her beloved husband.

"He was a good man, Allie-Cat, and Bessie loved you as her own. We'll always keep them in our prayers."

"I know Daddy. You never quite get over it. You just slowly learn how to go on without them."

Alex turned and walked into the arms of Colton and Madison. Together, the Rymans were a family which had faced the depravity of man, and survived.

THANK YOU FOR READING DEVIL'S HOMECOMING and THE BLACKOUT SERIES!

If you enjoyed it, I'd be grateful if you'd take a moment to write a short review (just a few words are needed) and post it on Amazon. Amazon uses complicated algorithms to determine what books are recommended to readers. Sales are, of course, a factor, but so are the quantities of reviews my books get. By taking a few seconds to leave a review, you help me out, and also help new readers learn about my work.

And before you go…

SIGN UP for Bobby Akart's mailing list to receive special offers, bonus content, and you'll be the first to receive news about new releases.

eepurl.com/bYqq3L

VISIT Amazon.com/BobbyAkart for more information on his next project, as well as his completed words: the Doomsday series, the Yellowstone series, the Lone Star series, the Pandemic series, the Blackout series, the Boston Brahmin series and the Prepping for Tomorrow series totaling nearly forty novels, including over thirty Amazon #1 Bestsellers in forty-plus fiction and nonfiction genres.

Visit Bobby Akart's website for informative blog entries on preparedness, writing, and a behind-the-scenes look into his novels.

BobbyAkart.com

READ ON FOR A BONUS EXCERPT from

PANDEMIC: BEGINNINGS
Book One in The Pandemic Series

Best Selling Author of The Blackout Series

BOBBY AKART

BEGINNINGS

THE PANDEMIC SERIES ❦ BOOK ONE

Prologue

You are free to make your choices, but you are not free to choose the consequences.

Western Africa

They were dragging Dr. Francois Alexis through a dark, dusty hallway. He'd become confused at how long he'd been held in the tiny cell, without light, and no sustenance. For days, he'd been bound and gagged. A dark hood was pulled over his head, which also made it difficult to breathe. Dr. Alexis had become completely disoriented in a world of blackness and terror.

Between the beatings and the fitful attempts at sleep, Dr. Alexis was unable to determine whether he'd been held captive for two days or ten. Many events were impossible for him to discern in this starved, sleep-deprived state. *What do they want from me?*

All he could remember was leaving the International Medical Research Centre in the former French colony of Gabon on the West Africa coast late Friday night. He stopped to pick up a sandwich and was hit in the back of the neck with a powerful blow, forcing him to the ground. He remembered the black hood being pulled over his head and he was whisked away in a vehicle to an unknown destination. His attackers never uttered a word throughout the abduction.

The Center for International Medical Research where he worked, known as the CIRMF, was staffed by one hundred sixty-seven scientists and had an annual budget of over five million dollars. Based in Franceville, a city of one hundred thousand in southeast Gabon, the facility boasted a biological research infrastructure, which was rare in Africa, including a biosafety level 4 laboratory. A BSL-4 represented the highest level of biosafety precautions and was designed for working with the world's most dangerous pathogens.

Dr. Alexis was one of a dozen scientists focused on emerging infectious diseases like Ebola, Marburg, and the three varieties of plague. The facility's primatology center was among the largest in the world. Containing five hundred primates, half of which were housed in a jungle enclosure, the CIRMF was ideally suited for testing and researching viruses in their natural hosts.

With his mind racing, seeking answers as well as anticipating what was happening, Dr. Alexis struggled against his captors while peering through the bottom of the black hood, which continued to obstruct his vision.

The more he struggled, the harsher he was treated. When the hood was removed, enabling him to see the floor, he stopped his resistance.

He was forced through an entryway into a brightly lit room, where a variety of power cords and cables spread across the floor. One of his captors yelled at him in Arabic and pushed him into a nondescript wooden chair in the center of the room.

Another man issued orders, barking the words in a guttural language he couldn't interpret, and the room lit up with artificial light, causing Dr. Alexis to wince despite his limited vision. He adjusted his posture in the chair and two strong arms pulled him upright in the chair. Then his hands were strapped to the back of the chair with zip-ties. His legs were bound in a similar manner, which effectively immobilized him. He'd become one with the chair.

The room became eerily silent. There was no speaking. No shuffling of feet. Only the faint sound of an internal fan on a computer or other electronic device, which whirred in the background. The anticipation added to Dr. Alexis's anxiety. His heart was pounding in his chest. He tried to speak, but the gag prevented the words from coming out. *What is happening?*

ZING!

The screeching sound of metal on metal filled the room. The

noise was familiar, but Dr. Alexis couldn't place it in his agitated state of mind. Horror overtook him as he frantically looked from side to side to locate the source of the sound.

Suddenly, an arm wrapped itself around his forehead and pulled his head back, exposing the pulsating veins in his neck. The young Frenchman felt the cold steel of the blade press against his flesh. He looked down past his nose to catch a glimpse of the weapon. It was a sword, polished chrome glimmering in the light of the room.

He attempted to voice his protest, but that caused his neck to swell and press closer to the sharp blade. His captor let out a throaty laugh, harsh and raspy, which caused the blade to move from side to side ever so slightly.

As if in the hands of a surgeon, the sharp blade pierced his skin, slicing slowly across his neck. His captor's precision was remarkable—not too deep, but enough to produce the desired effect. Warm blood trickled slowly out of the wound, marring the finish on the sword and dripping down onto his partially exposed chest.

I'm going to die today, Dr. Alexis convinced himself as he closed his eyes. *I'm about to become the lead news story on France's TF-1.*

His mind raced to his beautiful wife and two young daughters. Josephine had encouraged him to take this job. His pay was doubled because he was away from home, but she thought it would help them provide for their young family. She'd remained behind in Paris while their darling preteen girls went to the finest schools his salary could afford.

They never were concerned about the risks of his working abroad. Gabon was predominantly French and the city of Lawrenceville was relatively crime-free. The biggest concern for Dr. Alexis was mishandling one of the infectious diseases while working in the laboratory. The facility had a spotless accident record and Dr. Alexis was meticulous in his precautionary measures. He was only six months away from returning to Paris with a powerful reference on his résumé.

The blade pressed closer to his neck, opening the wound a little further and drawing more blood. In English, a man instructed his associates to turn on the camera. *This is it*, thought Dr. Alexis. He closed his eyes and apologized to his wife and children. Then he prayed to God to protect his family and forgive him for his sins.

Without warning, more lights were turned on, momentarily blinding him again. His head was snapped backwards and the blade dug into his throat a little bit more. He clenched his eyes shut this time and braced for the impact that would end his life.

The voice of his captor hissed into his ear, "You will only die today, Dr. Alexis, by your own choice. Now open your eyes!"

*****

"Where am I?" asked Dr. Alexis as he struggled to find the words and regain his vision. He wasn't sure if he was allowed to speak, but he tried nonetheless.

A fist full of hair caused his head to instantly jerk back, once again stretching his neck and bearing its vulnerability to the blade. This time a sword wasn't the weapon of choice to inflict pain upon him, a cup of salt did the trick. Dr. Alexis screamed out loud as the stinging pain from the table salt met the open wound on his throat. Tears ran down his face. He had never experienced pain like this, much less the brutality of his captors.

"Pay attention, Dr. Alexis," whispered the man behind him while he forced the Frenchman's head to look at the fifteen television monitors mounted on the wall. Only one monitor was on, and it was streaming images of the front of his home in suburban Paris.

Dr. Alexis stared in shock as the single monitor played surveillance video of his house. "What? That is my home! Why are you filming my home?" he shouted at his captor and attempted to wriggle out of his restraints.

A heavy hand covered in salt immediately began to choke his throat, causing him to scream in agony. The man gruffly rubbed his rough hand to grind the salt into the wound. He calmly spoke into Dr. Alexis's ear. "You will not speak until it is time. Do you understand? My next method of pain will be far worse."

Dr. Alexis managed a nod but was unable to vocalize the word *yes*. His throat was incredibly dry from fear.

"Turn them all on," instructed the faceless man, who continued to stand behind him. He gripped the doctor's head in both his hands and firmly turned his attention to all the screens.

"Oh no," moaned Dr. Alexis.

"Do you see, Doctor?" the man whispered in his ear. "Do you see your wife and children as we do?"

Dr. Alexis shook his head as tears streamed down his face. He began to sob as the videos were played on all fifteen screens. His children were walking into school together. His wife, naked, was entering the shower. All three girls were watching television. Every aspect of his family's life was played out in front of him.

Dr. Alexis's chin dropped to his chest, despite the searing pain from the wound. He gasped for air as he tried to speak. In Arabic, his captor asked for the pitcher of water sitting on the table to their right. He grasped his captive by the hair and poured water over his head, down his throat, and over his wounded neck. Dr. Alexis coughed violently in an attempt to clear his airway.

"Why? What do you want from me?" he begged.

"It is very simple for a man of your intelligence and position," came the reply. "You are going to do your job in Franceville, but now, you will take your instructions from me. But remember, we will be watching you, and them."

*****

Gabon, where the BSL-4 laboratory in which Dr. Alexis worked was located, was not exactly a hotbed of terrorist activity. Unlike Northern Africa, which was predominantly Muslim, Gabon's population was largely Christian and only five percent of the population was Sunni Muslim.

In the nearby country of the Democratic Republic of the Congo, formerly called Zaire, Islamic State terrorists had created a stronghold as it continued to expand its presence around the world.

Unbeknownst to Dr. Alexis, the DR Congo arm of ISIS was designed for this specific operation.

In the aftermath of the abduction and the revelation that his family was in grave danger, Dr. Alexis considered his options. He feared his movements were so closely tracked that unthinkable harm would come to his wife and young daughters. He became a recluse out of fear of saying or doing something that might be misconstrued by his handlers. He'd focus on the assigned task, and then as soon as practicable, he'd rush to Paris, gather up his family, and head for the Alps to hide.

As instructed, Dr. Alexis positioned himself to work with the team assigned to a recent outbreak of plague in Madagascar. Two of the districts in Madagascar had been declared by the WHO, the World Health Organization, as endemic for the plague bacteria. The most recent outbreak was blamed for sixty-two cases resulting in a fatality rate of eighty-five percent.

Dr. Alexis could not grasp how his ISIS captors came by this information, but their intelligence was correct. The strain of plague that Dr. Alexis was to work with was the deadliest form of the plague known as pneumonic plague, not its more recognizable sister, bubonic plague.

For weeks, he performed his duties in isolation, despite the fact that he was part of a larger research team. He'd become gloomy and unsociable. His co-workers didn't want to associate with him. He maintained limited contact with his family to mask his troubles. He was singularly focused on one thing—complying with his handler's directives.

By analyzing case studies of the dead, Dr. Alexis determined that the Madagascar strain of *Yersinia pestis*, or *Y. pestis* for short, the bacterium causing plague, could be *improved—enhanced.*

His handler's directives were crystal clear, but the choices he had to make were clouded by the love for his family. The moral fight raged within him. There was no one to talk to. The choice was his to make.

Plague was one of the oldest diseases known to humans and had caused over two hundred million deaths worldwide. There was no preventive vaccine. The plague could be treated. However, if it was modified and weaponized…

Sixty days later…

Part One

Week One

Chapter 1

Day One
Guatemala Jungle near El Naranjo

"It's too early in the morning for interviewing dead people," mumbled Dr. Mackenzie Hagan as she sloshed her way through the wet jungle path, which was well worn at this point from activity. She attempted to duck under the low-lying branches of a thorny lime tree and was almost successful before it grabbed her ponytail, which protruded through the strap of her cap.

She had taken a hodgepodge of modern transportation from Atlanta overnight, bouncing from a packed-like-sardines Delta flight, to a single-wing Cessna, and finally a decades-old Jeep J8 Patrol Truck, which was utilized by the Guatemalan military for its *special guests*. With only six percent of the Guatemalan population owning a vehicle, she felt lucky that her options weren't more unconventional. She had only wished the soldier escorting her to the site would keep his eyes on the road and quit trying to sneak a peek down her blouse.

June was one of the wettest months of the year in Guatemala, and this particular day did not buck the norm. A heavy downpour had just ended as the sun began to rise, causing the plant life to wake up in all its glory and the humidity to kick into high gear.

Mac, as her friends called her, was not an early riser. She often joked she either needed twelve hours' sleep or just four hours', although the latter generally resulted in a socially challenged epidemiologist.

After they arrived, Mac stepped out of the Jeep into the wet, soggy jungle. The sounds of chattering monkeys filled the air, as well as a light sprinkle dropping through the tropical foliage. The soldier led the way up a well-worn path created by foot traffic and hand carts carrying the CDC's gear.

Her escort pushed back an areca palm and opened up a gateway to a clearing that stood in contrast to the third-world vistas that made up the northern part of the country. Her counterparts from the Centers for Disease Control and Prevention, the CDC's Central American Regional Office in Guatemala City, had arrived twenty-four hours prior.

White tents surrounded the village, which was nestled into the eastern edge of the Laguna del Tigre National Park on the country's northern border with Mexico. A score of native settlements, dwarfed by the rising hills, lay scattered throughout the jungles of this region, which used to play an important political and economic role in the ancient Mayan world.

Like the nearly two million Indians that made up half of Guatemala's population, the residents of these outlying areas spoke various dialects of the Maya-Quiche language, which evolved from the descendants of the Maya Empire. On this day, as Mac interviewed the dead, the language barrier wouldn't be a factor.

Mac caught her first glimpse of the dead wrapped in colorful body bags and lying unceremoniously on the soggy ground. Signs of village life still remained—tools to cultivate corn and primitive back-strap looms used to create colorful and complex textiles designed to differentiate the village from others nearby.

This village was small by comparison. Only twenty to thirty small adobe houses were compactly grouped around the central square—where most of the bodies lay.

No roads connected this village with others in the jungle. The inhabitants traveled on foot and occasionally on horseback, along narrow paths that wound around precipitous hillsides. They owned no vehicles except for the hollowed-out canoes fortified on each side by clapboards. Mac could visualize a canoe's occupants paddling from a standing position, the one in the stern expertly steering the vessel along nearby Santa Amelia lake.

What is wrong with me? She never got distracted on an investigation as serious as this one. Perhaps it was the juxtaposition of a village set in an era a thousand years ago, but now surrounded by modern technological advances. Or it was the sadness of an entire group of people—families, with children, lying dead in their primitive village.

She took a calming breath. She seriously needed to buckle down. Taking her eye off the ball in a situation like this would not be prudent. She let out a tense breath and closed her eyes for a moment.

Mac bit her lip as she studied the scene again, taking into her imagination what life looked like in this desolate village before death came knocking. Several large raindrops snapped her out of her daze as well as the smell of something familiar.

Chapter 2

Day One
Guatemala Jungle near El Naranjo

"Dr. Hagan, I presume?" asked a lanky technician with a British accent. He extended his arm to shake hands with Mac, who opted instead to adjust her white cap with the letters CDC embroidered in blue across the front. She had abandoned the custom of shaking hands with others years ago. She had seen too much.

"Good morning, Sherlock." Mac chuckled, attempting to bring herself to the land of the living. "Please tell me that's coffee."

"Indeed, ma'am," replied Lawrence Brown, one of the career epidemiology field officers, or CEFOs, stationed in Guatemala City. "A little bird told me that you liked it black, full strength, and piping hot."

"A little bird?" Mac asked, tipping the warm brew into her mouth. She instantly received a waking jolt of energy.

"Tweet, tweet, Mac!" announced a female voice from behind her. Mac turned to view a friendly face. It was one of the EIS officers from Atlanta, Janelle Turnbull, a former veterinarian whom Mac had worked with in the past.

Created in 1951 during the Korean War, the Epidemic Intelligence Service was a postgraduate program established for health care professionals, physicians, and veterinarians interested in epidemiology. Both during and after their course work, these highly qualified individuals would study infectious diseases, environmental health issues, and other tasks within the purview of the CDC. Acceptance to the program was an honor that all of the nearly two hundred participants took seriously. Mac knew Janie to be a tireless worker and willing to travel to any part of the planet to perform her disease-detective skills.

Mac instantly beamed. "Janie, did you catch the wrong MARTA train?"

"No, the muckety-mucks wanted to make sure you had everything you needed down here," replied the petite brunette clad in a newly designed, military-grade biological suit created after the West Africa Ebola crisis. The suit used several zippers and fasteners to fall off and peel outward from the wearer, alleviating the need to touch any outer surfaces.

Prior to this new innovation created by a design challenge launched by the United States Agency for International Development, USAID, the EIS disease detectives would suit up with many layers of gear that took a partner and twenty minutes to dress. Even worn properly, the headgear didn't attach to the body suit, creating an opportunity for a miniscule virus one-billionth our size to slip into the suit.

In addition, the new suit featured an internal cooling system ideally suited for hot climates such as Africa and Guatemala. Air was constantly funneled to the headgear through an air chamber, which helped keep the brain cool. Cooler heads prevented heatstrokes and panic attacks.

"Are you about to go in?" asked Mac. She glanced around to observe the level of activity at this early hour. She also looked to the sky to gauge the possibility of more precipitation. This hot zone had the potential to be a hot mess if it rained much more.

"Yes, but I'd like to bring you up to speed first," Janie replied. "We can go in together after that. Come into the field ops tent. We'll get you dried off and then outfitted in your very own space suit."

Mac followed Janie into a large white tent, which contained an air-locked entry on both ends. The logistics involved in this type of investigation required preplanning and experienced technicians. When dealing with an unknown outbreak, mistakes could be deadly.

Mac got settled in after exchanging pleasantries with some of the field officers from CDC-Guatemala City. Janie quickly returned in her civvies with another cup of coffee for both of them. Disease detectives were very much like their law enforcement counterparts. Coffee fueled their day.

Janie settled in a chair next to Mac and opened a file folder, which contained several thick reports. Mac thumbed through the pages of reports as Janie spoke.

"I'll recap what you probably already know and then tell you what's transpired over the last twenty-four hours," started Janie, taking another sip of coffee before getting down to business. "Four days ago, a young man from another village came here on horseback with a load of yarn to trade. He found all of the villagers to be ill. He described them as being nauseated, weak, and with a high fever."

"How were we notified?"

"He returned to his village to give an account of what he'd seen. One of the village elders traveled into town to report the incident. According to the interview he gave a health care worker from the local hospital in El Naranjo, there were no deaths at the time. The local police and a nurse arrived here two days later. The entire village was dead."

Mac reached for the file full of reports and studied the findings. Eighty-one bodies were found throughout the village. There was evidence of vomiting and bleeding from the mouth.

"We need to conduct autopsies as soon as possible," said Mac. She rubbed her temple as she contemplated the magnitude of the situation. An entire village of eighty people, exhibiting flu-like symptoms, was dead within days.

"That's part of the update," added Janie. "Before we could mobilize and arrive on the scene, half a dozen bodies were removed to the hospital in El Naranjo. The local authorities took them early yesterday morning."

"Are you kidding me? They're not set up for something like this!"

"I know, Mac. I wish I had been here. We got it together pretty fast, but you know how these hot zones are. There's protocol. We've got to protect our own first."

Brown approached the two of them. Janie addressed him first.

"Well, Sir Lawrence, what say you?"

"We're gathering specimens now," he replied. "The good news is that the weather radar indicates this low-pressure system has moved past us. The hot zone won't be further compromised by rainfall. The bad news is that despite the fact the village is small by comparison to American towns, it's big enough that it can't be completely contained."

"Surely to God we can keep onlookers out of the zone," barked Mac. While containment was not within her scope of responsibility, she didn't want to be bumping into looky-loos while she assessed the scene.

"No, ma'am. The problem isn't people, it's the spider monkeys. The jungle is full of them. The military tells us that the village was crawling with them when they first arrived. By nature, the monkeys are scavengers. In addition to being overly curious, they're also looking for food."

"Food that might carry the disease!" Mac raised her voice, drawing the attention of technicians throughout the tent. She took a deep breath to calm down her anxiety. At the same time, as if on cue, the HEPA air filtration for the tent kicked on, causing the walls to quickly expand and then deflate as stale air was forced out to make way for fresh, filtered air.

"We've asked the military to help, but there aren't enough assigned to our location and the ones that are don't want to come anywhere within the outer perimeter of the village," replied Brown. "They're afraid of getting too close."

Janie, who was fluent in Spanish, added, "They're calling the village *Cerro de Muerte*—the Hill of Death."

Mac thought of her escort who'd led her up the path earlier. As soon as they reached the clearing, he'd stopped and left. *He didn't want any part of this detail.*

She contemplated for a moment and then gave Lawrence instructions. "Is there any place to land a chopper up here?" The village was in the midst of dense jungle vegetation. Mac hadn't seen a clearing.

"I'll find out or send someone to locate an opening," replied Brown. "Do you want me to take the bodies to Guatemala City? I'll need to get approval from their government for that."

"Why wouldn't they approve?" asked Mac. "They called us in, right?"

"True, but they assumed we would deal with the investigation here. They're in the midst of a presidential campaign. President Morales would like to see this kept out of the media. In fact, my understanding is that the military will raze the village, together with the bodies, as soon as we're done here."

Mac considered her alternatives. Transporting dead bodies carrying an infectious disease was a dangerous proposition, as she and others had learned during the Ebola outbreak in Guinea, Liberia, and Sierra Leone. Containment was a challenge anyway, but tribal burial customs, which included a final kiss of the deceased loved ones, had assisted in the transmission of the Ebola virus throughout the West Africa region.

After the first cases of Ebola were reported in Guinea in 2013, containment practices were instituted by the World Health Organization, which published a road map of steps to prevent further transmission. These steps were not always followed, and within a year, Ebola had exploded. Mac was not interested in a repeat of those failures.

The nearest U.S. military base was in El Salvador, which was too far away to ferry dead bodies by helicopter. There weren't any good options. She gulped down the last of her coffee and stood, ready to examine some of the bodies for herself.

"Well, we'd better get to work. But, Lawrence—" she paused briefly before continuing "—keep the monkeys out of the village. We don't need this disease spread all over the country."

CHAPTER 3

Day One
Guatemala Jungle near El Naranjo

At five foot ten, Mac was accustomed to donning protective gear designed for men. Her slender, athletic build was part genetics, part training. She found working out and participating in athletic events to be an excellent way to relieve stress. Daily, she faced the possibilities of a global pandemic. Some people feared nuclear war or economic collapse. Mac lost sleep over the myriad of possibilities that would result in a large number of deaths like those lying at her feet, multiplied by millions.

Mac had seen the worst of the worst. She had been to Zimbabwe in Southern Africa to investigate an outbreak of Lassa, a viral hemorrhagic fever first identified in Nigeria decades earlier, but had never been seen outside of West Africa. The natives were exhibiting symptoms common to most diseases—high fevers, severe diarrhea, vomiting, and rashes.

The first investigators on the scene from the World Health Organization made a diagnosis of Marburg disease, commonly known as the green monkey disease. Under the microscope, Marburg was distinctive with its long snakelike loops and twists. Lassa was similar in look, but different in treatments. Mac was able to lead researchers at the WHO to a different diagnosis, ultimately saving a lot of lives.

From that experience and others, Mac never accepted an initial hypothesis. She was known to check and recheck specimens. Her personality suited long hours in the lab, avoiding social interaction with co-workers or potential suitors. Mac had no use for the dating game. She enjoyed a quiet evening at home with a cold beer and a science journal.

Janie took Mac on a brief tour of the village to allow the entire picture to come into focus. As specimen gatherers knelt over bodies, carefully extracting tissue and blood samples, Mac would pause to observe.

She approached one of the technicians. "Have you seen any signs of lesions, pustules, or discolored skin tissue?"

"No, ma'am," he replied.

Mac nodded and left the man to his work. She continued her walk with Janie, periodically looking into the small adobe homes. The mostly rectangular structures consisted of block walls, thatched roofs, and only a few rooms. Bodies were found in beds or at times near makeshift latrines behind the homes.

She stopped for a moment and looked toward the perimeter, where two soldiers were jousting with a group of spider monkeys who were attempting to get into the village. "Have you found any dead animals in the village? You know, monkeys, rats, bats, etcetera?"

"Only a dairy cow that was still tied to its post near a barn. The horses, which were kept in a small barn up the hill, were unaffected."

"Have you seen any fleas since you arrived on the scene?"

"No. No mosquitos either. All of the typical carriers of disease appear to be absent except for the monkeys."

Mac motioned for Brown to join them. "Sir Lawrence," started Mac jokingly, "will you coordinate with our soldier friends to capture half a dozen monkeys for analysis? Also, we're gonna need to send our teams out to the surrounding areas to interview anyone who has come in contact with this village."

"I'm already on it," he replied. "Well, one more thing. I want to question the boy who reported the illness. He may be able to shed some light on the condition of the villagers before they died. Sadly, he might also be infected."

Brown hustled off, so Mac and Janie continued. "Why wouldn't they go for help?" queried Mac aloud.

"They just don't believe in modern medicine," replied Janie. "They have their own forms of homeopathic treatments, which obviously didn't work in this case."

"I've spent a considerable amount of time in Africa," started Mac. "Those of us who live in the modern world wouldn't believe that primitive people like this still exist. Despite what happened here, it does prove that mankind can exist without the conveniences of smartphones and fast food."

The two spent another hour surveying each body and discussing the initial findings with members of the CDC team. Brown secured more troops from the Guatemalan military and they were winning the battle in repelling the curious monkey population.

After completing their decontamination process, Mac and Janie returned to their civilian clothes and entered the administration tent to compare notes. As they entered the tent, a man was standing over the shoulder of a microbiologist while studying the file that Janie had provided Mac earlier.

Mac immediately approached the man and firmly snatched the file from his grasp. "May I help you?"

"Well, actually," he started as he removed his Ray-Ban Aviators from his head and tucked them into one of the pockets of his khaki cargo pants, "I was doing just fine until you rudely snatched the file out of my hands."

"Now, hold on, mister," protested Janie. "This file is not for public viewing. Maybe you should identify yourself."

"Sure, Nathan Hunter, Defense Threat Reduction Agency."

"Wait," interjected Mac. "DOD? Why would the Department of Defense be interested in this?"

He didn't respond, but instead stuck out his hand to shake. "And you are?"

As always, Mac avoided shaking hands, drawing a puzzled look from Hunter. "My name is Dr. Mackenzie Hagan with the CDC. This is my associate Janie Turnbull. Now, why are you here?"

Hunter acted sincere and apologetic. "I'm sorry, Miss, um, Dr. Hagan, if I've overstepped my boundary. I'm a soldier, of sorts, so I follow orders. Someone at Fort Belvoir thought it necessary for me to visit, so I'm visiting."

"How about some credentials," said Janie bluntly. Hunter glared down at her for a second before reaching into his shirt pocket and producing an ID issued by the Defense Threat Reduction Agency.

Janie handed it to Mac, who returned the laminated ID card to Hunter. Because of her mother's background, Mac was familiar with the DTRA, which was an agency within the DOD. Their main function was countering weapons of mass destruction, which included chemical, biological, and nuclear threats.

Hunter continued to focus on Mac, who was momentarily mesmerized by his steel-blue eyes. The man was an intruder into her realm, but he was handsome and built like he was carved out of granite. She seriously doubted this Mr. Hunter's sole responsibility with the DTRA was bird-dogging an isolated disease outbreak.

"Seriously, I don't want to get in your way," said Hunter. "I happened to be in the region and was asked to stop by to get an update. My superiors are interested in this sort of thing."

"Well, Mr. Hunter, *this sort of thing* can have catastrophic consequences just as much as Assad's chemical weapons program or Putin's nukes," said Mac, who handed the file over to a scowling Janie, who still had smoke coming out of her ears. "I'm hoping this incident doesn't give rise to a *thing of concern* to the DTRA."

"I agree." Hunter motioned for them to sit at an empty table. The three got settled and he got down to business. "Is there anything you can tell me? I realize that you're just getting started. I mean, you arrived this morning, correct?"

Mac hesitated before responding. How did he know that? She shook off the urge to challenge him and decided to respond. She wanted to get this over with so she could travel into El Naranjo. She wanted to see the results of the autopsies.

"Well, you know, I don't think that this situation will be one of interest to the DTRA. Normally an arenavirus doesn't rise to the level of a WMD."

"An arenavirus?" asked Hunter.

"Yes," continued Mac. "An arenavirus comes from the Latin word for sand. Under the microscope, the virus particle is round, and with further scrutiny under an electron microscope, the particle appears to contain grains of sand."

"Okay, good to know," said Hunter somewhat sarcastically.

Mac set her jaw and studied the man sitting across the table from her. *If you didn't want an explanation, you shouldn't have asked.* She continued. "Several of the diseases that are caused by an arenavirus fall under the broad category of hemorrhagic fever, like a dozen other infections from members of different viral groups such as Ebola, Lassa, and Marburg—three very deadly viruses. Make no mistake, in its most critical form, hemorrhagic fever can be as dramatic and relentless as anything you'll ever see in medicine."

"Based upon your observations, what leads you to a preliminary conclusion that an arenavirus is involved here?"

Mac leaned back in her chair and crossed her legs. She adjusted her blouse and took a quick glance down to make sure there were no distractions. It was warm in the tent and she was a little sweaty, but she resisted the urge to undo another button on her shirt. One set of groping eyes was enough for the day.

"The impact of hemorrhagic fever on the body is swift and severe. It comes on abruptly and leads you on a downward slope as you feel worse and worse with scattered symptoms being felt throughout your body's vital organs. The sense of fatigue is numbing, as though you were crushed under a boulder. Fever saps your will to work or go about your daily activities. Your skin becomes flushed and so sensitive that you don't even want your bedsheet to touch it."

"It sounds brutal. Almost like a really bad case of the flu," said Hunter.

"But much, much worse," added Janie. "Unfortunately, a patient stricken with hemorrhagic fever doesn't know the specifics of what is going on inside them. The liver begins to rot away. Internal bleeding will impact the kidneys. Surfaces of the patient's internal organs will show signs of hemorrhaging as plasma oozes out."

With each sentence, Hunter grimaced more. Mac sensed that Janie knew this and was therefore piling on the gory visual. She decided to join in the fun.

"Janie's right. The small bleeding points are one of the key features of hemorrhagic fever. They are the visual evidence of the many sites of damage to the tiny blood vessels located throughout the body, including on the surface, like your eyes and gums. As the soft mucosal surfaces of your gastrointestinal tract begin to break with the slightest provocation, like after eating too many Tabasco-rich burritos, blood will enter your mouth and eventually leave your body as you experience coughing fits."

Janie jumped in. "And the eyes. Yes, the eyes are a telltale sign. The small blood vessels will burst the first time a patient rubs them out of sleepiness or due to an allergy. The eyes usually bleed first. It can be gruesome."

Hunter studied the women for a moment, seemingly visualizing bleeding eyes. "Is that what you have here—hemorrhagic fever?"

Mac chuckled. "Well, we don't know, Mr. Hunter, because we haven't performed an autopsy yet. You see, hemorrhagic fever is just one of a dozen or so possibilities, all of which will be considered once we get on with our work."

"There's nothing you can give me at this point?"

"Nope, I've been on the scene for all of six hours," Mac responded. "There's a lot to do before I can satisfy the curiosity of the folks at Fort Belvoir."

Chapter 4

Day One
El Naranjo, Guatemala

Sister Juanita Gomez was an experienced, skilled nurse. Having come to Guatemala as part of the Catholic Church's outreach program, she found a home in El Naranjo, where she brought her New World skills to a third-world country. Over the years, she'd performed her job dutifully, and she was sure God smiled upon her accomplishments.

As time passed, she learned more about medicine and began to study postmortem examination of cadavers. This earned her the opportunity to work with the traveling pathologist, as he was affectionately called by the circuit of small hospitals dotting the Guatemalan landscape. These hospitals, challenged by minimal budgets, were accustomed to sharing specialists with other facilities. Without a pathology department per se, the hospital at El Naranjo utilized nurses like Sister Juanita to undertake the occasional rare forensic autopsies.

Sister Juanita still enjoyed her job, but after thirty years in the same place, she was growing weary of the routine. Plus, at sixty years old, the fourteen-hour days had taken their toll. In her younger years, prayers gave her the strength and determination to work the long days at the hospital. With age, however, prayers didn't have the same impact as they did during her more energetic years.

Over time, the physicians had gone their way, but Sister Juanita remained, dutifully performing her tasks even though, like a rock, she'd become worn down. And with wear and tear, any machine, the human body included, becomes fatigued. And with fatigue came mistakes.

Sister Juanita knew what to be wary of. More people died of lower respiratory infections caused by parasitic diseases than any other cause of death. Over the years, thanks to sexual promiscuity interjecting itself into Guatemalan culture, a new killer had taken root—AIDS. Like other infectious diseases, the precautions during autopsies in dealing with dead bodies inflicted with the AIDS virus were set in stone.

As with the plagues of old, all that a medical professional could do with these potentially deadly diseases was to protect themselves. AIDS was always on Sister Juanita's mind when she assisted the pathologist during a procedure. But this time, the deceased was a seven-year-old boy. He was too young for sex and not as likely to be a carrier of the AIDS virus.

The bodies delivered to them by the military convoy came without advance warning or explanation. In fact, no one had formally requested that the autopsies be performed. It wasn't until Sister Juanita learned that the American CDC was going to be involved did she take an interest in the six villagers who rested in their morgue.

As it happened, a new, young pathologist was making his rounds and happened to be in El Naranjo before he left for the much larger city of Poptún located to their east. They determined to undertake the autopsy out of concern for the local villagers. If there was some form of contagion, including malaria or yellow fever, which had been present in the jungle, it was a matter of time before other citizens became infected. Sister Juanita wanted to help protect God's children.

Typically, the morgue and the pathology rooms were quiet during all times of the day. Sister Juanita liked its basement location and the cool air it contained. While the pathologist scrubbed and donned his protective gear, Sister Juanita prepared the young boy for the autopsy. She set up the tools of the trade and provided all of the customary necessities for the pathologist to do his work.

The doctor arrived and immediately began the procedure. He was new, inexperienced, but methodical. It took him twice as long as the doctors she was used to working with.

He examined the outside of the boy's body, noting aloud anything out of the ordinary like droplets of blood, signs of bruising, or open wounds. Next, he would normally obtain simple X-rays, which was not possible at the El Naranjo hospital. Small facilities did not have the luxury of digital radiological equipment, so this part of the autopsy would have to wait for the mobile radiologist to visit in two days.

The pathologist took several blood and tissue specimens and then began examination of the boy's body cavity. Using his scalpel, he made a large Y-shaped incision from each shoulder across the chest and down to the pubic bone. Sister Juanita didn't flinch as the body's internal organs were revealed. She'd practiced the incision herself on unclaimed patients.

As one hour stretched into two, Sister Juanita's mind wandered to an upcoming church social. The pathologist reported his findings into a small recording device in his monotone voice—a voice that lured Sister Juanita into boredom and then sleepiness.

The pathologist asked for a 10 blade in order to make a small incision in the lungs. Sister Juanita snapped out of the doldrums and fumbled through the instruments neatly aligned on the tray. He handed her the larger used scalpel in exchange.

Only the slightest accidental prick of her finger by the bloody tip of the used scalpel brought her back to being fully alert. Sister Juanita didn't notice it at first, but then a droplet of blood oozed through the tip of her glove and she immediately ran to the wash basin to rinse the wound.

The pathologist attempted to comfort Sister Juanita by assuring her that the quick reaction to irrigate and clean the wound protected her from any disease. But then, whether Sister Juanita's cut was potentially fatal wouldn't matter to him, as he would be traveling for months and not see her again until the fall.

Chapter 5

Day One
El Naranjo, Guatemala

Mac and Janie rode down the mountain to El Naranjo to learn the results of the autopsies. The two got a kick out of the Guatemalan soldiers arguing over the honor of escorting them in one of the available Jeeps. Ultimately, rank overtook practicality and the acting officer on duty drove the pair himself. After they had an opportunity to meet with the pathologist, Mac planned on catching a flight back to Atlanta while Janie would travel to Guatemala City to begin the meticulous process of shoe-leather epidemiology. Janie would provide Mac a full report every morning.

"Good afternoon," a receptionist greeted the women with a heavy accent. Janie conversed with the receptionist in Spanish while Mac observed their surroundings. There were very few locals in the lobby. Two uniformed police officers stood near the entrance. Whereas in America, the presence of armed personnel meant protecting a medical facility from possible terrorism, in a Central American hospital, the concern of law enforcement was a raid upon the hospital in search of drugs. Narcotics could be transported to America for a huge profit. Antibiotics could be sold on the black market within Southern Mexico for even more.

Janie approached Mac, shaking her head in disgust. "Well, there won't be much to learn here, I'm afraid."

"Why's that?" asked Mac.

"Apparently, the nurse assisting the pathologist cut herself during the procedure and was too distraught to continue. As a result, the *prima donna pathologist*, who, I'm told, has only been on the job for three months, refused to continue without an assistant."

Mac rolled her eyes and shook her head. "Where does that leave us?"

"He did one autopsy today, on a seven-year-old boy."

"That's something," said Mac. "Where's his office? We'll learn what we can from today's work."

"That's just the thing," Janie added. "He's a traveling pathologist. He left for another town. There won't be a new pathologist on duty for many weeks."

"C'mon," said a frustrated Mac. She wasn't qualified to conduct an autopsy, even if the locals would allow her in their morgue. If she could get the chart, even if the findings were handwritten notes, they could narrow down the disease. But could she trust them?

Janie stopped them before they headed down the stairs. "You know what? I'll go find the chart. Wait here and try to keep the receptionist busy. I'll be back in a jiffy."

Mac smiled as Janie slipped off down a hallway toward the stairwell. Mac chatted up the receptionist and tried some of her conversational Spanish she'd learned years ago when she was growing up. The receptionist seemed to enjoy the opportunity to talk with an American, so she tried out her broken English as well.

On the end of the building opposite the stairwell that Janie took to the basement, Mac caught a glimpse of a man walking back and forth across the light pouring into the west wing of the hospital from the setting sun. The glare of the tile floor blinded her somewhat, but she could make out the clothing of Nathan Hunter from the DTRA.

What's he doing here? Mac noticed a restroom sign near the entrance to the hallway and asked the receptionist if it was okay to use it. With a wave of the arm as approval, Mac slipped away to get a closer look at Hunter, who appeared to be talking on the phone.

Mac slid behind the wall at the entrance to the hallway and eavesdropped on Hunter. He continued to walk back and forth, talking only sporadically. Janie emerged from the stairwell behind Mac and began to speak.

"Of course, the pathologist is gone, and there's no sign of his findings. I was alone down there, having my way with their filing system, but I found nothing."

Mac encouraged Janie to keep her voice down and pulled the smaller petite woman against the wall with her. "I think I know where the autopsy report went."

"You do?"

"Yeah, look down the hallway," replied Mac. Janie slipped past Mac and studied the pacing figure. "There's our new friend Hunter. Doesn't it look like he's got a clipboard tucked under his arm?"

"It sure does!" exclaimed Janie under her breath. "What's he up to?"

"I don't know, but the DTRA suspects something. I'm not buying his explanation that he just happened to be in the area."

"But what?" asked Janie.

Mac took Janie by the arm and led her back into the main lobby. "Okay, listen. We have to get these bodies back to the States, where a proper autopsy can be performed."

"What can I do?" asked Janie.

"Clear the removal of the remains to our custody through the Guatemalan government," replied Mac. "I'll call the higher-ups in Atlanta and get approval to use the CDC private jet to pick up the bodies. I wouldn't trust the autopsy of a part-time pathologist anyway. We need to re-examine these remains in a way this rookie pathologist never contemplated."

Janie nodded toward Hunter. "What about him?"

"I intend to find out what he's up to as well."

Chapter 6

Day Two
Flight from Flores, Guatemala, to Atlanta, Georgia

Mac was about to board the single-wing Cessna aircraft that was to transport her to Belize City and her Delta Airlines flight home when she received a phone call from Janie. The Guatemalan government refused to release the bodies for transportation to America. They stubbornly insisted that native Guatemalans should be buried on Guatemalan soil.

Mac quickly arranged for a pathology team to fly the CDC jet into Flores, Guatemala, a much larger city than El Naranjo. This required her to spend the night, which gave her an opportunity to clear her head and provide written instructions to the team.

She was particularly interested in the condition of the lower respiratory tract, which includes the trachea, the lungs and bronchioles. The symptoms described by the boy who found the sick villagers sounded like a form of pneumonia or bronchitis. Evidence of a bloody mucus mix around their mouths indicated a number of options, including *streptococcus*, *tuberculosis*, and *Y. pestis*—the plague.

She typed out her instructions and prepared an email to Dr. Kathy Farrow, the head of the pathology team. Dr. Farrow was a seasoned veteran of the Ebola battles in Africa and Mac trusted her completely. Nonetheless, she wanted to make her requirements clear.

```
LOWER  RESPIRATORY  TRACT—sterile,  screw-
capped  containers,  store  and  transport  at
2°C-8°C
```

BLOOD—transfer at ambient temperature, no refrigeration!

TISSUE/BIOPSY SPECIMENS—sterile container, add two drops of sterile normal saline to keep moist, keep chilled at 2°C-8°C

SWABS OF TISSUE—Don't bother, transport time too long

"I'm not going to follow in my mother's footsteps," muttered Mac as the jet containing the team touched down at the Mundo Maya International Airport. She made her way to the gate area servicing executive aircraft and waited for her associates to disembark. It was unseasonably cool after the low-pressure system crossed the Yucatan Peninsula the day before. Sixty-three-degree temperatures felt like fall in Atlanta.

As Dr. Farrow led the way across the tarmac and into the waiting area, Mac's mind began to wander back to those days when she was first exposed to fieldwork in the battle against infectious diseases. The West African Ebola virus disease was the most widespread outbreak of EVD in history. She and Dr. Farrow were at ground zero of the epidemic, while her mother was at ground zero of the political firestorm.

"Hi, Mac!" Dr. Farrow greeted Mac heartily with a wave and then a genuine hug. Dr. Farrow was a willing and competent mentor during those days, as well as someone Mac could vent to.

"Hey, Kathy, here we go again, right?" asked Mac with a chuckle.

"Are we? I mean *going again*?" replied Dr. Farrow with a question of her own.

"I don't know, Kathy. The situation is odd. The village was isolated from the world—no transportation, little interaction. They were only susceptible to one of the usual carriers of disease—the spider and howler monkeys."

"Maybe it's zoonotic," speculated Dr. Farrow. "I got your email, by the way. One thing bothers me about this. There are some loose ends to tie up such as the boy who discovered the sick villagers. Has he been located? Also, do we have any of the primates to study?"

"No, yes, maybe. How's that?"

"You learned that from me." Dr. Farrow laughed in response. "The unit in Guatemala City should be able to study the monkeys. Are they looking for the boy too?"

"We've assigned that task to the military, which has been marginally helpful," Mac responded. "They don't want any part of the disease. The soldiers assigned to the site kept their distance, which resulted in the invasion of the curious spider monkeys. Our specimens could have been compromised because of their lack of control."

Dr. Farrow paused as she waited for an announcement to be made over the airport's public address system. "You need to get back to Atlanta. We can discuss this more later. It's gonna take us the rest of today to travel. We'll hit it hard tomorrow and the next day. I'll have the lab notify you when they've received the samples from our autopsies."

"Thank you, Kathy. We'll see what the pathology tells us."

The two women shared an embrace and Mac approached the gate. Two of the ground personnel assisted her with carry-ons and led her up the stairwell into the Learjet. She would have the plane to herself for the flight back to the Peachtree–Dekalb Airport in Chamblee, just northeast of Atlanta.

As the aircraft taxied down the runway, Mac's mind wandered back to West Africa. Before she was deployed to Liberia, her mother had called her and encouraged Mac with these words, "Never read too much into things. Stay focused, disciplined, and inquisitive. Above all, never give up."

Chapter 7

Day Three
CDC
Atlanta, Georgia

Ordinarily, Mac avoided leading the Disease Detective tour at the CDC Museum like the plague, but today she felt like a day of transition from what she observed in Guatemala was a good idea. Besides, Dr. Farrow's team wouldn't be back with their findings for at least another day or so and Janie was constantly sending her text message updates.

Today's group was made up of high-school-age kids and their parents. The teens were participating in the Disease Detective Camp at the museum as part of the CDC's mission of educating the public about their work. Each week, for a period of five days, the campers were exposed to the inner workings of the CDC in order to give them a broad understanding of the agency's role in public health.

Every year topics varied, but ironically, this summer, the focus was on infectious diseases. Mac was a perfect candidate for leading the tour. She took the group through a series of exhibits that pointed out the specifics of a particular disease and how the CDC helped solve the mystery surrounding it. After the midway point, she opened up the floor for questions.

A parent, naturally, was the first to speak up. Mac often wondered if the Disease Detective Camp should have an adult version. "What's the difference between an outbreak, an endemic, and a pandemic?"

"That's a great first question," replied Mac truthfully. "Understanding epidemiological technical terminology can be confusing—especially with the fact they are misused so often in the media. Oftentimes, reporters throw around these terms without realizing they have very different meanings."

The group tightened their circle around Mac as she continued. "An outbreak refers to a number of cases that exceed the norm for a given region or disease. Based upon our data, if a disease is common to a particular geographic location, a slight increase in the number of afflicted patients would be deemed an outbreak.

"Now, if you take that same disease in the same geographic area and it continues to exist without eradication, then it rises to the level of an endemic. In other words, the disease is perpetual."

One of the young detectives raised her hand. "Do you have an example?"

"Dengue fever," Mac quickly replied. "Dengue fever is a very painful, debilitating, mosquito-borne virus that is typically found in tropical locations like the Philippines and Thailand. In those regions, there are mosquitoes carrying the disease and transmitting it from person to person. Dengue fever has remained in those regions since the middle of last century; thus it's classified as an endemic.

"Recently, we saw an outbreak on the Big Island of Hawaii. Somebody entered the country who was infected with dengue fever, got bitten by mosquitoes, which then created local chains of transmission throughout the Big Island. In this case, it was declared an outbreak due to the fact the disease was imported with subsequent transfer."

Three other hands rose. She picked a young man in the rear of the group. "Why didn't they just stop the person with dengue fever from entering Hawaii?"

Wow, Mac thought to herself. *Be careful with this question.*

"Well, for one thing, he or she may not have been exhibiting symptoms at the time. If the person was showing signs of illness, oftentimes they mirror those of the common cold or flu. In the United States, we haven't shown a willingness to quarantine people for cold or flu symptoms."

More hands flew into the air. "What if the disease was more serious? You know, like Ebola?"

"Okay, let's finish with our definitions first," replied Mac, avoiding the question. "We've discussed outbreaks and endemics. A pandemic is when there is an outbreak that affects most of the world."

"You mean like the plague?" queried the young man with a follow-up question.

Mac led them down the hallway toward a display titled *Plague—The Three Great Pandemics*.

"Yes, that's one example. In recorded history, there have been three world pandemics of plague recorded." She pointed to a timeline of events that also depicted estimated death tolls.

Mac continued. "In medieval times, like the year 541 and later in 1347, the plague ravaged the world, causing devastating mortality rates in both people and animals. The disease was so widespread that it travelled rapidly across nations and onto other continents. Both of these events were spread largely by human contact. The third great plague pandemic, which began in 1894, originated in China, then spread to India and around the world. The most prevalent disease host of the plague organism was the rat. Throughout Europe, for example, there were open sewers and ample breeding grounds for rats."

Mac took another question. "How long do the plagues last?"

"The plague pandemics increased and decreased over time. The third plague pandemic was officially declared over in 1959, although outbreaks of the plague occur from time to time, most recently in Madagascar, an island nation east of Africa."

"Has the plague come to America?" asked one of the parents.

"Plague was introduced into America in the early 1900s when steamships carried infected rats into our ports. Today, we receive reports of a dozen or so cases per year, primarily in the rural areas of Western states like New Mexico, Arizona, and Colorado."

Mac laughed to herself. Every time she conducted one of these tours, the questioning always turned to the plague. Every child had heard about the plague, the Black Death, from cartoons or television shows. Of all the diseases that posed immediate dangers to their everyday lives, they wanna talk about something exotic and rare like *Y. pestis*.

THANK YOU FOR READING THIS EXCERPT OF
PANDEMIC: BEGINNINGS, book one of The Pandemic Series.

The entire four book series is available on Amazon.com.

You may purchase signed copies, paperback and hardcover editions of Bobby Akart's books on www.BobbyAkart.com.

Printed in Great Britain
by Amazon